BELIEVE

"Entertaining and emotionally satisfying . . . McCarthy's signature clean writing style and an easy-to-follow story line make it incredibly easy to become involved in this book . . . A sweet new adult love story that takes us on a journey of friendship, self-discovery, forgiveness, and love."
—*Smexy Books*

"I was completely caught up in this story." —*The Book Pushers*

"A great love story filled with steamy romance and drama."
—*Dark Faerie Tales*

SWEET

"[A] riveting addition to the rising new adult category."
—*Library Journal*

"A sexy, romantic, emotional coming-of-age new adult that uses a different approach to defining the romance than the usual NA offerings. Crisp writing, indulgent humor, and a smooth flowing story line make it incredibly easy to become fully invested in this book . . . A wonderful love story that takes us on a journey filled with love, laughter, growth, and angst." —*Smexy Books*

"Full of steamy romance and entertaining banter . . . [McCarthy's] writing is very captivating." —*Dark Faerie Tales*

"A wonderful second book to the True Believers series. I love the characters that McCarthy has created." —*The Book Pushers*

"Sweet and fun . . . Erin McCarthy has a real gift with creating real stories." —*Ticket to Anywhere*

continued . . .

TRUE

"McCarthy's entry in the burgeoning new adult subgenre is a page-turning, gut-wrenching success . . . Their troubles are real, their love True, and readers will root them on past the very last page."

—*RT Book Reviews*

"A sweet, romantic, dynamic coming-of-age new adult that takes a much-needed detour from the usual emotionally draining, overly dramatic offerings . . . Crisp writing and a smooth story line make it incredibly easy to become fully invested in this book."

—*Smexy Books*

"By turns sweet, steamy, gritty, and heartbreaking, *True* is an outstanding read."

—*On a Book Bender*

PRAISE FOR NOVELS OF ERIN MCCARTHY

"Sizzling hot, jam-packed with snappy dialogue, emotional intensity, and racing fun."

—Carly Phillips, *New York Times* bestselling author

"A steamy romance . . . Fast-paced and red-hot."

—*Publishers Weekly*

"Characters you will care about, a story that will make you laugh and cry, and a book you won't soon forget." —*The Romance Reader*

"Priceless!" —*RT Book Reviews*

"Quite a few chuckles, some face-fanning moments, and one heck of a love story." —*A Romance Review*

"Readers won't be able to resist McCarthy's sweetly sexy and sentimental tale." —*Booklist*

"[McCarthy] is fabulous with smoking hot romances!"

—*The Romance Reader's Connection*

Titles by Erin McCarthy

A DATE WITH THE OTHER SIDE
HEIRESS FOR HIRE
SEEING IS BELIEVING

The Fast Track Series
FLAT-OUT SEXY
HARD AND FAST
HOT FINISH
THE CHASE
SLOW RIDE
JACKED UP
FULL THROTTLE

The Vegas Vampires Series
HIGH STAKES
BIT THE JACKPOT
BLED DRY
SUCKER BET

The Deadly Sins Series
MY IMMORTAL
FALLEN
THE TAKING

The True Believers Series
TRUE
SWEET
BELIEVE
SHATTER

Anthologies

THE NAKED TRUTH
(with Donna Kauffman, Beverly Brandt, and Alesia Holliday)

AN ENCHANTED SEASON
(with Maggie Shayne, Nalini Singh, and Jean Johnson)

THE POWER OF LOVE
(with Lori Foster, Toni Blake, Dianne Castell, Karen Kelley,
Rosemary Laurey, Janice Maynard, LuAnn McLane, Lucy Monroe,
Patricia Sargeant, Kay Stockham, and J. C. Wilder)

FIRST BLOOD
(with Susan Sizemore, Chris Marie Green, and Meljean Brook)

ERIN McCARTHY

BELIEVE

B

BERKLEY BOOKS, NEW YORK

THE BERKLEY PUBLISHING GROUP
Published by the Penguin Group
Penguin Group (USA) LLC
375 Hudson Street, New York, New York 10014

USA • Canada • UK • Ireland • Australia • New Zealand • India • South Africa • China

penguin.com

A Penguin Random House Company

This book is an original publication of The Berkley Publishing Group.

Berkley trade paperback ISBN: 978-0-425-27505-4

An application for cataloguing has been submitted to the Library of Congress.

PUBLISHING HISTORY
InterMix eBook edition / January 2014
Berkley trade paperback edition / November 2014

PRINTED IN THE UNITED STATES OF AMERICA

10 9 8 7 6 5 4 3 2 1

Cover design by Rita Frangie.
Couple © Forewer/Shutterstock.
Interior text design by Kristin del Rosario.

CHAPTER ONE

ROBIN

I SPENT MY SOPHOMORE YEAR IN COLLEGE PARTYING. I wasn't even original about it. Just the totally typical pattern of skipping class and going out every single night. If there was a keg party, I went. If there was a shot, I drank it. If there was a guy, I made out with him. I wore short skirts, showed as much cleavage as I could, and I felt sexy and confident while having the time of my life. I threw up in more than one toilet, made out with a taxidermied deer on a dare, and came home without my shoes, dorm key, or phone on a regular basis.

Later, I tried to look back and figure out why I had slid so easily into party girl, but all I could come up with was maybe I just wanted a louder voice, and drinking gave me that. I wanted some attention, I guess, or maybe just to have a good time where there were no rules. Or maybe there was just no reason at all.

It all seemed normal. What you do in college, right? You party. You make superficial friends. You drink. Do stupid things that you laugh about the next day and take pictures that will prevent you from ever being a senator.

It wasn't anything I felt bad about. I mean, sure, I could have done without some of those hangovers, and I did end up dodging a few guys who wanted to date after I spent a drunken night telling them they were awesome, but nothing to make me feel ashamed.

Until I hooked up with one of my best friends' boyfriend when she was out of town.

Then I hated myself and the existence of vodka. Because I wasn't one of *those* girls. Or I hadn't been. Never, under any circumstances at all, would I have come even remotely close to doing anything with a friend's guy sober, so why would I do that? How could alcohol make me cross a boundary so high and thick and barbwired? I wasn't even hot for Nathan. I never had been. I mean, he was cute, whatever, but it wasn't like I nurtured a secret crush or anything.

So how did I end up waking up next to him on his plaid sheets, his arm thrown carelessly over my naked chest? I came awake with a start, head pounding, mouth dry, for a second wondering where the hell I was and who I had had sex with. When I blinked and took in the face above that arm, I thought I was going to throw up. Getting to the apartment, sex, it was completely a black, yawning hole of nothing. I didn't remember even leaving the party. No idea how Nathan and I had wound up in bed together. All I had were a few flashes that suddenly came back to me of him biting my nipple, hard, so that I had protested, my legs on his shoulders. Nothing else.

As I lay there, heart racing, wondering how the hell I could live with this, with myself, the horror slicing through me like a sharp knife, Nathan woke up.

He gave me a sleepy, cocky smile, punctuated by a yawn. "Hey, Robin."

"Hey." I tried to sink down under the sheet, not wanting him to see me naked, not wanting to be naked.

"Well, that was fun," he said, his lazy smile expanding into a grin. "We should do that again before we get up."

The thought made my stomach turn. "But Kylie," I said weakly, because I wanted to remind him that while his girlfriend was back at her parents' for the summer, she still very much existed. His girlfriend. My best friend.

"I love Kylie, but she's not here. And we're not going to tell her." He shrugged. "I didn't expect this to happen, but it did and we're still naked." He pulled my hand over his erection. "No reason we shouldn't enjoy it."

And he leaned over to kiss me. I scooted backward so fast, I fell off the mattress onto my bare ass. "I'm going to puke," I told him.

"Bummer."

Grabbing my clothes off the floor, I stumbled into the hall-way, hoping his roommate Bill wasn't around. In the bathroom, I leaned over the sink, trembling, eyes that stared back at me in the mirror shocked, the skin under them bruised. I didn't get sick. I wished I would. I wished I could vomit out of myself the horrible realization that I had done something terrible, appalling, unforgiveable, mega disgusting.

I couldn't use vodka as an excuse. And now I knew Nathan was an asshole on top of it all.

Without asking him if I could use the shower, I turned on the water and stepped in, wanting to wash away the night, the dirty, nasty smell of skank sex off of my skin. I felt like a slut, like a bitch, like someone I didn't even know, and my tears mixed with the steady stream of water from the shower as I scrubbed and scrubbed.

I spent the rest of the summer sober, far away from parties, guilt nibbling at my insides, making me chronically nauseous, and I avoided everyone. I begged Nathan to stop when he kept sending me sexy texts, and I ignored my friend Jessica, who had stayed in town for the summer and who kept asking what was wrong.

By August I was consumed by anxiety and the fear that someone knew, that someone would tell, that I would be responsible for Kylie having her heart broken.

I slept whole days away and I couldn't eat. I thought about getting meds from the doctor for sleeping or for anxiety or for depression or for alcoholism or for sluttiness. But what was done was done, and a pill wasn't going to fix it. Or me.

When Jessica called and said Nathan's friend Tyler was picking me up whether I liked it or not and we were going to hang out, I tried to say no. But then I decided that I liked to be with myself even less than I liked to be with other people.

Besides, once Kylie got back in a week, I wasn't going to be able to be friends with any of them anymore, and this might be my last chance to spend time hanging out. I couldn't be in the same room with Kylie and pretend that I hadn't betrayed our friendship in the worst way possible. I wasn't going to be able to sit there and have her and Nathan kissing on each other, knowing that he had spent all summer trying to hook up with me again.

I was going to have to find a new place to live, and disappear from our group of friends.

If only it had been that simple.

If only I had walked away right then and there.

Then I never would have met Phoenix and my life would never have changed in ways I still don't understand.

TYLER WAS A GOOD PERSON TO CATCH A RIDE FROM, because he didn't need to talk. He just drove and smoked, and I stared out the window, my art supplies in my lap. I had promised to paint a pop art portrait of Tyler's little brother Easton, and I had to do it tonight because I might never see him again if I had the guts to follow through with my plan to move out of the apartment. I hadn't painted all summer. I wasn't inspired. And I didn't want to now, but I had promised I would back before the morning after with Nathan.

So since I couldn't explain any of that, I stayed mostly silent. I did say, "Rory gets back tomorrow."

It was a stupid comment. Of course he knew his girlfriend was coming back to school. But I wanted to make some sort of effort. It was hot, even for August, and the windows were open, air rushing in and swirling his smoke around in front of me.

"Yep. I missed her. A lot."

I didn't doubt he had. And I didn't think for one minute he would have betrayed her the way Nathan had Kylie. Even if he wasn't living with his brother and Jessica, who were also dating.

Tyler just wasn't that kind of guy. Both Riley and Tyler were loyal, and I wondered why I always seemed to attract the wrong kind of guy. The liars, the cheaters. My boyfriend freshman year had been a douche, flirting with other girls in front of me, laughing it off when I complained. My high school boyfriend had told me he wanted a girl who had her life together, who had goals. What kind of goals was I supposed to have at seventeen? At that point I already knew I was going to college to study graphic design, wasn't that good enough? So apparently his way to fix my deficiency was to hook up with his ex at a party and humiliate me.

It was hard to believe that someday there would be a guy in my life who would love me the way my friends' guys loved them.

Of course, I was never going to find that guy at a keg party. Another reason I had stopped going to the frat house all-nighters. I didn't have the stomach for the so-called living-in-the-moment fun since I had woken up next to Nathan. So maybe I didn't have my life all mapped out, but I knew that I was done with the superficial crap. I knew that I had crossed a line I never wanted to cross again and if that meant giving up alcohol forever, then that's what I was going to do because I had gone from being cheated on to the cheater, and I could barely live with myself.

And if I couldn't live with myself, what guy would want to?

When we went in Tyler's house, there was someone sleeping on the couch. I couldn't see his face since he was turned away from the room on his side, but he had black hair and a serious lack of a tan. "Who is that?" I asked Tyler.

"My cousin, Phoenix. He's crashing here for a while." Tyler kept walking past him to the kitchen. "Do you want a beer?"

"No, thanks." I hadn't had a drink in ten weeks and I didn't even miss it.

Jessica was in the kitchen, heating up food in the microwave. It was weird to me that she lived there with her boyfriend and his three younger brothers. I had never been to her parents' house, but I knew she had grown up with a lot of money, and this was no spacious colonial in the suburbs. The house was small and dark and hot and run-down, but truthfully she seemed the happiest she'd been since I'd met her. Riley came in from the patio and kissed the back of her head, looking at her like he thought she was the most beautiful creature the world had ever created.

"Want some?" she asked me, dishing up rice and vegetables onto four plates.

"I'm good."

She switched out plates in the microwave and said, "Then let's go in the other room. I want to talk to you alone." She touched Riley's elbow. "Can you put these in for the boys?"

"Got it."

I followed her back into the living room, and she sat on the floor by the coffee table. "Sit. I want to talk to you about what the hell is going on."

I did want to tell her. I wanted to get the awful truth out and ask her what I was supposed to do about Nathan. But I couldn't. All I could tell her was a small portion of the truth. I looked nervously at the sleeping cousin. "He can hear us. I feel weird talking in front of him."

"He's totally out. He just got out after five months in jail and he's been sleeping for two days."

"Jail?" I whispered, a little horrified. "For what?" How could she say that so casually, like it was no big deal?

She scooped rice into her mouth. "Fuck me, that is so good." She closed her eyes and chewed. "I'm going to have to step up the workouts, but I think carbs are worth it."

I didn't say anything, sitting down on the floor next to her, drawing my knees up to my chest. I was wearing a sloppy T-shirt, and I dragged it over my bare knees, making a tent, cocooning myself.

"Okay, so what is going on? Seriously. You won't drink, you won't go out. You've lost weight. You don't answer my texts. You're even dressing differently. I'm totally worried about you."

I was worried about me, too. I couldn't seem to drag myself out of the anxiety that had been following me around. "I'm moving out of the house as soon as I find a new place to live."

"*What?* Why the hell would you do that?"

Tears came to my eyes before I could stop them. "I just have to. I need to stop drinking."

"But, it's not like Rory is a big drinker. And I'm sure Kylie would respect it if you said you wanted to chill with the alcohol." She looked hurt. "We would never pressure you to party, God, that's so not us."

"I know." It made me feel even worse. "It's just I feel like I need to be alone for a while. I was even thinking about moving home and being a commuter. It's not that far to my parents', only like a forty-five-minute drive to class."

"You would seriously want to move home? That just blows my mind." Jessica stared hard at me, tucking her blond hair behind her ear. "Besides, this is going to leave Rory and Kylie with a whole house to pay for since we've both bailed on them. I feel really bad about doing that."

So did I. But I felt worse about screwing Kylie's boyfriend. What would I do when Nathan came over to hang out? I couldn't play it cool, like nothing had happened. I wasn't drawn that way. "Didn't Tyler say he wouldn't mind moving in with Rory?"

"Yeah, but I don't know if he can actually afford it." Jessica frowned, picking up her fork. "I guess I can ask him. I guess maybe Nathan could move in there, too, with Kylie. Bill is moving into the engineering frat house."

I dropped my knees, alarmed. That was not what I wanted to happen. I didn't want Kylie to become even more dependent and more in love with Nathan.

"This is so weird," she said. "This is totally not what we planned. It's like a complete roommate shuffle. What happened?"

Rory fell in love with Tyler. Jessica fell in love with Riley. I blacked out and had sex with Nathan.

Not exactly the same happy ending for me. I wanted to tell her so desperately I swallowed hard and clamped my mouth shut. Telling her would only mean she would have to keep a secret from Kylie. From Riley, too. Telling Kylie would only hurt her to appease my guilt.

I couldn't do it.

Shrugging, I said, "Things change."

"Robin."

"What?"

"If you got attacked or something, you would tell me, right? You know you can tell me." She reached out and touched my arm, expression filled with concern.

And it went from bad to worse. Now she thought I was a victim. I nodded. "I would tell you. It's nothing like that, I swear."

"Because it seems like you started acting strange after the party at the Shit Shack. Something is obviously wrong. So if that Aaron guy did something to you, tell me."

"No, he didn't." I shook my head emphatically. Aaron had just been a guy I had danced with, flirted with, kissed. Before he ditched me and somehow I ended up going home with Nathan.

"Did something freaky happen? Did you do something you regret, like anal?"

Not that I was aware of. I couldn't prevent a shudder. "No. No anal." Though I did do something I regretted, more than anything else I'd ever done. The person who said that life was too short for regrets clearly had never done something super shitty.

"Jessica!" Jayden called her name from the kitchen. "Can you come here?"

"Yeah, I'll be right there, buddy." She set down her fork. "Be right back."

Jayden was eighteen, but he had Down syndrome, and I knew that Rory and Jessica both cut him a lot of slack. If he asked for attention, they gave it to him, and I was totally grateful for the interruption. I wasn't sure how much longer I could lie to direct questions.

As Jessica went into the kitchen, the guy on the couch suddenly coughed. I turned and saw dark eyes staring at me. He had rolled onto his back and was sitting up on the arm roll, his hair sticking up in front. My palms got clammy, and I stared back, horrified.

Not only was he completely and totally hot, he had obviously been awake for more than thirty seconds. He looked way too alert to have just opened his eyes.

"Uh, hi. I'm Robin," I said, my hands starting to shake. What had we said? Nothing incriminating, I didn't think. I hadn't admitted anything. Though I had said "anal" out loud and that was awkward enough. All those nasty jokes about prison popped into my head and my cheeks burned.

His expression was inscrutable, but he nodded. "Phoenix."

"Nice to meet you," I said, because that's what you say even if there was zero truth to it. It wasn't nice to meet him. He was a criminal and I was a lying cheat, and I was way too preoccupied with my own self-hatred to have anything interesting to say to him.

"Yeah. Sure." He sounded about as enthusiastic as I felt.

Agitated, I sat down on the coffee table next to the couch, wiping my hands on my denim shorts. "Sorry if we woke you up."

He shrugged. "No big deal."

I wasn't sure what to say after that. He wasn't wearing a shirt, and like his cousins, he had tattoos covering his chest and arms. The one that caught my attention was the bleeding heart. It looked severed in two, the blood draining down his flesh toward his abdomen. It was beautiful and creepy and bold. Was it a metaphor? It seemed a little poetic for the average guy, but something about his steady stare suggested he was no ordinary guy. His dark hair stuck up then fell over one eye, so it felt like he had an extra advantage, that he could watch me from behind that cascade of hair.

Jessica hadn't told me why he had been in jail, and I decided

I really didn't want to know. Phoenix was trouble and trouble was exactly what I was trying to avoid.

"I'm not a big fan of anal either," he said.

Giving or receiving? I couldn't tell if he was making fun of me. He didn't seem to be trying to lighten the mood with a joke for my benefit since he still looked stone-faced. It made me super uncomfortable.

"We thought you were asleep."

"What difference does it make? You didn't confess to a crime."

Thank God. "I don't like just anyone hearing my personal business. You don't even know me."

"You're right, I don't." He threw back the blanket that had been covering him below the waist and he stood up. He was in his underwear, black boxer briefs that clung to his thighs. "Robin." He added my name at the end like it was an accusation.

His body was lean and wiry, yet muscular. He looked like he worked out constantly but had been born with a raging high metabolism, so he would never be bulky. Every muscle was obvious, the V of his hips so defined it made my mouth thick with saliva in a totally inappropriate way for the situation. He bent over and picked up a pair of shorts off the floor, stepping into them and drawing them up. But he left them partially unzipped and the belt clanked against his thighs as he moved out of the living room and down the hall into the bathroom without another word to me.

I watched him, unnerved. There was something hard about him, mysterious. His name suited him, unusual and intriguing. Annoyed with myself, I went into the kitchen, where Jessica was clearly laying out the situation for Tyler.

"So what are we going to do? Kylie and I were supposed to share, and Rory and Robin each had their own room, but now there's an empty room completely."

"Can you guys just break the lease?" Riley asked. "I mean, what difference does it make? Everyone can move out."

"My dad and Rory's dad are the ones who signed the lease. I don't think either one of us needs to piss our dads off any more."

Riley frowned. "No. That's no good." He looked at me. "I guess you should find a replacement, since you're the one moving out."

Hovering in the doorway, I crossed my arms over my chest, miserable. "I'll just move home and I'll pay my portion of the rent. I can cover it with my paychecks from waitressing."

I was trying to be fair. To not stick them with either a bigger rent or with a roommate they didn't know and may not get along with, but Jessica's eyes narrowed in suspicion.

"Wait a minute. So you'd rather live at home with your parents who are, like, sixty years old, and your ancient, evil-eye-giving grandmother, while paying rent on a place you don't live in, than room with Kylie and Rory? Okay, I call bullshit. What the fuck is going on?"

When she put it like that, it did sound insane. "Nothing is going on. I just need time to . . . reevaluate."

But Jessica was tenacious. "There is something going on and you need to tell me what it is."

Phoenix strolled into the kitchen, scratching his chest, and went to the fridge. "I think if she wanted to tell you she would have already," he commented.

That about summed it up.

"And who asked you?" Jessica said, whirling to glare at him as she yanked Jayden's empty plate out from in front of him and started scrubbing it aggressively in the sink.

"Just an observation."

"Well, mind your own business."

"I think Robin would probably say the same to you."

They stared at each other, and I felt the tension between them. Phoenix being in the house obviously upset the balance of Jessica being house princess. She was a strong personality, and she enjoyed being the only girl in the house, the one in charge. Somehow Phoenix was challenging her, and it was obvious to Riley, too. He held up his hand.

"Alright, chill out. Both of you."

"Please don't fight because of me," I pleaded, feeling even more horrible with each passing second. "Just please don't." And to my horror, I started crying, tears welling up and rushing out of both eyes silently.

Everyone looked at me in shock, and no one seemed to have a clue what to say. I wasn't known for being particularly emotional. Fortunately, Easton intervened. "Hey, aren't you supposed to draw me?" He tapped the canvas Tyler had propped on the floor next to the table. "When are you doing that?"

"Now," I said, taking an empty seat next to him and wiping my face, concentrating on drawing my breath in and out, slowly, evenly. "I just need some space."

That was definitely a metaphor.

Jessica went into the other room, clearly agitated, and Riley followed her, murmuring in a low voice. Tyler encouraged Jayden to go outside and shoot hoops with him. It left me at the table, methodically squeezing my oils into my paint tray, Easton across from me, bouncing up and down on his chair, and Phoenix leaning on the counter eating rice straight out of the container.

He was watching us, but I ignored him. Yellow, pink, blue. Squeeze, squeeze, squeeze. If I just focused on one thing at a time, I could function.

And it actually felt good to have my brush in my hand, the smell of the acrylics familiar and soothing. I felt calmer.

There was a knock at the back door, and Easton jumped. "Who is that?"

"It's probably my girlfriend," Phoenix said. "Or my ex-girlfriend, if this conversation doesn't go well. She's supposed to come over."

So of course the gorgeous bad boy had a girlfriend, despite his incarceration.

Phoenix opened the back door, and I have to admit, I tried to pretend I was busy working, paintbrush in my hand as I used a bold magenta to do the outline of Easton's head. But I snuck a glance up at the girl who walked into the kitchen and I tried not to be judgmental. She looked hard. Older than she probably was. Bad dye job, turning naturally brown hair bleach blond, drying out the texture. Lots of eyeliner. Bad skin. Her jeans were too tight in the waist and too big in the butt. Not the prettiest girl I've ever seen but maybe she was super sweet. And who was I to judge?

"Hey," she said, and tried to kiss Phoenix.

He shifted out of the way and rejected her effort. "Why didn't you come see me when I was locked up?" he demanded with no other greeting. "Not once. I didn't know what the fuck was going on, Angel."

Oh, God, seriously? Her name was Angel? I threw up a little in my mouth. I couldn't think of a name less suited to a girl who looked like she could beat the shit out of me if I looked at her wrong. Carefully, I set down my paintbrush and pushed back my chair. Clearly this was a private conversation, and I had enough drama of my own. I didn't want to be involved in someone else's.

"Who are you?" she asked angrily, shooting me a glare as the noisy scraping sound of the chair made her aware of my presence.

"I'm just going in the other room," I said carefully, not wanting to go a round with her. I had no doubt I would lose, especially in my current emotional state. Easton obviously felt the same way. He bolted into the living room without a word.

"Good," Angel said, playing with the ring in her nose.

"She doesn't have to leave," Phoenix said, gesturing for me to stay. "This is only going to take a minute. So what did you want to tell me, Angel?" He crossed his arms and leaned on the kitchen counter.

I stood up anyway, despite his words.

"I'm pregnant."

I couldn't prevent a gasp from leaving my mouth. Yeah, I should have left the room. But Phoenix didn't react at all. His face never revealed any surprise, and the only movement he made was to flick his eyes over her flat stomach.

"You don't look six months pregnant to me."

"I'm not. I'm only two."

He'd been in prison more than five months. Jessica had said that. I knew that. What I didn't know was why I cared one way or the other about it being his baby, but I felt horrified for him that he'd been cheated on, and a little bit of relief that he wasn't the father.

"Then I don't need to know that." Phoenix went and opened the door. "Bye, Angel."

"Don't you even want to know what happened?" She looked disappointed. "Who the father is?"

"No. All I wanted was to know for sure that we're broken up, and we clearly are, so good luck. Lose my number."

"You're an asshole," she said.

I wasn't sure how he qualified as the jerk in this situation, but I kept my eyes on the canvas as she stomped out the back door, and he slammed it loudly behind her.

"Well, now I guess we're even," he said.

I glanced up, curious to see if he was going to rage or look upset. But he didn't. He looked . . . neutral. "Even how?" I asked.

"Now we both know each other's personal business."

I finished my brushstroke. "True. And I'm going to stay out of it, like you did with me." I just wanted to paint, to lose myself in the wet sound of sliding paint.

He came over and looked down at my canvas. "You don't need Easton here to paint? You're doing it from memory?"

"Yes."

"Cool."

He watched me for a minute, and I didn't actually mind. I didn't need quiet or solitude to paint pop art, and it felt good to lose myself in the narrow focus of creating lines on canvas. But while I wanted to respect his privacy, I also knew that it had to have hurt him that his girlfriend hadn't visited him in prison, that she had cheated on him. I also felt guilty that I was a cheater, that if it ever came out, I would be the one causing pain. I hated that.

"I'm sorry," I told him, glancing up, hoping he would understand.

"For what?"

I didn't want to be specific. I didn't think he would appreciate that. "For what I heard. For what you heard."

"That you heard it? Or because it happened?"

"Both. But mostly that it happened. It hurts, I know. And I'm sorry."

Phoenix shrugged. "I'll live. I've survived worse."

I wanted to say that she wasn't good enough for him anyway, that she was a liar and a cheat and a shitty girlfriend who didn't deserve him, but did I really know that? And if I was no better than her, did I have any right to say anything?

"Sometimes we do stupid things." Very stupid things. Sometimes we needed forgiveness.

"Yeah. Some of us more than others." Phoenix pulled out a chair and sat down across from me. "I've never painted before. I sketch. It must be hard to get the subtlety of the lines and the shading in paint."

"You sketch?" I asked, amazed, then not sure why.

He nodded. "And I do tattoos. I guess the difference is with oil paint you layer on top, right? With a tattoo you do a little, but mostly it's about precision and shading."

"Do you have pictures of your work?" I asked, curious to see it. The idea of tattooing someone with a needle scared me. There was no retracting a mistake.

Sort of like life.

"Nah. But I did the original design for my cousins' arm tat, the one they all have, and I did Tyler's dragon on his leg."

"Cool. That dragon is beautiful."

"Thanks." He drummed his fingers on the table. "We're a fucked-up family, you know. We haven't always gotten along, depending on whose mom was hooking the other on what drugs."

"Why aren't you living with your mom?" I finished the outline of Easton and started shading in his strong features. Even in the brilliance of yellow and magenta, I wanted to capture the deep sensitivity of his eyes.

"I don't know where she is. She didn't leave a forwarding address."

So not only had his girlfriend cheated on him when he was in jail, his mom disappeared and neglected to tell him? I wasn't sure I could be so casual about it. In fact, I knew I couldn't. My parents were all about family. They loved me and my older brothers in a way that was almost smothering, and I was grateful for it. "Oh my God, I'm sorry."

He shrugged. "She'll turn up eventually. But Riley and Tyler are being cool and letting me stay here."

I wasn't sure what to say. "Family seems important to them."

Those fingers increased their rhythm, but the rest of him stayed completely still. The only movement seemed to come from those anxious fingers and the intensity of his stare as his eyes raked both over me and the canvas. I was never still. My mom had always commented on that. I fidgeted and shifted and couldn't stay in a chair longer than ten minutes without creating a reason to get up for a task before sitting down again. I struggled to sit through movies and I hopped up and down off barstools, going out on the dance floor and outside to smoke cigarettes, which I didn't even like. Even now I was bouncing my knee up and down rapidly and chewing hard on a piece of gum. His immobility fascinated me.

Which may explain why I said, "Do you want to paint? I have another canvas and brush."

Again, there was no reaction. I wondered what it would take to draw emotion out of him. "Nah, I don't want to waste your supplies."

"It's a cheap canvas. It was only five bucks."

But he just shook his head. Then a second later he asked me, "Do you have a boyfriend?"

"What?" I almost dropped my paintbrush. "No. Why?"

His phone slid across the table toward me. "Then give me your number."

"Why?" I said again, which was a totally moronic thing to say. But I didn't get any vibe he even liked me, let alone was interested in me.

For the first time, I saw the glimmer of a smile on his face. The corner of his mouth lifted slightly before he controlled it again. "Why do you think?"

For a split second, I felt like myself, and I said the first thing that popped into my head. "So you can send me honey badger videos?" I joked, because it seemed like a safer response. He was just out of prison, and he had just broken up with his girlfriend ten minutes earlier. So not a good idea to get involved with him. I wasn't up for dating anyone, let alone him.

"Yes. And kitten memes."

"Well, in that case." I took his phone because I wasn't exactly sure how to say no. It seemed super rude, and I doubted he was actually going to ask me out. He would probably send me a typical guy text of "hi" or "what's up?" and I could say "hi" back or "nothing" and we'd be done with it. Guys put no effort at all into communication or pursuing a girl. If you didn't go into a huge, long text of explanation of what you were doing and dug deep into their text to get an adequate response back, the conversation just died. A big old waste of time, that's what most texting with guys was.

So I typed my number into his phone with my name. It was an old smartphone, with a cracked screen, like he had dropped it on the pavement. I set it back on the table.

Tyler came back into the kitchen and looked over my shoulder at my work. "Hey, that's cool so far. You got Easton's nose just right."

Out of the corner of my eye, I saw Phoenix palm his phone and put it back into his pocket, tossing back his hair. Then he just stood up and left.

My phone buzzed in my own pocket as Tyler went to the fridge and started rummaging around. I pulled it out and saw it was a text from a number I didn't recognize. When I opened it, there was a honey badger video. At your request was the message.

I smiled for the first time in what felt like weeks.

Way better than writing "hi."

CHAPTER TWO

PHOENIX

WHEN I WAS IN THIRD GRADE, I REALIZED TWO THINGS: THAT the doctors thought something was wrong with me, and that my mother loved drugs more than she loved me.

Because while the doctors kept asking me questions and taking scans of my brain and giving my mother prescriptions for me to take, I never swallowed a single one of those pills. She would take me to the pharmacy, collect the pills, then sell them to a guy behind the gas station who smelled like my grandmother's basement. Then she would use that money to buy little plastic bags from a different guy, the one I thought looked like a Ninja Turtle because he always wore a bandana around his forehead. Then those bags would open and the needle would come out and she would lie on the couch for hours and hours, scratching her arm and drooling, eyes unfocused.

When she was like that, I could do whatever I wanted, and I didn't really mind that she was checked out, not exactly. I could watch TV and drink chocolate syrup out of the bottle and go play down the street until way after dark and she wouldn't notice any of it and there was a cool sense of freedom.

But I didn't like it when she would forget to buy groceries or make me lie to the doctors and say that even though I took all the pills the way I was supposed to, I still felt angry, I still couldn't concentrate. Because it wasn't true. I hadn't taken those pills, and I didn't feel angry.

It wasn't until later that I figured out that my meds had a black market value as appetite suppressants and she could exchange them for heroin.

At eight, I just knew there was something wrong with both of us because I was supposed to have the drugs but she was the one who couldn't go a day without them.

So I shouldn't have been surprised that she had disappeared during my stint in jail, but I was. I kept waiting for the day when she actually gave a shit about me, and she kept proving over and over that she didn't.

It wouldn't have mattered so much except that all my stuff was at her apartment, and the landlord had cleaned it out when she ditched on the rent. There was no question in my mind that she hadn't bothered to pack up my clothes and the miscellaneous crap from twenty years to take with her. An old yearbook, the only one I'd ever had the money to buy, with the inscription from Heather Newcomb of "Stay Sweet, Phoenix," which I had thumbed my finger over a thousand times, wondering what it meant. A Little League trophy for Best Pitcher. A watch my grandmother gave me. Nothing of value. Stupid stuff, but *mine*. All I had. Gone.

Wearing nothing but a pair of shorts I had borrowed from

Tyler, I texted the girl painting in the kitchen, Robin. I shouldn't, I knew that. She was way out of my league, I knew that, too. Girls like her didn't look twice at guys who didn't even own the shirt on their back. Or, in my case, the shorts on my ass. But for whatever reason—good manners would be my guess—she had given me her number and I was going to use it, because I needed a distraction. Someone to talk to about nothing.

I thought maybe she did, too. There was something . . . bruised about the way she looked. She kept her head down when talking to Jessica and held her arms across her chest a lot. Jessica, who was fucking bossy in my opinion, kept poking at her, and Robin didn't protest, but she didn't answer either. Not really.

There was something about the way she had sat in the living room while she thought I was asleep and hugged her knees to herself, stretching out her shirt to cover them, that made me feel just a little bit sorry for her. I'm a sucker for a sad girl, I can't help it. It's fucked-up, but it is what it is. Maybe because for once I feel like I actually have something to offer. Understanding, at least. There's a difference between sad and depressed, though, and even I know not to go there with a chick who is clinical, but I knew Robin wasn't because of the way her face changed when she started painting.

It was like her shoulders dropped and her forehead smoothed out. She was content with that brush in her hand, or at least not miserable. Pretty, too. She had a tiny nose and cherry red lips and dark hair that spilled over her shoulders and made me want to bury my face in it.

So I got her number and then she left the house and I texted her and she answered me twice and then nothing. That was that.

College Girl wasn't going to play with me, and hell, who could blame her? It had been an impulsive long shot. Disappointing, but I was used to that feeling.

Shoving the phone back in my pocket, I went into the kitchen to see if I could borrow Riley's car. I needed to see about getting a job, as fun as that sounded. When I came into the room, conversation between Jessica and Riley came to a stop, making it pretty freakin' obvious they were talking about me. I didn't quite understand the new dynamics in my cousins' house. When I had gone into jail, my aunt Dawn had still been alive, and everyone here walked on eggshells around her. Now she was dead, and Riley's girlfriend was in the house, and she was possessive and territorial, it seemed. She had done some home improvement shit like pulling up the nasty carpet and putting cookies in the cookie jar and washing dishes.

Weird. That's what it was. Disorienting. I think maybe she was what you call maternal, but I had such little experience with the concept I couldn't exactly be sure. All I know is that she was a bitch to me and I wasn't so crazy about her myself.

"What's up?" I asked, casual. Friendly. I could kiss ass and be nice. No one had to let me stay there, and Riley and Tyler were being cool about it, so I had to watch what I said. Besides, they were the only family I had, and I didn't want to lose them.

"You know that Riley just got custody of Easton, right?" Jessica asked, twirling her blond hair around one finger and looking nervous.

I nodded. I had been glad to hear it. The system would chew that kid up and spit him out. I knew Riley had worked hard to get custody and that his girlfriend, even though she and I rubbed each other the wrong way, clearly wanted the best for Easton and Jayden, too. I'd seen the family photos she'd hung in the hallway, like families who weren't fucked-up did, and I personally appreciated her no smoking in the house rule.

"Well, it's not out of the realm of possibility that a social worker could drop by at any time unannounced. And Tyler is already living here when he really shouldn't be."

That was all she said, clearly waiting for me to volunteer the conclusion.

So I did. No sense in beating around the bush. "So having two convicted felons in the house is maybe one too many?"

She nodded, biting her lip.

Riley looked pained. "Look, bro, you know you can stay here until you get a job and a place, but you probably can't stay here forever, that's all we're saying. I can't lose custody of Easton, not now."

"I understand." I did. I also understood that Easton was lucky, despite his shithole parents. He had his brothers.

Their bond was a steel cable. Mine with them was more like cooked spaghetti. We were family. They cared. They would help. But the loyalty wasn't the same, and I was jealous of that, I admit it. I felt alone.

My mom had figured out birth control after me, unlike my aunt. My mom made a point of telling me that once was enough for her and she wasn't taking any chances of making that mistake twice, unlike Aunt Dawn, who got drunk and forgot condoms existed.

So it was just me.

"I'm going to see about getting a job today, actually. Can I borrow your car for an hour?" I didn't have anywhere to go. No friends I trusted enough to crash with. But I could always go to the shelter if I had to. I didn't want to be responsible for Easton ending up in foster care. He was a cool kid. In fact, he kind of reminded me of myself at that age. And hey, I was a cool kid, right? Quiet, weird, prone to random outbursts, but whatever. I was comfortable in my own skin now, which was good, because it was about all I owned.

"Sure," Riley said, fumbling in his pocket for the keys, looking guilty.

It was obvious he felt bad that he was asking me to go, but I didn't blame him, and the fact that he had guilt about it gave me a warm fucking fuzzy, I'm not going to lie.

"Aren't you going to eat before you go?" Jessica asked. "There's still some leftover Chinese food. I can heat it for you."

I stared at her for a second, not sure what her angle was. Because there had to be an angle. There always was. "I'm okay, thanks." I couldn't imagine standing there while a chick heated up food for me. It was just weird.

But I did gesture to the painting that was propped up on the table against the wall, drying. Robin had managed to paint a graphic of Easton in, like, forty-five minutes. It was just a basic silhouette, but it did look like him, and there was something about the bright pink and yellow that smacked you over the head, but in a good way. "Your friend has talent."

"Yes, she does. She did that other piece, too, just for fun. We wanted to make it more . . . cheerful in the house."

Riley laughed. "That's a polite way of saying it was a dump here, babe. It's true, isn't it, Phoenix? Our mothers did not excel at housekeeping."

That actually made me cough up a rusty laugh. I hadn't laughed much lately. "That is true, cuz. My mom isn't much for decorating either." I actually thought that her reaction to an art piece that spelled out YUM in tiny pieces of old candy wrappers would be to rip it off the wall and toss it in the trash disdainfully. She didn't like the idea that anyone could be happy or enjoying something. "What does Robin like?" I asked, but it was too obvious.

Two sets of eyebrows shot up, and Jessica's mouth fell open. "What? Why?"

"Never mind." I shrugged. It didn't matter anyway. If she hadn't answered me in an hour she wasn't going to.

Jobless, soon to be homeless, with a criminal record and an ex-girlfriend who had stuck me with her cell phone bill before I went to jail, the last thing I needed to be fucking around with was a rich girl who looked like she might cry if I pinched her. Not that I would. Pinch her, I mean. It's just an expression. She just seemed fragile or something, and it would be stupid. A huge, dumb-ass, fucking idiotic, stupid idea to get involved with her in anyway.

So how come I couldn't seem to get the image of her bent over that canvas, pursing her plump lips in concentration, out of my head?

Because I was the guy who always ran headfirst into danger, and I usually wound up blacked out and bleeding, on the ground.

But in this case it wouldn't matter because she wasn't going to answer.

Riley narrowed his eyes. "How's Angel?" he asked.

"Pregnant. And no, it isn't mine. She says she's only two months along." I had to admit, my heart had almost stopped for a second when she'd made her announcement. But then I had known immediately it couldn't be mine because she wasn't showing at all, and yeah, I was relieved. Because what kind of father would I be? I'd never even touched a baby, and I didn't know jack about taking care of anything besides my mom's loser boyfriends when they outstayed their welcome.

"I guess that's good and bad. Sorry, man."

I shrugged again. It hurt more when she didn't see me in jail. It hurt that I had only had one visitor in five months and that had been Tyler, because he'd been there, done that. He knew it sucked.

Feeling suddenly angry, I concentrated on my breathing, slowing it down, drawing it in and out steadily. I made sure my entire body was still, that nothing twitched or shook or jiggled. It was a trick I learned a long time ago, that if I quieted my body, I could quiet my mind and the anger would escape like air from a balloon instead of a firework shooting off.

"It's no big deal," I said, which was a lie, and Riley knew it was a lie.

"I'm going in the basement to work out," he said. "You want to come down and hit the bag with me?"

"I thought you were going on a beer run," Jessica said, straightening the napkin holder on the counter, stuffed with paper napkins with cherries printed on them. Cherries? For fucking real?

Riley gave her a look. "I changed my mind."

Of course he had. He knew. "Sure," I said. "Then I'll see about a job afterward if you don't mind me borrowing the car."

"Not at all. Come on, let's break a sweat."

"Sounds hot," Jessica said. "Can I watch?"

"You can't handle all the testosterone we'll be displaying," he told her, giving her a teasing pat on her ass.

"Oh, I can handle anything you've got," she said, and her expression wasn't subtle.

Neither was the flare of Riley's nostrils. "Later, babe, later."

I walked out of the room, heading for the basement door. I needed to punch something.

My phone vibrated in my pocket.

It was Robin.

It didn't even matter what she wrote. The smiley face at the end was enough to have me unclenching my fists.

Not good. Or damn good, depending on how I looked at it.

But just to be sure and in control, instead of answering, I slammed my fist into Riley's boxing bag at the bottom of the stairs and felt the adrenaline rush through me.

Only drug I've ever needed. Pain.

CHAPTER THREE

ROBIN

"THANKS FOR DOING THAT," TYLER SAID TO ME AS HE DROVE me home. "You know, it's cool for Easton to feel kinda special."

"Sure. I was happy to do it." I felt my phone vibrate in my lap, and I pulled it out, seeing it was another text from Phoenix. I hadn't saved him as a contact yet but I knew it was him. I had sent him a kitten pic back in response to his honey badger video. Just a fluffy white kitten with a black mane of fur around its face. It was the first kitten I found when I did an online search and it didn't actually say anything. It was just the kitten drinking from a tall glass of milk.

I opened the text. It said, Is this you? I see the resemblance.

Furry? I tapped back.

Milk drinker.

Feeling like I might smile when I shouldn't, I shoved the phone back in my pocket without responding. But I did ask Tyler, "What's the deal with your cousin?"

"What do you mean?"

"Is he . . . I don't know . . . nice?" That wasn't what I wanted to ask exactly but I didn't know how to really express myself.

But something about what I said seemed to tip Tyler off. He turned and glanced at me. "Oh, no. No, no, and no. You are not allowed to be interested in my cousin."

"Why?" I asked, stung by his vehemence. "Not that I am, but I mean, I know I'm, like, a total mess and I'm not exactly hot these days but . . ." I stopped speaking, appalled by what was coming out of my mouth. And because there was no "but." I could no longer claim to be a fun party girl, or a loyal friend, or someone with a healthy dose of self-respect and confidence. I had none of those things anymore.

Nor did I bother doing my nails or getting a bikini wax or wearing anything other than saggy jean shorts and huge T-shirts anymore either.

"Robin, that is not what I meant, Christ." Tyler shook his head. "I meant you are way too nice of a girl to be getting involved with him. Phoenix, well, he has problems."

Didn't we all.

"What kind of problems?"

"Big ones. He just . . . it's just . . ." Tyler shook his head. "Just don't go there with him, seriously. You'll regret it."

"But he's your cousin," I said, my phone vibrating again to remind me I hadn't answered Phoenix's text. "And I'm not going anywhere. I was just asking about him."

"I care about Phoenix. I do. But he's not easy to get close to."

"What do you think about his girlfriend? Angel?" I knew I should have dropped the subject, but I couldn't seem to help it. I was morbidly curious.

"I'd never even met her before tonight. But he usually picks head cases. Like his mother. Freud would have something to say about that."

"Freud was full of shit," I said, because I was annoyed with the whole conversation. I didn't want to be talked out of feeling a little twinge of pleasure at the fact that Phoenix had shown interest in me. Whether it was just to be friends, or something more, was irrelevant. I just wanted someone to look at me, in all my pale, non-drinking glory, and think I was someone they wanted to talk to. That's all.

"You know you're going to have to move into the house you all rented," Tyler said, totally changing the subject. "Unless you're mad at Rory or Kylie, there is no reason you can't. So either clear the air or drop the whole thing."

I bit my fingernail, and stared out the car window as we pulled into the driveway of the house we had rented for the school year. "I'm not mad at anyone." Except myself.

"Then why do you want to move out?" Tyler parked the car and stared at me. "Seriously."

"I don't know," I lied. It wasn't even a lie of effort. It was just a lame shrug off.

But Tyler didn't let it go. "It's because of Kylie, isn't it?" he asked.

Startled, I turned to him, my heart rate kicking up a notch. "What do you mean?"

"Look, Robin, I saw you and Nathan making out at the Shit Shack at that party that night, the one where Riley got into it with the frat dude. You were in his car and you were kissing and I saw it."

Mortification caused a blush to stain my cheeks. I wasn't sure what to say. "I don't remember that," I told him honestly. "I blacked out that night."

"But you know you did, don't you?" Tyler held out his hand. "Look, I haven't said anything to anyone, not even Rory, so just be honest with me."

"Please don't," I begged him, terrified he would tell the truth and Kylie would be devastated and everyone would hate me. "I would never do that sober, I would never hurt Kylie. I feel *awful* about it. It's the worst thing I've ever done, and that's why I can't live there. I can't even look at Kylie without thinking I am the worst sort of friend ever."

Tyler drummed his fingers on the wheel, taking one last drag of his cigarette before tossing it out the open window. "It was just that one time, right?" he asked.

"Yes." I nodded vehemently. "It was vodka, plain and simple. It will never happen ever again."

"And that's why you haven't been drinking."

"Exactly." I looked at the house, tears welling up in my eyes. "I just can't act like nothing happened . . ."

"But you have to," Tyler told me. "You have to try to be normal or it's all going to come puking out and then Kylie will just be hurt. You know Jess. She's like a dog with a freaking bone. She won't let this go. So the best thing to do is to stay in the house like you planned. That way you won't fuck Kylie over twice by sticking her with extra rent, too."

"I was going to pay the rent," I protested weakly, stung by his use of the phrase "fuck Kylie over." It was the truth, the unintentional truth, and it was horrible.

"Robin." Tyler's voice softened. "We all make mistakes. Don't make another one."

"This wasn't a small mistake." I dug my fingernails into my thighs, wanting the distraction so I wouldn't cry.

"Neither was me breaking up with Rory on Christmas." He gave me a smile. "I mean, that was a *huge* mistake."

I gave a watery laugh. "That wasn't your finest moment, I'll admit that."

"I know you think you're doing the right thing for Kylie, but seriously, the right thing is to stick to the plan."

I wasn't sure what I was going to do anymore, but I did appreciate that he wasn't screaming at me that I was a drunken slut. "Thanks, Tyler."

When I got out of the car, I paused on the big, wooden front porch and watched him back out and pull away. Sitting on the steps, I let the hot sun seep into my skin, and I twisted my hair up into a messy bun that I tied off with my own hair. Then I pulled out my phone and answered Phoenix, unable to resist, bad idea or not.

There was too much time in my own head, too many minutes to turn around and around what I had done and why and what it said about me. Too much time to feel the guilt weaving its way into the fabric of me, so that if I tried to tug it out it would unravel all of me.

The urge to talk to someone who was a total stranger, who knew nothing about me, was irresistible.

Milk does a body good. ☺

Then I immediately thought maybe that was too flirty. So I added a second text.

What are you doing?

Which then seemed like a stupid question to ask. What was he going to say? Nothing. And would he think that was suggestive or something? And why did I care?

It seemed like I didn't remember the rules anymore, the normal way to talk to a guy without parties and booze and hookups. Or maybe it was just I didn't know how to talk to a guy like Phoenix.

It was ten minutes before he responded. I wasn't doing anything, just lolling in the sun, cradling my phone and trying to work up ambition to take a shower.

When he did respond, it surprised me.

Working out. Thinking about you.

A shiver ran through me. There was no mistaking that message.

Thinking what?

That I want to see you. Busy tonight? Want to hang out?

There was no question that I wanted to. But should I?

I glanced out at the street, at the cars lining up and down Ludlow Avenue. We had the second and third floors of an old house, and I did like the neighborhood. But it was lonely living in the house solo for the summer, and I had no plans for the night. I could go inside and watch a movie by myself or I could watch a movie with someone else. Someone who just might understand what it felt like to be lonely.

Sure. Want to come over? Watch a movie?

I didn't think he had any money and I didn't have any ambition to change my clothes. I didn't want to go *out* out. I didn't want it to feel like a date, and I didn't want there to be alcohol around. I just wanted to feel comfortable again.

He sent me a picture back. It was a cat, leaping through the air. THIS, it said.

I laughed. He had a quiet sense of humor that I liked. Is that yes?

Yes. Address? I'll take the bus.

I can pick you up.

Maybe that sounded a little pathetic or overeager, but I was exhausted with the games I had been playing with guys since I had turned thirteen and sprouted breasts. I was tired, hot, and I wanted company, and he was offering it, so why I wait an hour and a half for him to take the bus when I could pick him up? The key to successful distraction was to not have time to talk yourself out of taking the distraction.

So while I felt a reflexive twinge that I shouldn't make it easy for Phoenix, I got over it.

You have a car?

Yes.

K. Meet me at the corner of Riley's street in the CVS parking lot in an hour.

He wanted me to pick him up at the drugstore? So he clearly didn't want anyone to know he was going to be with me. My first instinct was to be insulted, but then I thought about what Tyler had said to me about Phoenix and staying away from him. It didn't make any sense for me to piss off the one person who knew the truth about Nathan, so I probably shouldn't be seen with Phoenix anyway. It felt weird that after worrying all summer that someone would find out, I now knew that Tyler had known the whole time.

It made the shame feel fresh and throbbing.

I wanted to run away from it.

Ok. See you then.

With forty-five minutes to kill, I flipped through a magazine but it bored me and I wound up staring into space again, biting my fingernail as my thoughts absorbed the time. Glancing at my phone, I decided I should leave or I'd be late. Not bothering to change or even put on lip gloss, I walked down the driveway to my car. I wasn't going to primp for him. This was it. Me. Sober. Hanging on by a thread.

When I pulled into the parking lot at the drugstore, he was leaning against the wall, waiting, one foot back on the stucco. His hair was in his eyes again, and he was wearing a black T-shirt and the cargo shorts he had pulled on earlier, when I had been cataloguing his tattoos. I noticed now there was another one on the back of his calf, but I couldn't tell what it was. He wasn't my type at all. I was usually into guys who had a lot of bulk, who made me feel petite and feminine next to them, and who were loud and chatty, the communications and marketing majors.

Phoenix looked dangerous. An elderly woman gave him a wide berth when she shuffled from her car to the store, eyeing him with suspicion. Unlike his cousins, though, he didn't have any accessories, no chains, no studded bracelets. Riley and Tyler would make the metal detector at the airport lose its shit, they were always that covered in hardware. But Phoenix was bare except for his tattoos.

There was something beautiful about him. I knew I shouldn't think of a guy in those terms, but he was. He had a strong jaw, cheekbones that a model would kill for, and that dark hair that fell with an ease that normally required a pro blowout, when I knew in reality he had probably just finger-combed it. I wasn't sure if what I felt as I watched him was attraction, or simply appreciation that he was good-looking in a different way, one that spoke to me now, at this particular point in my life.

The outsider intrigued by the outsider.

Because that was how I felt—a self-imposed outsider in my former life.

I waved, and he pushed himself off the wall, raising a hand back in greeting.

When he opened the door and got into the passenger seat, he nodded slightly to the right, the corner of his mouth turned up in amusement. "Woman in the car next to you is debating calling the cops. She thinks you're here to buy drugs from me."

Glancing past him, I saw there was a middle-aged woman with two kids in the backseat, and she was shaking her head in disgust, cell phone in her hand poised in front of her face, like she was debating whether or not it was worth it.

"Do I look like a meth addict?" I asked, glancing down at my grubby clothes. "Maybe I should have changed."

"It's not you, it's me. People in this neighborhood can smell when you've been on the inside, I swear." He gave me a shrug, his dark eyes indecipherable. "If I wasn't so recently out, it might be entertaining. But I don't want to deal with cops and their bullshit."

I pulled out of the spot, glancing over at him. "You don't have drugs on you, do you?" I hadn't thought about that at all. I didn't know if he was a user or not. Maybe those were the issues Tyler was talking about. The thought of having drugs in my car terrified me. All it took was one cop and I could find myself in serious trouble.

"No. I don't do drugs. Or sell them. I don't drink. I don't smoke." His knee came up to rest on the glove box of my car. "I'm a regular fucking Boy Scout, that's what I am."

It didn't sound like sarcasm, but I wasn't entirely sure if he was being serious or not. "I don't do drugs. Or sell them. Or drink. Or smoke. But I did quit Girl Scouts in third grade once I realized they wanted us to sleep in a tent."

He gave a half laugh. "Seriously?"

"Seriously. Nature makes me uncomfortable. And I was very concerned about using an outhouse."

"Valid concern." There was a pause then he asked, "So you don't drink ever?"

"No. I used to, but I felt myself getting out of control with it, so I cut it out of my life." It wasn't something I needed and I didn't mind telling Phoenix that. In fact, it felt empowering to say this was the way it was. I didn't drink. Ever.

"How long has it been?"

"Ten weeks and three days." The fact that I knew to the day surprised me. I guess I had been mentally ticking off each day without being entirely conscious of it.

"That's awesome, seriously."

As I drove back toward my house, I was very aware of the space he took up in my car, how he didn't move at all, but his eyes were trained on me the entire time. For a second, I wished that I had worn a different shirt, one that didn't have a coffee stain on the stomach area. But it didn't matter. That's not what this was about.

And I found myself weirdly excited that I had met someone who didn't drink either. Someone who wasn't going to be a preachy asshole about it. "Thanks," I said. "I feel good about my choice. It's working for me."

"I don't think I've ever met anyone else who was totally clean," he said, sounding intrigued by the idea.

I laughed. "Me either. We could form our own club. The Clean Club. Like the Clean Plate Club, only without the plate."

He didn't say anything, and when I shot a glance at him, his nose was scrunched up. "No?"

"I don't know what the Clean Plate Club is, sorry. Though I'm down with being in the Clean Club. Membership two, huh?" He held his fist out to give me a bump, and at the red light I did, reaching out to him with a quick tap with my knuckles.

"The Clean Plate Club is what my mother always told me I could be in if I ate all of my dinner. It's some bizarre attempt by parents to force kids to eat foods they don't like or to essentially overeat, in my opinion. So your mom didn't do that, I take it?"

He made a sound, like that was hilarious. "Hardly. Most of the time my mother forgot to buy food. I guess I was automatically a member of the club."

God, that sounded awful, and I felt like my foot was jammed up in my mouth. Pulling into my driveway I parked the car and turned to him. "I'm sorry. I didn't mean to make you uncomfortable."

But he shook his head. "No. Hell, no. Don't do that. That's not why I brought it up. I don't want or need pity. I'm just telling it like it is."

Was there pity on my face? I guess there was, because I did feel a profound sympathy for his childhood. It wasn't fair that some kids got awesome parents and some got shitty ones. But that wasn't really the same thing as pity. "Injustice makes me feel sad. It's not personal."

A ghost of a smile flitted across his face. "Cool. This your place? You got any milk? That would be my drink of choice for the night."

"Are you serious?" I asked, again not really sure. I turned off the car and palmed the keys nervously.

"Well, I'm pretty confident *you're* a milk drinker. So am I."

"Why, because of the kitten? That wasn't a subliminal message." Though he was right. I did drink milk. Behind coffee, it was my favorite drink. I wasn't big on soft drinks. They left me hungry with an aftertaste in my mouth.

He just shrugged. "Because I can sense it. You have chocolate syrup, too, don't you?"

"Of course. I have strawberry, too. Even milk needs a little variety now and then." And were we really talking about milk? It seemed so random and innocent.

As we climbed the front porch, I hesitated at the front door. I realized I still didn't know why Phoenix had been in jail and my assumption that it was drug- or alcohol-related was clearly wrong. But if he were a serial rapist or a girlfriend beater, Tyler would have said that. Neither would Riley let him stay in the house with Jessica living there. Pushing my key into the lock, I studied him like his cheekbones, his eyelashes, could reveal the truth about him.

But only his lips could do that, and he wasn't volunteering, and I couldn't ask. It seemed too personal.

He flipped his hair out of his eye. "What? Having second thoughts about hanging out with me?"

I shook my head slowly, because I really wasn't. I was just curious. "Just thinking that life is weird." Every decision, every choice, altered the course of our lives, and it was sort of mindblowing if you stopped and really thought about it.

"Life is like waiting in line at the grocery store. You wait, you slowly move forward, you pay the price, then you exit unsatisfied and broke."

Shoving the door open I frowned, disturbed by his description. "That's cynical."

"I'm not cynical. I'm realistic. And hey, if you choose to be patient, content, then it's all good. You don't mind the line."

"I'm not exactly sure what I am, but I don't think I'm cynical," I told him as we started up the stairs to the second floor and my apartment.

"Optimism is a luxury not afforded to the poor."

I so did not agree with that. "That's not true. Without optimism no one would ever achieve upward mobility. Without the belief that you can have more, you don't reach for it."

The corner of his mouth turned up.

"What?" I asked now. I opened the door to the apartment.

Phoenix carelessly shrugged his shoulder. "Nothing other than I appreciate that you have an opinion. Nice place." He moved into the apartment, hands in his pockets. "So who lives here?"

"Rory, Tyler's girlfriend, and our friend Kylie." I tossed my keys on the kitchen table. "Jessica was supposed to, but then her parents cut her off and she decided to live with Riley."

"So why does she get to be on your ass about wanting to move out when she was the first one to ditch?"

Good question. "I guess she feels like she had a good reason. Her parents wanted her to major in religion and marry a guy from their church and when she said she wasn't interested and that she was with Riley, they cut off her money. So she's too broke to stay here. I don't have any excuse."

Yanking the fridge handle, I winced at the hypocrisy of that. I did have a good reason, just not one I could share with anyone.

Fortunately, he didn't call me out on it. "What's Rory like? I can't see Tyler digging the same kind of girl as Riley."

Pulling the milk out, I set it on the counter. "She's totally different even though she and Jessica are tight. Rory is sweet and very logical. She doesn't play games and she really loves Tyler. She thinks he's the bomb-dot-com."

"Must be nice."

"Yeah. It must." I set two plastic tumblers down and said, "You pour. I'll get the chocolate syrup."

He tossed the tumblers in the air in an attempt at juggling or fancy bartending. He was actually pretty good at it, managing to have them spinning while he switched them from hand to hand.

"Wow. Impressive."

"I'm good with my hands."

If another guy had said that, I would have either rolled my eyes or giggled, depending on my level of interest, assuming he was flirting. But Phoenix didn't seem to be flirting in any way. He just seemed like he had needed to get out of the house and I was a convenient way to do that. Like he was mildly curious about me, but not much more than that.

He used the chocolate syrup sparingly, tinting the white milk a soft caramel color. "What's the point in using any at all?" I asked, squeezing hard to create an inch of chocolate sludge at the bottom of my glass.

"Subtle flavor, that's all. Just taking the milk up a notch, not drowning it out." Then he raised his glass in the air and waited for me to do the same. "To the Clean Club."

"Cheers." We tapped glasses, and I thought that I should feel uncomfortable around him, considering how little I knew him and how different he was from other guys I'd known, but I didn't.

We sat on the couch, and the space between us felt natural, a foot or two so we weren't touching, but not an awkward gap of huge proportions where we both hugged the arms. Scrolling through our movie options, we settled on an action movie and we watched, silent, drinking our milk. I drew my feet up under my legs, and he propped one foot on the coffee table and slumped down in the couch.

It was entertaining enough to hold my interest, and when it was over Phoenix said, "That didn't suck."

"So generous in your praise."

"Cynic. Told you."

I smiled. "That means its time for a romantic comedy."

"Really? Do I have to?" He gave me a pained look, but I wasn't buying it. I had seen how long he had lingered on a Julia Roberts movie in the queue when I had let him have the remote to scroll.

"Yes. It's mandatory. Like taxes and Taco Tuesdays."

He gave a laugh. "What? How the hell are tacos mandatory?"

"Because my grandmother says so, that's how, even though we aren't Puerto Rican." I smiled back, pleased that I had amused him, and happy that I actually had wanted to crack a joke. I felt almost . . . normal.

"She the boss in your family?"

"Oh yeah. She has always lived with us and she is totally in charge. She's my dad's mother, and she was born in Puerto Rico, though she came here when she was four."

"So you're half Puerto Rican? What's your last name?"

"Yes, though it drives my grandmother crazy how totally American my dad is. Basically the only Latino thing about him is his religion and our last name—DeLorenzo. My mom's family is a mix of European."

"That's a cool name. And now I see where you got your dark hair." He pointed to my head.

"Where did you get your dark hair?" It was as dark as mine.

"My mom and my aunt Dawn both have—well, Dawn *had*—light brown hair, but my grandmother's hair was black, so probably from her. I couldn't tell you about my father since I've never met him and I've never seen a picture of him. My mom didn't even give me his last name, nor did she ever tell me what it was. I'm a Sullivan."

"How did you get the name Phoenix? We're both named after birds. How random is that?" Reaching forward, I drained the last of my milk, which was warm, and licked some chocolate off the rim.

"I wasn't named after the bird. My mother just had a thing for River Phoenix, and he died right before I was born." Phoenix rolled his eyes. "Nothing like being named after a dude who OD'd on heroin and cocaine. Seems right for my mother, though."

"It's still a cool name," I said truthfully. "It makes you unique."

"Or a freak."

"There's that cynical thing again."

He smiled slowly. "I'm a lost cause."

"You'll change your mind after you've watched *Mamma Mia!*" I lifted the remote.

"You're really going to make me watch this?"

"Yes. 'Dancing Queen' will change your life. But first, we need refills." Taking his glass and mine, I went for more milk, plus chips and salsa.

Then we watched the movie, and I didn't resist the urge to sing along. I probably never would have done that with a guy before, but now, in grubby shorts and a T-shirt, no makeup, my hair in need of some serious shampoo, what difference did it make? So I sang the crap out of every number while Phoenix steadily munched tortilla chips.

"What did you think?" I asked him when it was over.

"I only wanted to commit suicide three times, so it was a success, I think." He looked at me from under that lock of hair. "I admit, I was watching you more than the TV. I dig that you dig those songs."

"Thanks." I took the comment at face value. "You can pick the next movie." It was after midnight, but I wasn't tired. I had slept so much all summer, and I felt awake for the first time in two months.

He picked a drama about a mentally ill couple and it made me cry. Watching them fall in love, two lonely people in a world that didn't understand them, was sort of the ultimate statement of optimism, and my heart both broke and felt happy for them. I expected Phoenix to make a crack or tease me, the way the usual guys I hung out with would have. But he didn't. He just said, "I need to think about this one before we discuss."

"It was sad," I said, wiping my eyes.

"Yeah, but there was hope. Interesting." He stared at a chip in his hand before tossing it back down uneaten. "I guess I should call a cab. It's too late for you to drive me home."

"It's only two. I'm not even tired. I can drive you home or you can just crash here on the couch. Since no one else has moved in yet, it won't matter." I didn't want to be alone. I didn't want the thoughts, the guilt, to crowd back into my head. With Phoenix around, I could ignore those feelings, my personal recriminations.

"Are you sure?" He had taken off his shoes and was now almost lying on the couch and he looked totally comfortable.

I nodded. "It's no big deal."

"Okay, cool." He laughed. "I don't really have money for a cab. I was going to walk to the bus stop. Which is stupid, because the bus only runs on the hour at this time of night."

"So why would you tell me that then?"

"Because I didn't want to be a jerk and make you drive me back to Riley's."

For some reason, that touched me. The guy that old ladies shied away from at the drugstore was worried about inconveniencing me. Me. I hadn't felt worthy of consideration lately.

"I don't think you're a jerk."

"You don't, do you?" He seemed puzzled by that. "You don't seem scared of me either."

"Should I be?" I eyed him directly, boldly, wanting the truth.

But he just shook his head slowly. "No. I don't want to hurt you."

I believed him. I also knew that he couldn't hurt me any more than I already hurt myself.

So we stayed on the couch together, talking a little, mostly watching TV, for another three hours, until my eyelids were droopy and I finally felt ready for sleep.

"Are you okay here on the couch?" I asked him as I stood up and stretched.

"Is there another option?"

That was a loaded question, and I didn't know the answer.

CHAPTER FOUR

PHOENIX

SEEING ROBIN'S FACE FREEZE, I REALIZED I SHOULDN'T have said it like that. I wasn't talking about sex, but that was obviously what she heard.

It was easy to read her expressions. She wore them all on her face clearly, and what amazed me about her was everything she said seemed so honest and totally free of bullshit. The other thing I noticed was that she seemed as totally lonely as I was. I couldn't figure out why.

"I'll be fine on the couch," I said. "I've slept in worse places, trust me."

That eased the tension in her shoulders a little, but now the pity was back, which I hated. I didn't want her to feel sorry for me, for my shitty childhood, or my criminal record.

"I guess so. Let me get you a blanket and a pillow."

When she eased past me, my hand shot out before I could stop it, and I grabbed hers. "Thanks." For the pillow. The blanket. For answering my texts. For talking to me. For the milk and the movies. I didn't say any of those things, but I stared at her, hoping she could read it in my eyes.

"Sure." She nodded. "It's not a problem."

"I got a job tonight," I said, having no fucking clue why that popped out of my mouth, other than that I clearly wanted to impress her or at least prove I wasn't a total loser. "I'm going to apprentice at a tattoo parlor I used to work at. Gave the owner a call and he said I can start on Monday."

Her face softened, and her hand, so small and warm in mine, relaxed, fingers entwining with the callused ones that belonged to me. "That's awesome," she said, and I knew she meant it.

I also knew that I shouldn't have stayed so long.

Because now all I wanted to do was pull her down onto my lap and taste her lips. I wanted to see how her eyes would change then, with passion or with something more.

It was dangerous but oh-so-fucking tempting.

That she was as chemical free as me was only the beginning of what I found amazing about her.

I hadn't expected her to have an opinion on much of any-thing, but she did, and a solid one, too, every time.

I had also counted on the fact that she was a suburban col-lege girl and I would be intimidating to her, the dude just out of jail, so it would be easy to stay disconnected. But she hadn't been nervous, and she hadn't been bothered by my sitting next to her. She hadn't glanced at the clock on her phone or worried that I was going to attack her in a fit of lust or rage or both. She didn't even ask why I was in jail in the first place.

But she wasn't flirting either. Or just flat out going after me, the way Angel had. I had ended up dating Angel because she had decided we were going to date, and I appreciated the effort. Of course, the lesson with a girl like that was the loyalty was short-lived.

Somehow, I didn't think Robin would be that kind of girl. The sad girl was always a loyal one. It's why she was sad.

"I'm looking forward to it," I said, because I was. Not only did a job mean money so I could pay my cousins back for helping me out and feeding and clothing me, but I was going to be able to draw and play around with tattooing any customers in the shop who would let me do it for free. I had worked there for just a few weeks before I'd gotten arrested, so I was seriously glad Bob, the owner, had been willing to rehire me. But why the fuck did Robin want to hear about it at five in the morning?

I let go of her hand. "Good night." Look, don't touch. I couldn't afford to buy this model. I had to remember that.

"Good night, Phoenix." For a second, she looked like she was going to say something else, but then she just went down the hall.

A minute later she reappeared with a blanket and a pillow. I stripped off my shirt and punched the pillow. She hovered in front of me for a second, then she gestured to my tattoo on my chest.

"It's tragically beautiful," she said, eyes on it, not my face.

Like her.

I didn't say anything, just watching her, feeling a warning clanging loud and clear in my skull. If I had any fucking sense I would walk back to my cousins' house, because a dark room and a girl who looked this vulnerable and pretty was dangerous.

Then she seemed to realize she was staring, because she spun on her heel and walked away, turning off the light on her way, leaving me alone in the dark. Lounging on the couch, I pulled my phone out and scrolled through it checking news headlines, the weather, social media, anything to attempt to distract my thoughts from Robin. I was too keyed up to sleep. Jail hadn't been great for getting a solid eight hours. I had felt like I had slept with one eye open most of the time, given that my cellmate was a crazy motherfucker with wide eyes and a twitch. So when I got to my cousins' I had crashed for almost forty-eight hours.

But now I couldn't. I was wide awake.

The cell phone was Riley's old smartphone that he had dropped at a construction site, shattering the screen. It worked still, so I had borrowed a hundred bucks from him and reactivated my account. I was in, like, three hundred bucks easy to Tyler and Riley, and I owed them big time. Going through my contacts list, I deleted Angel. I didn't want to hear from her ever again. Then I deleted another five people who hadn't bothered to text or ask how I was the whole time I was away. If they didn't give a shit, why should I?

It left my list pathetically small. But it was hard to make friends I could trust. We had moved every year or so most of my childhood, and I changed schools constantly depending on which block of the neighborhood our new apartment was in. My sophomore year in high school I didn't even start until November because my mom kept forgetting to get my vaccines updated and the school wouldn't admit me. I'd had a group of guys I'd hung out with until the last year or so, but with us all being out of school, some working, some not, and me spending time with

Angel, we sort of lost touch. More of my contacts were girls than guys. Girls who wanted to be the one who got some sort of emotional reaction from me.

I was a challenge.

It was unintentional. I had a tight rein on my emotions. I had to.

I did have a text from Tyler. U ok, man?

I wasn't used to having anyone notice I wasn't there, that I hadn't come home.

Yeah, thanks.

There was no way I was going to tell him where I was. Tyler had come home from dropping off Robin and had hinted that I was to stay the hell away from her. He would be pissed if he found out I had been texting and making plans with her while I was listening to his lecture. I wasn't offended by his warning. He was right—I shouldn't be talking to her.

But I couldn't help it. Nor could I help standing up and going down the hall to see if her bedroom door was open.

Moving silently, I picked my way carefully through the dark, knowing if she woke up and saw me watching her in the dark she was going to think I was a fucking creeper. Maybe I was. Did creepers know they were creepers? I felt normal enough, but hell, maybe I wasn't. If abnormal is your normal, you feel normal, right?

Her door was slightly ajar, and I pushed it open a little further so I could see her bed. There was a stream of moonlight coming from her window. She hadn't closed her blinds. The light illuminated her curled up on her bed, on her side, her comforter wedged between her legs so that I could see the long shape of her calves and her thighs. She had changed into a tank top, and her hair spilled in dark layers across her white sheets.

Maybe part of me wanted her to wake up. Maybe I wanted to see fear in her eyes. Not because I wanted her to be afraid but because when someone is scared of you, you're no longer vulnerable. They don't have any power over you.

"What is it?" she whispered suddenly, surprising me.

She didn't look awake. Even now, her eyes were still closed, and I wasn't sure how she had known I was there. She definitely didn't look afraid, and she clearly trusted me enough to keep her eyes closed.

Naive, that's what she was.

It made me angry with her. What if I was there to hurt her? She'd be in serious trouble before she could even think to fight back. She needed to be smarter. Tomorrow I needed to talk to her about that.

"I can't sleep," I told her. "Sorry. I was just looking for company." That was only half of the truth.

"Me either."

"You look asleep."

Her eyes finally opened, and her soft lips parted. "Am I talking in my sleep? Or dreaming then?"

I shook my head slowly. "No. I don't think I would be the man of your dreams." Then without waiting for permission or an invitation, I ignored the intent behind my words and went over to her bed.

She drew in her breath, startled, when I lay down next to her. How could I explain to her that I didn't want to be alone? I couldn't. So I just lay on my back and stilled my body so I wouldn't scare her. "Do you mind?" I finally asked.

"No," she whispered.

"Night."

"Lift your head," she said.

"What?" I turned and saw she had one of her pillows and she was offering it to me. I lifted my head and she tucked it behind me.

I looked away. God, this was so bad. Things were stirring in me, things that shouldn't be.

Resolutely, I closed my eyes and counted backward from one hundred. I got somewhere around fifteen when I lost consciousness.

Dreaming about Iggy, my mother's latest piece-of-shit boyfriend, the knife in his hand when he threatened her, I felt the anxiety crawling up my spine, my fists clenching. When a hand touched my shoulder, I jerked awake and instinctively sat up, hand going out to grab the throat of my cellmate in warning to stay the fuck away from me.

Except I wasn't in jail.

I was in Robin's bed, and I was only inches from her throat with my outstretched hand. I dropped it quickly at the look of stunned horror on her face. "Sorry, sorry. Jesus, I'm sorry. I was dreaming. I thought I was still in jail."

Her expression smoothed out. She was standing next to the bed, hair tumbling forward as she leaned over me.

"No, no, I shouldn't have touched you. I'm sorry. I was just awake and going to make coffee and your phone keeps buzzing.

I wasn't being nosy, but when your screen lit up I could see that Tyler has texted you, like, four times." She crossed her arms over her chest. "Sorry."

I shook my head, swallowing hard and tossing my hair out of eyes. I still felt groggy. "No, it's cool. Thanks. I hope I didn't scare you." I knew I had, though. She had curled back up inside herself, and when I moved to push the sheet back, she flinched.

My thought had been that it would be easier if she was afraid of me, but it wasn't. I despised it.

"No, it's fine. Do you want coffee?"

"Sure. Thanks." I searched her face. For what, I wasn't sure. "You hungry? I could make you breakfast."

"You cook?" Her arms dropped. "Really?"

I gave her a half smile, pleased that she seemed to have forgotten her fear. "It was either that or starve, so yes, I can cook. Sort of. I'm no Iron Chef, but whatever."

"Oh. Cool. That would be great. I'll start the coffee."

Swinging my legs out of bed, I reached for my phone as she went down the hall. There were four texts from Tyler. He seemed to think I was in trouble since I hadn't come back to the house. I appreciated the concern, but I wasn't going back until Robin was sick of me. This might be my only chance to hang out with her.

It's fine, bro. I'm with a girl.

He just didn't need to know which girl.

She was in the kitchen, and now that she was wearing a tank top and tiny stretchy shorts, I could see her body much better than when she had been swimming in that T-shirt and denim shorts. It was enough to get my blood pumping without coffee.

She didn't seem to realize how hot she was, though, just giving me a shy smile as she reached for two mugs, the tank riding up to expose her smooth skin.

Fuck.

I went into her fridge to see if there was any food in there at all I could do something with and to get a blast of cold air. Plus hide my hard-on.

"Do you ever eat?" I asked her, eyeing the pathetic selection in her fridge. It was mostly filled with condiments and string cheese. There were eggs, though, and a loaf of bread that, when I squeezed it, felt a little stale.

"Of course I eat. I just don't cook. I eat simple stuff."

"Do you have syrup?"

"Yes. For my frozen waffles."

"Those taste like cardboard," I told her, pulling out the eggs and bread. "I'll make you some French toast then."

"Really?" She looked dubious.

"Sure, why not?"

As I cracked eggs into a bowl I found in the cupboard, she poured out the coffee. "Do you want cream and sugar?"

"No. Just black."

"So do you have to do anything today?" she asked.

"No. I can find a ride home, don't worry about it." Even if I was making her breakfast, I had probably outstayed my welcome.

"I was just thinking that if you're not busy, maybe we could go to Eden Park. There's a free concert there, and I was going to go and sketch."

My hand stilled as I was about to dip a slice of bread in the egg. "I don't have any plans, no," I said, my throat suddenly tight. "That sounds cool."

She shifted a coffee mug toward me on the counter, and when I looked up at her, she was smiling. "I have an extra sketchbook if you want to borrow it."

Oh damn, I was in trouble. If I had any sense at all, I would get the hell out of there and never come back. But a cactus isn't going to tell a rainstorm to go fuck itself. I had never had anyone offer me this sort of innocent friendship. I wanted it like the greedy motherfucker that I was.

"Cool. Thanks." Then I took a huge sip of my coffee, knowing I was going to scald the shit out of the roof of my mouth. I wanted to. I wanted the pain to ground me. "Shit," I cursed, when the liquid burned tender flesh.

"Are you okay?" She looked alarmed. "Do you want some ice?"

"I'm fine." Which wasn't true at all. Focusing on scraping my tongue over the raw spot, I finished making the French toast, flipping it from one side to the other as it cooked, then dropping to the kitchen floor to do some sit-ups to burn off the anxiety I was feeling.

"What are you doing?" She gaped at me.

"Just some crunches." I liked to sweat, to work out. It made me feel above my body. I pushed hard, knowing she probably thought I was a complete tool, but figuring this was the reality of it. I shouldn't hide the fact that I was not a well-adjusted, middle-class college student like the guys she probably usually hung out with.

But for some reason, she just bent over and touched my knees. "You're moving too much. My high school track coach would make you redo all of those."

"You were on the track team?" I asked, slowing down my crunches and sucking in some air. She was right. It was harder when you couldn't move your legs at all.

"Yep. Distance runner." Her hands were firm on my skin, showing the strength I didn't expect her to have given she looked so fragile.

But as I bent up, my abs burning, I spotted using her lips, those perfect plump, cherry lips that made me want to suck on them. She was smiling, and she didn't look vulnerable. She just looked beautiful.

"Think you can do a hundred?" she asked, the challenge in her voice unmistakable.

I would do it or die trying. "No problem."

"Let me turn the burner off." With one hand she reached back and turned the knob. "Okay. Go. One. Two."

"I already did at least fifteen," I protested.

She readily agreed. "You're right. Okay, sixteen, seventeen."

But somehow that meant I had a point to prove. When she reached a hundred, I was in pain and out of breath, but I pushed on to a hundred and fifteen to make up for the ones I copped an attitude about.

When I came to a stop, laying down on the cool floor, breathing hard, she eased her grip on my knees. "Wow, that was awesome. Good job."

"Thanks." I peeled myself off the floor, knowing I was going to be wincing every time I moved for the next two days. But at least I had proved I was badass. Mental eye roll.

Robin transferred the French toast to plates and put them on the table. I carried our coffee mugs behind her. The kitchen was huge, with one wall sporting a cutout that overlooked the stairs. Robin's bedroom was on the third floor with the living room and a bathroom, but the kitchen and two larger bedrooms were on the second floor with another bathroom. Robin's room was tiny, and it seemed to me that she had a lot of privacy even if the living room was down the hall from her, because how often would her roommates go out of their way to come upstairs? They would probably end up spending half their time hanging out in the kitchen.

The fact that she didn't want to stay seemed to be a mystery to everyone and I was curious about it, but I wasn't going to pry. She was respecting my privacy and not asking ten thousand questions about my record. I could give her the same space.

"This tastes amazing," she said enthusiastically as she took several bites. She ate quickly, but then seemed to fill up super fast. She was only halfway through one piece when she set her fork down and put her hand on her stomach.

"You done?" I asked her, raising my eyebrow.

She nodded. "I can't eat too much at once, it gives me a stomachache."

I had two pieces already, but I reached out and stabbed the remains of her piece. "I'm not letting that go to waste."

She laughed. "Such a guy."

"Last time I checked, yep."

Robin's nose scrunched up. "I'm going to take a shower if you don't mind."

"Nope."

As she went upstairs I shoveled food and coffee into my mouth and tried not to think about her naked.

That worked for about five seconds, then the hard-on was back with a vengeance. Five months was a long time to go without sex, and unlike some dudes, I wasn't up for jacking off in my cell. Then the memory of prison brought a hot, metallic taste to my mouth, and I immediately lost my arousal.

A girl like Robin didn't deserve to be tainted by me.

Which made me selfish.

But even knowing that, I still just stubbornly sat there and ate French toast.

Everyone was entitled to some fucking French toast now and then, weren't they?

I thought so.

CHAPTER FIVE

ROBIN

GETTING READY TO GO TO THE PARK WITH PHOENIX SENT me into ambitious activity, displaying more energy than I had all summer. I grabbed a blanket for the ground, packed a cooler with water bottles and energy drinks, along with chips and string cheese, and collected my pencil kit and two sketchbooks. Then I applied sunscreen to my nose and cheeks. I had even shaved my legs in the shower, though I didn't bother to blow-dry my hair. I just towel dried it, then let it do it's thing.

Phoenix showered after me while I was packing things up, and he came back downstairs just as I had everything by the door to go. His hair was wet and dangling in his face, but he had put his shirt back on, which was good. I had decided at some point during the last twelve hours that, why yes, I was in fact attracted to him. Very much so. The realization had come to me sometime between midnight and five a.m. and was absolutely undeniable when he had come into my room and laid down beside me. I had been aware of every inch of my body, yet he had never made a single move toward me.

As far as I could tell, Phoenix just wanted a friend.

So it was better if he stayed covered because there was something totally drool-worthy about his muscles and all that skin displaying his bleeding heart tattoo. It covered so much real estate, it must have hurt like a bitch to get that done. Given that his shorts were too big, they tended to strain down, exposing the ab muscles I now understood how he'd gotten. He had been tenacious doing those crunches. But I was determined that I could ignore any reactions my body made toward his and embrace a new friendship.

I liked his company.

I didn't want him to leave.

I wasn't really sure why but I figured it didn't matter.

For the first time all summer, I wasn't spending the majority of my time hating myself.

"Here, let me carry that," he said, taking the small, soft cooler from my hand. He also picked up the blanket and tucked it under his arm. He gave me a smile. "Are we going on a picnic? Man, I never thought I'd be doing this."

"Too lame?" Maybe it was too tame of an entertainment for him. I admit I was a little disappointed.

"No. It's just no one has ever invited me on a picnic before. Once when I was about ten my mom and my aunt took me and my cousins to the fair, but they got high behind the grandstand, and Riley got busted for stealing a hot dog for Jayden. The cops cuffed him for twenty minutes to scare him before letting him go. I don't think Easton was born yet. Or maybe my aunt was pregnant with him at the time. I don't know, I don't remember. I just remember thinking that it was like a whole fairground full of families doing normal shit and having fun and eating craploads of food, and I couldn't have any of it." Phoenix made a face. "And I have no idea why I just bored you with a shitty story like that."

What did I say to that? I knew he didn't want my pity. And he seemed to be musing about the past more than anything. "I don't have any hot dogs," I said. "But I can pretty much guarantee insects and oppressive sun, so you'll get the genuine picnic experience."

Phoenix gave a short laugh. "Thanks. That's nice of you."

"When I was ten I had a bird shit on my head at the fair. I tried to wash it out in the bathroom but it was still gunky and I cried for an hour before insisting on sitting in the car alone sulking." The memory made me smile. "I was kind of a jerk about it. And my brothers called me Shithead for the rest of the summer."

"Brothers are good for that. Probably the only reason I'm glad I don't have any. Are they older than you?"

"Yes." We started down the stairs. "They're thirty and twenty-seven. I was born when my brother was in kindergarten. I think I was a bit of a surprise." Though I was pretty confident it was a happy surprise. My mother had always wanted a girl, and one of her favorite things to do was take me for a mani/pedi.

"Why is everyone so surprised by pregnancy?" Phoenix asked. "If you have sex, the probability is there."

Wondering if he was thinking about Angel, I locked the front door behind us. "True. But my mom is sixty now. I think she thought she was too old to get pregnant again."

"I don't know how old my mom is," he said as we walked

down the driveway. There was a frown on his face. "I guess she has to be about . . . forty-three?"

"How old are you?" I asked him, starting to hate his mother. She sounded awful. We got in my car, Phoenix loading the cooler and blanket into the backseat.

"I'm twenty. My birthday is September second."

"That's in a week and a half. Do you have plans?"

"I plan to sit outside somewhere and appreciate my freedom. Maybe I'll buy myself a Dilly Bar at DQ."

It had been a stupid question. What kind of plans did I expect him to have? A big event at a restaurant? A party bus? "That sounds awesome. Can I steal that idea for my birthday in November? It'll be my twenty-first, too, and I know everyone is going to expect me to go out and party and get loaded and it just isn't my thing. Not anymore."

"It's your birthday. Do whatever you want. Fuck 'em."

"I have a feeling you're better at living that philosophy than I am. I worry too much about what people think." Part my personality, part the way I'd been raised, I was definitely a people pleaser. I wanted everyone to be happy. To like me. I backed down the driveway and paused at the street, but as I looked left and then right, I saw Phoenix was doing it again, staring at me in a way I didn't understand.

"We're pack animals. It's natural to want to belong. But some of us never will. We're meant to be alone."

Was that me now? God, I hoped not. I was so lonely I ached with it. But here, in the hot car with Phoenix, I felt like at least one person understood what I felt like, and I wondered if two loners could make each other less lonely. So far, the answer for me was yes.

"Do you want to drive?" I asked, putting my car in park. I didn't want to have to focus on the road. I wanted to watch him, and I wanted to feel . . . I don't know . . . taken care of.

But he shook his head. "I don't have any insurance." Then for some reason he laughed. "Actually, I don't even have a license."

"You don't have a license? I thought you said you borrowed Riley's car. Why don't you have a license?"

"Long story." He was smiling. "But the gist of it is you need actual proof of who you are to get a driver's license. I don't have any of that. No birth certificate, no Social Security card. Just my criminal record. And I might have possibly been breaking the law in driving up the street, but don't tell my parole officer."

It didn't seem like being unable to drive or breaking parole was all that hilarious, but he looked good smiling. I couldn't help but grin back. "I guess I'm driving then."

"Good plan."

The park was only a few minutes away. I found a spot in the lot, and we climbed out and moved past the reflecting pool where kids were dipping their fingers and dogs were drinking. It wasn't as hot as it had been, and the sun felt good on my bare shoulders as we staked out a spot and Phoenix spread the blanket. The band playing in the gazebo was some kind of big band–style quintet, and the majority of the guys I knew would think it was seriously corny, but Phoenix didn't say anything. He just laid down on the blanket and stripped his shirt up, balling it behind his head. His foot tapped up and down to the music and he lounged.

"Look at the sky," he said.

Using my hands to cradle my head, I lay down on my back next to him and stared upward at the vast blue umbrella of the atmosphere above us. I felt a lazy contentment I hadn't had in months. The breeze ruffled the sundress I had put on, not because it was a fashion statement but because it was loose and easy and didn't crawl up my ass like all those short shorts I had bought last year. My dress danced over my knees, and my hair ruffled softly, and the sun warmed my skin while the band played something bouncy and retro in the background.

"'The bluebird carries the sky on his back.' That's Henry David Thoreau." Poetry didn't always make sense to me, but the American transcendentalists we had studied freshman year told a simple message I could understand.

"'No one is free, even the birds are chained to the sky,'" Phoenix said. "That's Bob Dylan."

Turning my head toward Phoenix, I ran my tongue over my bottom lip, in a bit of awe of the moment, that I was here, like this, with him, someone I hadn't even known two days earlier, and that the jagged edges of anxiety were being softened. "Poor birdies," I whispered. "Chained, carrying the sky . . . so burdened."

"Yeah," he murmured, and his hand shifted, his fingers entwining with mine. His grip was loose but solid. "Poor birds. Sucks to be them."

We lay like that, holding hands, staring up at the sky, and for the first time in a very long time, I thought maybe I was going to be okay. Or at the very least like I wouldn't shatter into a million pieces upon contact.

* * *

PHOENIX AND I SPENT THE WHOLE DAY AT THE PARK. WE borrowed a Frisbee from a group of guys and tossed it back and forth. Phoenix played with a random German shepherd in an impromptu game of chase, followed by tug-of-war with a tennis ball. I sketched on the blanket and watched him, enjoying the way he was coming alive, opening up, losing that tight, controlled look. There was a food truck, and I bought us two coneys with cheese. He ate his in two bites.

"I owe you," he said, sprawling out on the blanket. "As soon as I get paid I'm going to buy you a bunch of groceries."

"You don't have to do that." I managed to eat half of mine before handing it to him to finish.

"And you didn't have to hang out with the jailbird, but you did." Phoenix lifted the rest of my coney to his mouth, but before he popped it in, he asked, "Why did you?"

I shrugged. It wasn't any sort of great mystery. He was offering companionship, and with him, I could be myself. "Because I wanted to."

"And I want to buy you groceries. It's simple."

I nodded. I understood what he was saying. He wanted to be nice to me for the same reason I wanted to be nice to him—because I liked him. It really was that simple and uncomplicated, and it felt relaxing, safe.

How ironic that I felt safe with someone who had just gotten out of jail. That probably made me stupid, but I just felt good. Normal.

I was sketching a bird. It just seemed like the imagery was

stuck in my head after our conversation. I didn't want to draw a phoenix, that was too literal. And drawing a robin would be just conceited or something. So I drew a simple sparrow, pulling up some images on my phone to see what they looked like. I felt more sparrow than robin anyway. Robins were showy. That wasn't me anymore.

After a while, Phoenix started to sketch, too, and I was curious what he was drawing. I admit to being a total girl and wanted him to be sketching me in a perfect ending to a perfect day. But when he showed it to me, it was a cobra, spreading its hood, looking super pissed off.

Okay, so he wasn't waxing poetic about my lips or whatever in charcoal.

It was still an awesome day.

Until Phoenix ran into a guy he'd known in prison.

We were cleaning up our wrappers and empty water bottles, and Phoenix had just tossed them in the nearest garbage can when a guy yelled, "Hey, brother, what's up?" and clapped Phoenix on the back.

He was a big guy, covered in tattoos, including on his face and shaved head, and while his smile looked friendly enough, I saw that Phoenix tensed immediately. "Davis," Phoenix said, shaking his hand. "Good to see you, man."

"Yeah, yeah, you too. When did you get out?"

"Tuesday."

Davis's eyes shifted over to me, and he gave a low whistle of appreciation that had me fighting the urge to cover a chest that wasn't even remotely exposed in my dress. "This your girl? Angel? As pretty as her name."

Nothing like hearing he had talked about his ex in jail to ruin whatever fantasy I had started spinning in my head. Or hearing that he'd been in jail, because I had almost convinced myself that hadn't happened. Or if it had, he had a good reason. Which I didn't really know.

"This is just a friend," Phoenix said, but he shifted his body so that he was more firmly between me and Davis.

Davis caught the message. He shook his head slowly. "Don't be like that, Sullivan. You still owe me."

"Yeah, I do." Phoenix nodded in agreement, but his entire posture had changed. He was leaning forward in aggression, clearly to show he wasn't afraid. Davis was twice his width, but Phoenix didn't look scared. "But that doesn't mean you can look at her."

Before I could even react, Davis's fist came out to grab the front of Phoenix's shirt, but he anticipated the move, so he did the same. They were both holding with a tight grip, faces inches away from each other. I was so shocked I jumped, but didn't make any sound. I couldn't. My throat felt closed with fear. For a second I thought they were going to head butt each other and go down in a flurry of fists.

Then Davis laughed. "Crazy-ass punk." He let go of Phoenix. "That's what I like about you, man."

Phoenix relaxed a little, and let go of Davis in return. "Sorry, bro, didn't mean to overreact."

"No worries. I'm not planning to take what you owe me out of your girl's ass. That ain't my style."

Oh my God. That did not sound like anything I ever wanted to hear. I made a strangled noise like a dying rabbit.

"Shit, I scared her, didn't I?" Davis asked Phoenix. "Sorry." He held his hands up toward me. "Don't worry, Angel, I actually like your pretty boy here. It's all good."

I nodded, too terrified to speak. My palms and pits were sweating with stress, and I felt about the furthest thing from badass to ever exist.

"You do have a way with the ladies, Davis," Phoenix said, rolling his eyes. He reached out and took my sweaty hand, squeezing it for reassurance.

"Fuck you," Davis said, but he didn't look offended. "But you know I like me a big girl, one who can handle all this man." He gestured to his girth.

Phoenix laughed. "A bull rider, huh?"

"Exactly." He reached out and gave Phoenix a fist bump. "I'll catch up with you later, man. I'll be in touch."

Phoenix nodded. "Take it easy."

But he didn't fully relax until Davis was a good fifteen feet away. Then when I looked at him, his expression was hard.

"What was that all about?"

"Don't worry about it. He won't hurt you, I promise." Phoenix let go of my hand and dropped to the blanket. "We should go soon. It's getting dark already."

I sank to my knees, not sure what to say. That wasn't a good enough answer for me. "Who was that guy? I mean, obviously you knew him in prison, but is he a friend? What do you owe him?"

Phoenix sighed, and he stared at me, his hand brushing over my knee. "Not friends. Allies. You need someone to watch your back in jail. That's all. Don't worry about it. It's got nothing to do with you."

"Why did you let him think I'm Angel?"

"Because he doesn't need to know your real name."

I let it go because I didn't want to ruin the day. I didn't want to see him retreat and close up any more than he already had. So I didn't ask all the questions that were burning in me. I ignored them and lay back down beside him. Phoenix pulled me close to him, and our bodies touched for the first time when he wrapped his arm around me and I leaned onto his chest.

"Look at that," he murmured, pointing up at the sky. "Fireworks downtown."

"The Reds must have won their baseball game." I relaxed onto him, letting my hand rest on his stomach. He was firm and warm, and I smiled a little in the dark, appreciating the irony of the fireworks display over us. So he hadn't sketched a picture of me. This was a close second for perfect ending. The fear Davis had inspired retreated, and I marveled at how peaceful it was, even in a crowded park. Phoenix's fingers found their way into my hair and he stroked the strands, causing goose bumps to rise on my skin.

"I missed the whole summer," he murmured. "But none of it would have been as good as today was anyway."

My heart swelled, and I found myself lightly stroking his stomach.

When we were encouraged by the cops to leave the park with everyone else twenty minutes later, we rolled up the blanket and walked to the car. There was no mention by either of us of taking him to his cousins' house. I just drove to my apartment and we went upstairs, tired and a little sunburned. Phoenix sank down onto the couch and patted the seat next to him.

It seemed safe to mention it now that we were in my place and we had implied he would be staying over by coming here. "I don't mind you sleeping in my bed again," I told him, which sounded bolder than I meant it to. I just meant that he didn't need to bother to start out on the couch, because the truth was, I wanted him sleeping with me. There was something comforting about his presence in a way that made no sense at all. I knew that. But it didn't make it any less real.

"Thanks. I'll take you up on that. But I guess I have to go back to Riley's eventually," he told me, taking my hand and pulling me up close to him. "I'm going to need to change my underwear at some point."

I laughed. "True. And I can't help you with that unless you like bikini style." Funny how I had abandoned the thongs when I had stopped wearing the tight Lycra dresses out at parties and clubs. No longer worried about panty lines, I had gradually shifted back to fuller coverage for comfort.

"I'm good with boxer briefs, thanks. Dental floss in my ass doesn't work for me." He reached for the remote. "You okay watching a movie?"

"Sure." I should have been sleepy. That was my constant state of existence lately. But I was wide awake.

Waiting for him to kiss me. That's what I was doing. But he didn't seem like he was going to do anything other than channel surf, with me leaning on him, his other hand stroking my hair.

It was stupid to want him, stupid to want more.

I should be grateful that he wasn't taking our relationship in that direction, that he was clearly just interested in companionship or something.

Because what the hell did I really know about him?

But what I knew was that he made me feel like I could look people in the eye again. He made me feel like I wasn't going to break into a thousand pieces at any given moment. He made my hands stop shaking and helped my breathing slow down.

He made me feel like a crumbling wall that has suddenly gotten new mortar between each brick and feels stable again.

And if he could make me feel that way, maybe I could make myself feel that way, too.

CHAPTER SIX

PHOENIX

SELFISH ASSHOLE, THAT WAS ME. I SHOULD HAVE GONE home. I should have deleted her number after we ran into Davis in the park, but man, when she looked at me like that—like she thought I was something amazing instead of a piece of shit—I couldn't help myself. I couldn't leave.

I couldn't stop myself from touching her either, though I was working damn hard at making sure it was nothing more than holding hands or my arm around her.

So maybe humping her head with my hand wasn't exactly keeping it cool, but I'd been dying to touch her hair since the minute I'd met her, so fucking sue me for going for it. She didn't seem to mind, which was insane. Why she wasn't terrified of me by that point, I couldn't figure out. No self-preservation at all.

Except since it was working in my favor, I couldn't exactly fault her.

When she started to doze, pressed against me, I shook her

hand a little. "Hey. Let's go to bed. You'll have a headache tomorrow if you sleep like this."

In the glowing light of the TV she glanced up at me, her eyes glassy and wide. She smiled. "Okay."

The urge to kiss her was so strong I felt my temple pulse as I clenched my free fist, digging nails into the flesh of my palm. I couldn't do that to her. I couldn't drag her down to my level.

"Come on," I said, trying to keep my voice steady, even. I led her down the hallway to her little room and she stumbled along behind me.

The bedroom was small, cell size. When I stepped inside, I felt the tension inside me getting ready to explode. The room surrounded me, trapped me, and I felt guilty for grabbing at her in my sleep that morning, for taking advantage of her niceness, for exposing her to a guy like Davis.

For enjoying spending time with her, for wanting her so bad I could practically taste her on my tongue.

She crawled onto the bed still in her sundress and peeled back the sheet. Once under it, she settled down onto her pillow with a sigh. Her hand reached out for mine. "Aren't you coming to bed?"

One, two, three small breaths out nice and slow. "In a minute," I told her, and my voice sounded completely normal. How, I had no idea. "I need to take a piss." I leaned forward and brushed her hair back off her forehead. When my hand started to shake I pulled it back.

"'kay." Her eyes were already closed.

I retreated slowly, trying not to make too much noise. I eased her door almost all the way shut, then went into the living room. Even though I wanted to punch the shit out of something, there was nothing to punch. Nothing to throw. So I did push-ups, at a grueling pace, three reps of thirty each. Then I went up and down the stairs twenty times, grateful for the old, dingy carpet so Robin couldn't hear me.

The doctors could take their meds and shove them up their asses. They'd made me take them in jail, and I hadn't felt any different. Intermittent explosive disorder? Go fuck yourself.

The only thing wrong with me was that my mom was an asshole and I'd been left on my own too much. Nothing else.

Someday I would fall in love like every other idiot did at one time or another. I just couldn't let it be with Robin.

But I knew how to control my emotions. I always had.

I went back upstairs, peeled off my shirt, and eased myself into bed beside Robin, still breathing hard. She was out cold, and I lay there and let my muscle fatigue become the focus of my thoughts. The way my shoulders burned, the strain in my calves. The pain crowded out the other thoughts, and I finally relaxed.

Careful not to move too much, I turned my head and watched her sleep. I hadn't had a lot of opportunities to sleep next to a girl. In high school my girlfriend had stayed over a few times when my mother wasn't home, but her parents had busted her and that had been the end of that. Angel had stayed with me once, but she had gotten pissed at me for taking too much space and had kicked me in the shins hard before stomping off to sleep on the couch.

But Robin seemed to like me in her space. She shifted toward me on the couch when we watched TV, she had turned toward me on the blanket in the park, and in bed she curled her legs up and tucked her hands under her chin, but always facing me.

I studied her face in the dark, wanting to memorize it, to sketch it later.

She was beautiful. She was naive.

She felt like my reward for surviving jail.

I stayed awake for an hour watching her, before drifting into oblivion.

ANOTHER NIGHTMARE SHATTERED MY SLEEP. IN THIS ONE I was watching my mother being raped by Iggy, half conscious from the beating he'd given her and from the drugs. Her body moved sluggish with each thrust, his grunts making my stomach roil, but there was a cell wall between me and her, so I couldn't help her.

Then it wasn't my mom anymore.

It was Robin, and her eyes were dead of any of the sweetness I'd seen, even void of the sadness she had shown me. They were just empty. Black holes. There was nothing there as that bastard abused her body in the most violating way possible.

I pounded on the cell walls, yelling, shaking the bars until my throat was hoarse and my hands were bleeding. I wanted to explode outside of myself and kill him for hurting her.

I had done this to her. I had killed her soul.

Then suddenly I fell through as the glass wall dissolved into nothing and I was free, but Robin wasn't there anymore . . .

Waking up with a start as I fell, I half sat up. I must have made a sound because Robin jerked awake, too.

"Shit," I muttered, heart pounding, sweat all over the back of my neck, the image of her still floating in front of my eyes. "God."

"Are you okay?" Her hand stroked my arm, then my back, her touch warm and small and caring.

And suddenly I didn't give a fuck that I was bad for her. She was letting me be there, right? She was offering comfort and I was going to take it, because I couldn't stand the way she had stared at me in my dream, like I wasn't there. Like I didn't exist.

"Yeah," I whispered, wiping my forehead as I eased myself back down onto the mattress. "I'm fine."

She touched my cheek and pushed my hair back. "Are you sure?"

Nodding, I shifted closer to her so that our faces were aligned. She was so beautiful, so sweet, so trusting. I ached with want, the need to touch her greater than my self-control. I needed to see her smile, see her willingness to kiss me. *Me*. Her eyes, still heavy with sleep, darkened as I watched her, running my fingers down her cheek to her lips.

She knew what I was about to do because her mouth drifted open, so that when I kissed her, she kissed me back. And of course, just to torture me, it felt as good as I had imagined. God. Those lips were plump and soft, and nothing had ever felt so simple and good and important. She gave a little sigh that had me pulling her leg up onto my hip so we could be closer, my other hand buried in her thick hair.

Robin was safe, I wasn't in a cell, and the kiss was perfect, our bodies pressed against each other, my tongue darting in between her lips. She opened for me without hesitation, and her hips started to rock against mine. Her skin, her breath, were warm, and my hands felt big, covering so much territory on her body at once. Our breathing got heavier, and I was inching under her dress, endorphins or whatever the hell they were called shutting down my ability to think rationally.

Which is exactly how we were when her roommate flung open the door and said, "Robin, sweetie, you awake—oh shit, sorry!"

Robin broke off our kiss and yanked her leg off of me, slumberous eyes now full alert. "Kylie?" she breathed, rolling onto her back and gripping her chest. "Oh my God, you scared the shit out of me."

"Sorry. I didn't know you had, um, a friend here." The blonde in the doorway eyed me with a naked curiosity that annoyed me. She started twirling her hair around her finger, and her hip came out as she leaned on the doorframe.

Shoving my hair out of my eye, I sat up, giving her a long look that hopefully would send her scurrying away. A little privacy wasn't too much to ask for, was it? Christ. Since she had just interrupted what was shaping up to be a fucking awesome moment.

Her eyes widened. "We can catch up later."

"What are you doing?" A guy's voice came booming down the hall, then a head appeared behind her. "What is going on here?" He took in Robin and me in bed, and he looked appalled. "Phoenix? Phoenix Sullivan?"

Fuck. I knew this guy. It was Nathan, Tyler's best friend from middle school on. I'd always thought he was a bit of a tool. "Nathan? What's up, man?" I gave him a casual head nod, reaching for Robin's hand.

Her cheeks were stained pink with embarrassment, and she had curled up into a ball.

"What the fuck are *you* doing here?" he asked me.

None of his business. I shrugged. "Hanging out with Robin."

"She's not just some chick you can screw around with." Nathan looked and sounded angry.

Robin made a small sound in the back of her throat, but otherwise she didn't say a word. She looked like she was fighting the urge to cry. She didn't seem anything like the girl I'd just spent the last forty-eight hours with. She looked like the girl I'd met in Tyler's living room, tenting herself inside her T-shirt. She was literally tucking her legs into her body right beside me. What the hell?

"Hey," I said, getting pissed off right back at him. "Mind your own business. You're embarrassing Robin. You don't know a goddamn thing about what is going on here, but I do think you know I'm not someone to fuck with." I'd mop the goddamn floor with him and his baseball scholarship. Thought he was someone because he was going to college. He could fuck the bat he swung to get there.

Since Robin's hand was tucked away, I couldn't squeeze it, but I did touch her hip when I stood up. I figured if I moved toward Nathan, he would back up. Which was exactly what he did.

"Does Tyler know?" he asked.

"Does Tyler know what?" My cousin appeared in the doorway, too, and when he saw me, the smile fell off his face. "Seriously? Phoenix, Jesus."

I stepped forward, but they all stayed crowded in the doorway. "Back up!" I demanded, irritated. "You're embarrassing her and it's really starting to make me angry."

Tyler knew well enough that angry was never a good look on me, so he tapped Nathan and jerked his head toward the living room. Once they cleared the doorway, I turned back to Robin and said, "It's all good, don't worry. Be back in a second." I pulled the door closed behind me so she could recover or whatever. She was starting to freak me out. She looked so upset, way more than the situation merited. We weren't even naked or anything. It was just a kiss. Well, kisses. It shouldn't be that big of a deal.

Other than the fact that I shouldn't have done it, but I didn't think she really understood that. This was something else.

"Is there where you've been the last two days?" Tyler asked me. A pale redhead put her hand on his arm, like she wanted to calm him down.

"Yeah."

"What about me saying it was a bad idea did you not understand?"

"The why."

Tyler clenched his fists. "Dude, it's like you want to screw yourself over. Why do you do that?"

"I don't know what you're talking about. We're just hanging out. It's not a big deal." But that was a lie. It *was* a big deal. I knew it was. It was a big deal in that they all knew just as well as I did that she was above my reach, but more important even than that, it was a big deal because I really, really liked her.

The door opened, and Robin appeared, arms across her

chest. "Why do any of you care?" she asked in a small voice. Then she went to the redhead and hugged her. "Hey, Rory, welcome back. I missed you."

Tyler got a sheepish look, but Nathan was still shooting me looks of instant death.

Then Robin went to the blonde and hugged her, too, hard, though she shifted out of the way when Nathan tried to hug her.

I was getting a bad feeling that I really wanted to ignore. "So is this move-in day?" I asked.

The blonde nodded. "Yeppers. I'm Kylie."

"Phoenix, Tyler's cousin. You need help unloading stuff?"

"Oh, God, yes, I have so much crap."

She wasn't lying. Her car was crammed with boxes, and we unloaded the car in an uneasy silence except for Kylie, who babbled like she had no clue she was with a group of pissed-off people. When both her and Rory's stuff was in the apartment, my cousin leveled a look at me. "Can I give you a ride back to the house?"

Since I was on day three of the same clothes, I didn't mind that he was about to go all paternal on me. Whatever. It was his personality, and I had been dealing with it for twenty years. "Sure."

Robin was in the kitchen helping Rory unpack some bowls or some shit, and I moved toward her. The look she gave me, man, it was like she was being abandoned in hell, and I felt like the worst jerk-off ever. "I need to go back and change. Want to come with me?" I asked, which hadn't been my original plan, but those eyes were killing me.

She shook her head. "I want to help here."

Moving my body so Rory couldn't see or hear, I bent over Robin and cupped her cheek. "What's going on?"

But she shook her head again.

There was no point in pressing her. She wasn't going to talk. "I'll call you."

She nodded.

Puzzled, and not liking the change in her, I hesitated but then Tyler yelled for me to come on, so I stroked her bottom lip with my thumb, remembering that amazing kiss, wanting her to remember it, too, before leaving.

"WHAT THE HELL?" TYLER ASKED ME IN IRRITATION AS WE went out to his car.

I didn't say anything. I didn't owe him any explanations.

"She's going through some shit, I don't think this is the time for you to be dicking around with her."

Yanking the car door open I narrowed my eyes at him over the top of the car. "I'm not dicking around. We're friends." I could see she was going through some shit, and it seemed to have something to do with their group of friends. She didn't want to live in the apartment and the minute everyone had shown up, her whole attitude had changed. "And how is me hanging out with her any different than you being with Rory or Riley being with Jessica? From what I hear, Jessica's parents cut her off for dating Riley and you all seem okay with that even though I think that would fall under the category of dicking around with her life."

With that I climbed in and slammed the door shut behind me. I was thirsty and hot and annoyed.

"Wow. You really like her, don't you?" Tyler started the car. "You sound about as rational as I did when I met Rory."

"Nothing I just said was irrational. And it's fucking hot as balls in this car. Don't you have air-conditioning?" I kicked off my shoes and stuck my arm out the window.

"Oh my God, your feet smell horrible, man. Look, if you really like Robin, then I can't say anything about that. It's just that something is clearly going down with her, and if you were just looking to hook up, I don't think I can be okay with that. She's a nice girl."

"It's never been my style to go after a chick. They usually come to me. So the fact that I am should tell you something."

"Yeah, that you're an arrogant douche bag." Tyler scoffed, amused.

It wasn't meant to be arrogant. But it was the truth, like I said. Girls wanted to get a reaction from me, so they flirted hardcore.

"Just, you know, maybe take it slow or something, that's all I'm saying." Tyler was fumbling in his dash trying to pull a cigarette out of his pack. "Dude, light a cigarette for me."

"No." I wasn't putting that poison to my mouth even for ten seconds.

He made a sound of exasperation. "I forgot, you're a purist. I respect that about you, but right now it's not helping my personal addiction."

"Robin is the only person I've ever met who is as clean as I am," I told him.

"Yeah, about that. She wasn't always that way. She was a regular on the party scene last year. So maybe it will last and maybe it won't. Just FYI."

"I know. She told me that." But it had me thinking. What had changed?

When we got back to the house, I showered and borrowed more clothes from Riley. I took all the dirty laundry from his and the boys' room downstairs and put it in the washing machine. Since I was bumming clothes off everyone, the least I could do was wash them. Though I wasn't sure who the SEXIEST BEARCAT tank top belonged to. It came out of Tyler's room, but I couldn't picture Rory wearing that, but what did I know?

Apparently not much. I sat out on the back patio where there was a decent breeze and I started doing some poking around on the Internet on my phone, checking out Robin's social media sites.

Tyler was definitely telling the truth. There were dozens of pictures of Robin posing with friends at parties with a glass in her hand, or sometimes a beer can. It didn't even really look like the girl I had met. She had big hair and lots of makeup on, and in every picture she was wearing tight and tiny clothes. Jessica and Kylie were with her a lot, and they were smiling and laughing and doing sexy poses. Douchey guys were photobombing half the shots or had their arms around the girls. There was only a picture or two with Rory in it, and she never dressed like her friends. They would be towering in high heels and miniskirts, and she would be wearing a floral dress with a lacy collar, looking out of place.

Robin definitely looked the party girl part in these pictures.

Interesting.

So which one was the real Robin?

I knew which one I liked better. The one I knew. The one who wore easy and loose clothes and who never had a single speck of makeup on her beautiful face. Those fake eyelashes crawling above her eyes in some of the pictures made me want to reach through my phone and yank them off. That wasn't her. I didn't think.

Where was the girl who studiously painted and sketched, her face a calm lake of concentration? Where was the girl who laid on the blanket beside me and quoted Thoreau to the sky?

It was disturbing, and after half an hour, I felt tense. There was only one recent picture of her up and it had a July date and had been posted by Jessica. Robin was wearing some kind of uniform and they were in a restaurant. The description was "We need tips, bitches!" written by Jessica. Robin was sitting down at the bar, bottles behind her, and she was leaning on her hand, like she was exhausted. The smile she gave the camera was luke-warm and forced, and there were circles under her eyes. I knew this face. Not the other ones.

Tossing my phone down on the picnic table, I tried to process what I was feeling. It was weird, but I already missed her.

And now I wanted to know what had changed in her life. What had happened.

When Tyler came and sat next to me to smoke a cigarette, I asked him, "Where's Jessica?" I knew she didn't know anything, given the conversation I'd heard between her and Robin, but I was curious what else she might be able to tell me.

"She and Riley took Easton to buy school supplies. Half an hour they'll be back and Riley will be bitching about how much paper costs and Easton will spend an hour rearranging his pen-cil case. Mark my words."

"Things seem good here, cuz." It did. They looked to have settled down into a life that was working for all of them.

"It is. Sad it couldn't really happen until after Mom died, but there it is. You know how it goes."

"I do." I propped my head with my hand. "I give it a month before my mom comes around looking for me or you to bum money off of. Just be prepared for it."

"I know."

"So what happened to Robin?" I asked, straight out. "Because something obviously did."

Tyler just shook his head. "I don't know. You said it yourself—if she wants to tell anyone, she will."

That wasn't good enough for me. Because I had a sneaking suspicion that despite what she had told Jessica, this was about a guy making her uncomfortable. And I also thought I knew who it was. "Was Nathan at that party? The one Jessica was talking about, back at the beginning of the summer?"

"Yeah." Tyler blew out a stream of smoke.

"Was Kylie?"

"No, she's been back home all summer."

"Who else was there?"

"I don't know. Bill, Nathan's roommate. Fifty other people. Robin was hanging around with some guy Jessica knows."

I didn't want to know what that meant. I could already feel the beginnings of jealousy. Frustrated, not sure why, I went to send a text to Robin. My first instinct was just to say "hey," but then I knew that wouldn't give me the response I wanted. So I started surfing for a kitten picture as Tyler watched me.

"Phoenix."

"Yeah?"

"If Robin isn't in a good place, if she isn't, you know, emotionally healthy or whatever, is that really the best person for you to be involved with? Don't get pissed. I'm just asking because we're blood. And I care."

He looked uncomfortable with what he had just said, and I appreciated the effort. "I don't know, man. But when has that ever stopped anyone from falling for a girl? Logic's got nothing to do with it." I shook my phone. "Hell, I'm searching for kitten pictures for her because she likes them. I mean, what the fuck does that tell you?"

"That you're whipped."

I gave my cousin a rueful look, not at all offended. "Exactly. Ty, you know what we did yesterday? We had a picnic in the park. A picnic. Who does that for me? No one."

"A girl who likes you." He shot me a grin. "Though God knows why."

"Kiss my ass."

"Did you shower?" He made puckering lips at me.

I recoiled. "Dude."

Tyler laughed so hard he started coughing. "I'm fine. Don't worry."

"I wasn't."

"Dick."

"Pussy."

Quality family time. That's what we were having. It felt good.

Jayden came out of the house with an unholy grin on his face. Then we got drenched with water as he let loose with a water gun. It actually knocked Tyler's cigarette out of his hand. I shook my hair out of my eyes and tried not to laugh.

"I'm going to kill Jessica for buying him that."

Tyler didn't really look mad. But he did leap off the picnic table and go after his brother, who screamed and ran into the kitchen, pulling the door shut behind him.

Wiping my now wet phone on my jeans, I sent Robin a picture of a cute and fluffy white kitten. I typed "you" in the message. Then I sent her a Grumpy Cat image. "Me."

Having saved two pictures of her off her page, the one of her at work looking so tired and an earlier one of her wearing a clinging red dress, spray tanned and arms up in the air as she danced, I was studying them side by side when she responded.

It was an image of two adult cats leaning shoulder to shoulder on each other. "Us," was all she had written.

Fuck me. I wanted that.

Despite what everyone seemed to think, I did have emotions other than anger.

I just didn't know what to do with them.

CHAPTER SEVEN

ROBIN

I WASN'T PLAYING IT COOL WITH PHOENIX. I KNEW THAT. I just didn't care. What did playing head games with guys get me ever? A boyfriend who cheated and a lot of casual dates. There was no flirt left in me. She seemed to have disappeared with the vodka. So I was just being honest with Phoenix and he seemed okay with it. Maybe in another three days he would get bored with me, but then whatever. It was better than pretending that I was too busy or too in demand to spend time with him.

But I did feel a twinge of embarrassment that maybe I had overreached with the cat picture. His response came right away, though, and had been to ask me if he could see me later, so I felt reassured. More than that. I felt pleased. Excited.

The way he had kissed me . . . like I was precious, fragile. Like he wanted to meld us together into one person. Like he genuinely liked me, like he looked at me and saw me and wanted *me*. It wasn't what I expected. It wasn't what I had ever experienced.

Then Kylie and Nathan had shown up and I had immediately felt guilty. Not only did I feel guilty about Kylie, but I felt guilty that Tyler knew and that Phoenix didn't. Plus I felt a little sick to my stomach at seeing Nathan, who had acted weird about Phoenix being there. I hadn't seen Nathan since that morning in his room, and I hadn't been with a guy since then, but here he had to go and see me in bed with someone? I knew he was thinking I was a slut and I didn't really blame him. There was no point in telling him the truth. I didn't want to talk to him and it didn't really matter what Nathan thought of me.

It couldn't be good. Not in the ways that mattered.

Having dinner with my parents tonight, I texted. Classes start 2morrow but maybe we could do something 2morrow nite?

I start work. 3 to 11. Lunch?

That was disappointing. I had wanted to see him tomorrow night and have him spend the night again. I liked having him there with me, especially with my roommates around. I was becoming resigned to the fact that I couldn't move out without causing huge drama. I was stuck. But it would be easier to see Nathan around the apartment with Phoenix there.

Which sounded so pathetic. And unfair. I hated myself for even thinking about it in those terms.

Maybe I didn't deserve to see him. Yet that didn't stop me from texting back.

I only have an hour free. 12:45 to 1:45.

I'll be there. Where should I meet you?

On campus. University center. Text me when you get there.

I wanted to add something. Like an "x" or an "o," or a heart or a smiley. All of which seemed too much.

K. See ya then.

K.

He didn't respond, because uh, why would he? And then I felt like a jerk.

Damn it. I decided right then and there that I was going to continue to do and say whatever I wanted with Phoenix. That this was my chance to have a totally pure experience with a guy, in the sense that I wasn't going to censor what I said or did. I was going to treat him exactly the way I would one of my girlfriends.

So I went for the smiley.

And he sent me back, get this, a rose. Swoon. Seriously, of all the guys I had ever dated, no one, not a single sucky one, had ever done that. It was simple. It was nothing much. Just a tiny graphic that required nothing more than him tapping it on the screen and hitting Send.

Yet it meant everything to me that the guy who was supposed to be such bad news was actually kind of charming. He reminded me of the Beast in the Disney version of *Beauty and the Beast*. Rough around the edges, a little bit grumpy, but well meaning. Sweet.

When I went off to my parents' house for dinner, I smiled as I sang along in the car to some Taylor Swift. The lyrics didn't suit my mood, but the upbeat tempo did.

The smile lasted even through my grandmother starting in on me about eating more.

"Skin and bones, it's disgusting. Men don't like a woman who looks like a chicken," she said to me, scooping more rice onto my plate.

"No thanks, I'm full," I told her, knowing I was offending her and, in her mind, offending my mother as well by refusing her cooking. But I was going to burst if I ate anything else.

She clucked. Her hair had gone gray before I was born and she refused to dye it. She also refused to say how old she was, but by my father's best geusstimation, she was eighty-nine, having had him at twenty-seven or thereabouts, because she had left Puerto Rico to come here for college and had married immediately. But whenever you asked her about any of it she gave vague responses and said things like, "Age is a state of mind. And muscle tone."

"I'm going to die before any of you are married," she said, looking tiny and forlorn in her chair at the foot of my parents' enormous and very traditional dining room table.

"Probably," my brother Eric said, which earned him a slap on the back of the head from my dad.

Dinner at my parents' every Sunday was a thing. You went unless you were vomiting from the flu or were recovering from major surgery. My aunt and uncle and cousins were there every week too, and my brother Marco had brought his girlfriend, Rebecca, for the first time, which was basically a sign of commitment. You didn't bring just anyone to Sunday dinner, but they both looked uncomfortable with the reference to marriage, and who could blame them? They'd only been dating a few months, but my grandmother had been sighing and giving them meaningful looks all afternoon.

For some reason, I'd been seated to the right of her at the table since I was about six, and it was a dubious honor. She was always overfeeding me and always criticizing me. My eyebrows were too thick, then too thin once I waxed them. I was too fat, too thin. Too outspoken, too quiet. I was silly to focus on my art, then silly to want to work in an office. She hated my clothes, no matter what they were. Yet I knew she would murder a man with nothing but her attitude and her handbag if he ever tried to hurt me.

"Robin Bernadette," she said, using my middle name like she always did, because it was a saint's name, whereas Robin was too English and pagan in her opinion. "You look like a girl who has had her heart broken. Tell your *abuela* who this rotten boy is."

Unfortunately, while Nathan might have proven himself rotten, it wasn't his fault. Not really.

"Mama, I think that's old news," my dad said. "Haven't you noticed she keeps sneaking looks at her cell phone under the table? And she's smiling today. There's a new boy." He tapped his temple, looking smug. "Trust me."

Well, since they had me all figured out, there wasn't much for me to say.

I wondered then about how we are raised, how it shapes us. Tyler and Phoenix had grown up with addicts, Rory without a mother, Jessica with a father who ran a huge church, while Kylie and I grew up in the so-called ordinary nuclear family. How had that made me who I was? Was it so very ordinary that I was ordinary?

I do know that when I applied to college I stressed over that damn entrance essay because what did I have to say? I couldn't outline how I invented an app for family members of cancer patients or did missionary work in Africa or was the daughter of a senator or had to navigate gang warfare to get to the community center where there was one teacher who believed in me. I lived in a middle-income, multicultural suburb of white, black, and Hispanic families where both parents worked as teachers, bank tellers, warehouse managers. Nothing other than ordinary people doing ordinary things.

My mother wanted me to milk my Latina heritage in my essay,

but it felt like bullshit to me, so I didn't. I wrote about expressing myself through art. My twelfth-grade English teacher gave me a "C" and suggested a rewrite. I didn't. But I got in to the design school and that was all I ever really wanted, so I figured it didn't matter.

Yet then I guess I fell off the rails, even though it didn't feel like that at the time. It just felt like a party. But now, it didn't feel like me.

Was it because I didn't have a strong identity or a real sense of myself? Was that what my high school boyfriend had meant? That I had a quasi sense of self?

I didn't know.

But I did know that today my father was right. I couldn't stop myself from smiling just a little. Despite my grandmother's comments about my disappearing breasts and my chicken wrists. Despite knowing that it was going to be hard to have Kylie and Nathan around the apartment.

"Leave her alone," my aunt Marguerite told my grandmother. "She looks beautiful, as usual."

"Actually, she looks hungover," Eric said.

That had me sitting up straighter. "I'm not hungover. I don't drink." That was one thing I did know. I wasn't going to be accused of doing something I was determined to stay away from.

The look he gave me was so skeptical that I made a face back at him.

My phone buzzed in my lap. When I glanced down I saw that Phoenix had sent me a text. Glancing down and up in the ridiculous hope that no one would guess what I was doing, I read the text.

Ink I want. What do u think?

It was his sketch of the snake from the park. I couldn't imagine where that was going to fit on his body, but I guess there were parts I hadn't seen yet. Yet? I felt my cheeks growing warm and when I raised my eyes I felt the beady-eyed stare of my grandmother. She said something in Spanish and I had no clue what it was.

But I didn't really want to know.

When I got back to the house around seven, Rory and Kylie were watching TV and they waved to me. "Sit." Kylie patted the couch next to her. "We totally need to catch up."

I should. I knew I had to. But I panicked. I couldn't sit there and pretend nothing had happened. I wasn't ready, or strong enough, and the scene from that morning was still fresh in my mind. The embarrassment I had felt when I had seen Nathan.

"I actually feel sick," I said. "I have super bad cramps. I need to lay down."

"Oh, bummer," Kylie said. "Take some Midol." She didn't look the least bit suspicious because Kylie never believed anyone had ill intentions. It was a gift she had, of pure happiness, all the time. Happiness I would destroy if she found out the truth.

Rory was eyeing me like she knew there was more to it than that, but she would never ask. She would think about it, analyze, study me. The one person I really had to avoid, truthfully, was Jessica. And, of course, Tyler. He knew almost all there was to know, but even he didn't know it went way beyond just making out in a car. Obviously Nathan wasn't going to tell, though I didn't want to see him either.

"Thanks. Glad you're both back," I said, forcing a smile.

Then I went down the hall and shut the door firmly to my little room. Sighing, I fell onto my bed and answered Phoenix.

We texted back and forth for three hours, about everything,

about nothing, until the TV in the living room went off and the line of light under my door disappeared. I felt safe in my room and relieved when Rory and Kylie went to bed. Classes started the next day, and I wasn't sure I was ready for the pressure of schoolwork, but at midnight, in the dark, with Phoenix distracting me, I thought I could deal.

He was funny, in a sly, side door kind of way.

He was also clearly interested in keeping the conversation going, and maybe it was me, maybe it would have been anyone who would talk to him, but I was grateful.

And even as I worried that developing feelings for a guy I felt grateful to was seriously pathetic, I couldn't stop myself.

Nite, I finally texted him when my eyes wouldn't stay open anymore.

See you tomorrow.

I closed my eyes, but I wished he was lying next to me, his quiet, steady breathing soothing me the way it had the past two nights.

It wasn't good. It wasn't good at all.

I knew I should cancel lunch with him. I knew I should pull away. That I couldn't let myself get pulled into a friendship I wasn't ready for, because I was still too raw, still holding on to my secret.

But I couldn't pull away.

Just the opposite.

WHEN I SAW PHOENIX WALKING ACROSS THE FOOD COURT IN the university center the next day, I bit my lip to keep from smiling too broadly. I was sitting at a table with plastic chairs around it, my backpack on the floor next to me. I had decided to wear another sundress again because they were so comfortable. My leg stubble was starting to grow back in, which meant I was on the edge of being a hippie, but the skirt was long enough that I had decided I didn't care. Phoenix was wearing jeans and a T-shirt, nothing weird, but without a backpack, he did look a little unusual. But what mostly struck me was the way he moved through the crowd, looking neither right or left, with a confidence and an aggressive walk that made people shift out of his way, probably without even realizing they did it.

He was swinging car keys around his finger, which meant he was ignoring his lack of a license again. I wondered why he didn't worry that if he got pulled over, he would wind up back in jail. When he got closer to me, the corner of his mouth turned up, and he was doing what I was doing—trying not to smile too much. We were both like a couple of middle schoolers making eye contact at a dance.

Flipping his hair out of his eye, he dropped into the chair next to me, his legs sprawling out. "Hey."

"Hey. You found me okay."

He smiled. "I have good tracking skills. You know, and the texts with the specific instructions like 'Next to KFC in the food court' helped, too."

"Good."

"Though I don't think you needed to point out what you're wearing. I'm pretty sure I'd recognize you whether your dress was floral or solid."

I wasn't sure why I had done that. He was right. We didn't recognize people based on their clothes, so why would I think he needed a description of my sundress to find me? "I overexplain.

Sorry. What do you want to eat? I have a ton of points on my meal plan and I never use them all, so lunch is on me."

"I can pay for myself," he said, even though we both knew he couldn't.

"But why should you when I have all this credit? Last year there was, like, two hundred bucks unused at the end of the year, and it doesn't get credited back to you." I didn't have a meal plan anymore since I wasn't living in the dorm, but he didn't know that. I had a swipe card that billed everything to a central account where my tuition and books showed up, too. I figured I would go in and pay the food expenses myself before my parents saw it and it would allow me to trick Phoenix into letting me pay for lunch.

"Okay," he said, but he looked reluctant. He did insist on carrying my tray back to the table after we ordered. I got a bowl of soup and he got a burrito the size of my head.

When we sat back down, the group of girls at the table next to us stared boldly. I knew one of them from my literature class, and the others I had seen at parties, but I didn't know their names. I smiled tightly at them when we made eye contact, but they didn't look away. I could hear them whispering.

"OMG, who is that chick Robin with? Is he like her bodyguard or something?"

I knew that Phoenix heard them, too, because his shoulders were rigid, but otherwise he showed no change in emotion. He was better, a thousand times better, at hiding his emotion than I was. I knew I probably looked uncomfortable. But I just sat there and spread out my napkin in my lap.

"Bodyguard? She doesn't need a bodyguard, she needs a stylist. She looks like hell this year. WTF happened to her?"

I paused with my spoon halfway to my mouth.

"I heard she has cancer, that's why. I mean, look at her. I'm surprised she's even here for classes."

"I heard she spent the summer at rehab. Drugs."

"No, it was for sex addiction."

Phoenix made a sound of disgust and he leaned over and touched one of the girls' arms. She jumped and looked at him like he was a zombie out for her flesh.

"I'm sorry to interrupt your gossip session," he said. "But we can hear every word you're saying and it's rude. In case you didn't realize that."

Their mouths all dropped open. Two had the decency to look shamefaced, but the third just sneered. "Sorry," she said, and it was about as insincere as you can get. "But now you can clear up the mystery for us. Who are you? I'm Frannie."

"Go fuck yourself, Frannie," he said in a very polite voice, a tight smile on his face. Then he picked up my tray and his and moved us three tables over.

They had no response, clearly as shocked as I was.

I followed him, their gasps of indignation washing over me, not sure how I felt. I was embarrassed that people were talking about me, that my appearance was so noticeably different it was grounds for gossip. But at the same time, I didn't really give a shit what they thought of me. They weren't my friends and never would be. They were bored girls with no real worries in their lives. I had been one of them. But now I knew I had no business judging anyone else.

I also wasn't sure how I felt about Phoenix feeling like he had to defend me.

"You shouldn't have to listen to that shit," Phoenix said, his jaw tense, his nostrils flaring. He moved back and forth in front of the table for a second before he yanked the chair out and sat down. I could see him pulling himself in, controlling his emotions and his body.

"It's okay," I told him. "It doesn't matter, and they are right, you know. I do look like hell. But I'm okay with it." I was. If it truly bothered me, I would put on makeup. But I couldn't work up the energy to worry about it. It was nice not to have to reapply lipstick every hour.

"You do not." Phoenix glanced away for a second, and when he looked back at me, my breath caught in my throat. He looked at me like I was important, special. "You're beautiful, you know."

To him, I was. I could see that and it had more impact than any bitchy comments from girls I didn't know. "Thank you," I whispered.

"Are they right, in any way?" he asked, and I realized his face was pale. "Do you have cancer?"

Oh, God. I shook my head rapidly, feeling guilty all over again. "No! No, of course not. I'm not sick at all. And no, I didn't go to rehab either, though I did stop drinking because I had one of those nights where I blacked out and it scared the shit out of me." That was as close to the truth as I could get, but I wanted him to understand that he shouldn't feel sorry for me. I didn't deserve his pity or sympathy.

He gave a sigh, one that seemed like relief to me, and he nodded. "I'm glad to hear it. For a second I thought, what if they're right?" He looked like he was going to say something else, but he didn't. He just shook his head. "Anyway. Eat your soup."

I took a spoonful, but my appetite was gone. I couldn't think of anything to say that wasn't either supercharged or totally generic chitchat, which seemed almost insulting. Conversation for strangers, and whatever Phoenix was, he wasn't a stranger. So finally I asked what I wanted to know. "Can I ask you something?"

He nodded, chewing his burrito. "Sure. But make sure you're prepared for the answer."

That was a good point. But I still asked it anyway. I needed to know before I let myself fall any further. "Did you love Angel? Do you still love her?"

His eyebrows rose. It obviously was not a question he was anticipating. But then he smiled and shook his head. "No. I never loved her. She was interested in me. I figured, why not? And I did care about her. But then for someone who claimed to want me so much, she couldn't be bothered to visit me when I was in."

"So you're more angry than hurt?"

"Yeah, I guess. But I suppose I'm not even all that angry, because anger on me is a lot louder and messier than what you saw."

It seemed like a warning. Or maybe I just took it that way. I didn't have a lot of experience with anger. Passive-aggressive behavior? Sure. But not pure anger. "Well, I'm still sorry that she wasn't an honest girlfriend to you."

"It's okay." Phoenix leaned forward, closer to me. "Can I ask you a question now?"

"Sure. Just be prepared for the answer," I parroted back to him, hoping he wouldn't ask me anything I felt like I couldn't answer.

"What's his name?"

"Who?"

"The guy everyone thinks did this to you."

"Did what?" I asked, heart starting to race. "No one did any-thing to me."

"What those girls noticed." He pulled his phone out of his pocket and started swiping at it. "I am being honest, you look beautiful to me, but you do look different. What happened at that party where you blacked out?" he asked.

Then he showed me a picture of myself from early in the summer. I was drunk, yelling, plastic cup in the air. I was in full makeup, cleavage out, hair hot-rolled into waves. My lip curled before I could stop myself.

"No one did anything to me. That is the truth. And even if they did, why would you want his name?"

"So I can beat the shit out of him."

I tore my eyes off his phone screen to stare at him. He sounded serious. He looked serious. Tightly wound, the caged tiger, ready to attack the minute the gate was raised. "I don't need you to do that, but even if I did, aren't you on probation or something? And why were you in prison anyway?"

"For beating the shit out of someone."

My jaw dropped. It made sense. I mean, if it wasn't drugs or driving under the influence, what would it be? I didn't think he was the kind for stealing. It just didn't match the behavior I had seen. But fighting? It wasn't that hard to picture. A five-month sentence seemed harsh for assault, though it wasn't like I really had any clue about sentencing and the justice system. Maybe I had been avoiding asking because while I wanted to respect his privacy I also just didn't want to have to face the fact that Phoenix had done something wrong. I wanted to hold on to the belief that like Tyler, he had been wrongfully imprisoned in some way, despite what Tyler himself had hinted at.

My pause where I processed that information grew too long, and he gave a sound of exasperation.

"Don't worry, I only beat the shit out of people who deserve it."

"Who deserved it?" I asked in a quiet voice, wondering if anyone ever truly deserved it.

"My mom's piece-of-shit boyfriend, who just happens to be a drug dealer. Some of his inventory went missing and he decided my mother took it. I caught him with a knife, carving up her stomach while he . . ."

I was horrified, and my face must have reflected that.

Phoenix cut his words off, shaking his head. His lips were pursed. "Never mind. But he deserved it for that and for all the times he hit her before that. And I'm not even sorry for it. I'd do it again if the circumstances were the same."

I saw that he meant it. All for a woman who hadn't bothered to tell him where she was moving while he was in prison for defending her. So I just nodded, because I had no idea what to say. I didn't understand that world and I didn't know what it would feel like to watch your mother being abused or how instinctive it would be to use violence to stop violence. I did think that it was the right thing to do to stop someone hurting another person, that in a situation where nothing was right, it was more wrong to walk away and pretend it wasn't happening.

A knife carving up her stomach. Good God.

Phoenix pushed his tray away. "I should probably just go."

"Why?" That upset me. I didn't want him to walk away with anything awkward between us. I wasn't even sure how I felt, but

I knew I didn't have any right to judge something I didn't know anything about.

"Because . . ." He looked away and shook his head.

"Why?" I repeated, both of our lunches totally abandoned.

"Because I like you." Phoenix turned back and met my gaze. "And I won't be good for you."

My throat tightened. "I think maybe you think I'm a better person than I am."

But Phoenix shifted his chair closer to me so we were sitting next to each other, and he took my hand. "Robin."

"Yes?"

"I'm no good for you. And you're probably no good for me. But we're going to do this anyway, aren't we?"

I nodded, because looking into his dark eyes there wasn't any other answer. I couldn't walk away from him, and I couldn't let him walk away from me. "Yes. We are."

"I thought so," he murmured, and he kissed me in the food court, a quick brush of his lips over mine.

My skin tingled, and I sighed.

Oh yeah, we were definitely going to do this.

It was the only thing I'd been sure of all summer.

When the truth was that an ordinary life with an ordinary family hadn't just made me ordinary, it had made me naive. Because in that moment, I genuinely thought that Phoenix's background, his anger, my secret, didn't matter at all.

It did.

CHAPTER EIGHT

PHOENIX

THE VERY MINUTE I KNEW I WAS DONE FOR? WHEN ROBIN asked me if I loved Angel. Because when a girl asks that, she wants to know if there is room in your heart for her. I knew that not only was there room for Robin, she could probably work her way through it until she was in every single crevice, spreading like octopus ink across the ocean floor. I got in to octopuses in fourth grade, checking out every book I could at the library about them and featuring them in all my reports and art projects. The teacher wrote a note to my mother about my obsessive behavior, which I never gave her. But I remember thinking, what is so wrong with digging octopuses? They have eight legs and suckers and spew ink—is it any wonder I was fascinated?

But there is a fine line our world dictates between an appropriate and healthy interest in something and obsession. If you express too little interest in anything in particular, you're lazy, a slacker, lacking in hobbies and liable to fall in with the wrong crowd. If you show too much interest, then clearly you're obsessive-compulsive, unnatural.

I had already been fixating on Robin, I knew that. But when she made it clear that she was interested in having me fall in love with her, or that she wanted to know if the possibility was there, I knew that I had moved into octopus territory. I wanted to know everything there was to know about her—I wanted to see her all the time, touch her, smell her, unlock the mysteries of her body.

There would be disapproval from somewhere—maybe everywhere—but I didn't give a shit.

I walked her to her class after she mostly didn't eat her lunch, holding her hand, which felt small and delicate in mine, ignoring everyone who glanced at us. "So what are you studying?" I asked her. "Art?"

"No. Art isn't practical. Graphic design. It's a way to be sort of creative and actually make a living."

"That makes sense." Still, I had a hard time picturing her in an office or whatever. I thought of her head bent over the kitchen table or her sketching in the park. That was when she seemed happy. "Did you ever wonder why you were born with a talent if you can't fully use it? I mean, we can't all be Michelangelo painting the Sistine Chapel, so why are we born with this burn to draw?"

"Maybe because we're people and we're flawed." She glanced up at me, her hair tumbling around her face wildly as we walked down the path, students rushing past us on bikes. "For every ten thousand people who have that talent, only one will fully realize their potential."

Sad but true. I didn't know anyone who had reached their

full potential. Most gave up long before that when the daily grind beat the crap out of them. "Life has a way of doing that. I mean, look at you and me. Neither one of us can pursue studying art. We have to be practical."

"Yeah. I used to want to run off to Italy or France and study the masters or at the very least have the courage to set up a stall in New Orleans or some place like that and sell my paintings. The starving artist's life. But I'm too . . . I don't know. Afraid, I guess. Plain and simple."

"It's harder to let go of fear when you have something to lose. Being fearless is easier if you have nothing to risk." In my case, I had absolutely nothing to lose. But I'd never had particularly grand ambitions. "I suppose I could just as easily be homeless in New Orleans as I can be here, so if I really wanted to do something like that I could, if I could figure out how to get there."

Her hand squeezed mine tighter. "You're not homeless."

For the moment. "Riley politely asked me to leave as soon as I can. He's worried about his custody of Easton. You know, the whole felony conviction thing." I was glad I had told Robin about why I'd been in. I didn't want her to find out from someone else, and I didn't want secrets between us if we were going to have a shot at a relationship. Granted, I hadn't told her the full truth, how I had found Iggy raping my mother, but she knew that yes, I was in fact guilty of the crime I'd been in jail for. I had nearly killed him, and I had done it for my mother, whether she appreciated it or not, because no man should be allowed to use his physical power over a woman.

Robin still had a secret, I knew that. Something had happened the night she had blacked out and she knew what it was.

She just wasn't ready to share, and that was okay. I was about 99 percent sure it had something to do with Nathan, because that made the most sense. It wasn't that hard to imagine she was wasted, his girlfriend was gone, he pushed her mouth down on his dick because everyone is always after what they can get.

I was going to get the truth, and then I was going to make Nathan pay for it.

But that was for later.

Right now, I just wanted to sit back and let Robin work her way inside my heart with her shy smiles and her big, brown eyes.

"Oh," she said, and she bit her lip. "I guess I can understand that, but it still sucks."

"I don't blame Riley or Tyler. They've done a lot for me." More than I had actually expected. But it did feel like with our mothers gone, the bond between us was stronger. "I'll figure something out."

"You can stay over with me whenever you need to," she said.

I smiled. The words were said casually, like she was being polite, but I knew better than that. She wanted me there. I wanted to be there. "Cool. Thanks. But I don't get off work until eleven and I don't want to keep you up."

She stopped walking. "This is my building." She gestured behind her to a glass monstrosity. "What are your days off work? Do you know yet?"

"Wednesday and Thursday. Weekends are big for tattoo walk-ins."

Her face lit up. "Those are my days off, too. Well, and Mondays and Tuesdays. I work Friday through Sunday."

"That works out then." I glanced up at her classroom building, knowing she had to go, not wanting to let her leave. I had never felt this, the compulsion to be with a girl every second I could, and I didn't know what to do with it.

"Have a good first day at work," she told me. "This is going to be a great opportunity for you."

"Thanks," I said, surprised. It was just a standard thing to say, I guess, but it wasn't what I usually heard. What might just be politeness sounded an awful lot like caring to me, and I was hungry to hear that. It might be what prompted me to say, "Tonight I'll probably be really tired, but can I stay over tomorrow night? What time do you go to bed?"

"I don't usually go to bed until midnight." She tucked her hair behind her ears. "Yes, you can stay over."

It was there again, that intriguing shyness she had, where she met my eyes, then glanced away, as if she were embarrassed by her willingness. I can't lie. I found it fucking adorable. It also increased my confidence in her feelings for me.

God only knew what she was seeing when she looked at me, but she was willing to give this a shot, and that was all I could ask for.

"Okay, cool. I'll text you later." I tucked her hair behind her ear after it sprung free again. She had thick hair. "Now you'd better go."

"Right. Talk to you later." She turned and jogged up the steps without looking back at me, her dress swirling around her feet.

At work as I booked tat appointments and watched artists doing ink on customers, I felt pretty goddamn grateful.

Exactly one week earlier I had been sitting in my cell in a jumpsuit praying my release didn't get messed up or delayed.

Now here I was, working at a cool shop where no one judged me, my cousins at my back, and a new girl who didn't seem to care where I'd been, just about who I was.

Pretty fucking awesome.

When I showed up at her house on Tuesday night around eleven thirty, Robin let me in with a smile. "Hi."

She was wearing pj shorts and a tank top that made my mouth water. Her nipples were clearly outlined beneath the cotton, and I wanted to suck each of them into my mouth and listen to her groan softly in my ear. We'd barely even kissed so far, but I had every intention of changing that in the next twenty minutes if she was down with that. I kept thinking about how it felt to lie in bed next to her, hearing her steady breathing, and I wanted to do that naked, her body as close to mine as it could be.

"How was work?" she asked.

"It's going good. I mean, it would be better if I could ink customers myself, but I can be patient. And maybe I can talk Riley and Tyler into letting me practice on them."

She was about to jog up the stairs to the third floor, but I pulled her to a stop in the stairwell and drew her into my arms. Her breath caught as I rested my palms on the small of her back, giving her a smile. "Hey."

"Hey what?" she asked, though she obviously knew what I was after. Her eyes were wide, and her fingers had crept onto my chest.

"How about giving me a kiss? I think that's a standard greeting."

"Not for just anyone," she whispered, but she went on her tiptoes and kissed me, her eyes drifting shut.

She kissed the way I liked, with soft lips and little sound, just the quick increase in breathing as her grip tightened on my chest. The kiss dissolved into a sigh, and she pulled back, her mouth still close to mine. "Is that a good hello?"

"Very good. Now show me how you say that you're glad to see me." I nuzzled into her neck, kissing her tender flesh there, my thumbs slipping under her waistband.

Her body shifted closer to mine, and I felt the press of her breasts on my chest, her tight nipples scraping across my T-shirt. Goddamn it, I wanted her so bad. When she kissed me again, pulling my mouth to hers for a deep kiss with a hot tangle of our tongues, I buried my hands in her hair to hold her against me. To keep her with me.

But when I started to grip her ass to rhythmically bump our hips together, she turned her head with a groan. "Phoenix. We should go to my room."

I took it as a green light, and my dick got harder in anticipation. Before work I had stopped at the drugstore and bought condoms with my under-the-table pay from the day before, and they were in my back pocket. Hopefully she was on the Pill for a double dose of birth control, but I still wanted to use a condom to show her that I cared about her and wanted to keep her safe. I didn't think I had anything skeezy, but it wasn't like I really knew that for a fact.

"Sure." I kissed her softly and took her hand. "Unless you want to watch a movie or something."

But she said, "No. I'm ready for bed."

There was a double meaning there, I was sure of it. She was telling me she was ready, if going braless hadn't already been a clue.

Or maybe I was reading it all wrong.

I was debating that as we went up the stairs, me leading her by the hand and into her tiny room. The answer was obvious when I went to turn the light on and she shook her head.

"Can you leave it off?" she whispered.

"Sure, baby, sure." Something shifted inside me and I didn't even want to think about what it was. So instead, I peeled off my shirt and kissed her in the dark, feeling my way across her body for the first time. Exploring her breasts and her ass and the hot V between her legs with my thumb, listening to her soft sighs and sounds of encouragement.

When my finger slipped inside her shorts and panties, into her wet heat, she gave a sharp cry of excitement and it almost undid me. After stroking her for a few minutes, learning the angle she liked best, finding her clit and brushing over it, I stepped back and lifted her tank top off over her head. She had breasts the perfect size, just enough for me to cup while I sucked at her nipple until her nails clawed at my bare back and her breath came in short gasps. Not wanting her to come just yet, I moved up and kissed her deeply, the taste of her flesh still in my mouth, as I took her hand and slid it across my cock over my jeans.

"Are we going too fast?" I asked her when her fingers jerked reflexively. "I can slow down." Unless it was good for her, it wasn't going to be good for me.

"No," she whispered, and I could feel her warm breath on my neck. "It's just that I don't have a ton of experience, and almost none of it was sober. It's stupid, but I'm nervous."

That she was trusting me to be the one here with her, totally sober, made me want to do anything to protect her, to make her happy, to please her. Love wasn't something I knew, or had felt much of before, but I was starting to wonder if it was possible for it to happen this fast, because what I felt for Robin was . . . more.

"Babe, it's fine." I kissed the corner of her mouth. "I'm glad you told me, and it's not stupid. What you feel is never stupid. We'll just do whatever you're comfortable with, okay?"

She nodded, and I felt the movement more than I saw it. Her hands were clutching the waistband of my jeans and I felt a complete wave of tenderness come over me. God, I was actually grateful for the dark myself because if the lights came on she was probably going to see me staring at her like a total jackass.

"Can I feel it first?" she whispered, her fingers teasing across the snap of my jeans.

Oh, hell, yeah, she could feel it. "You can do whatever you want."

I closed my eyes and clenched my jaw, getting control as she undid the snap and pulled my zipper down with trembling fingers. When her hand went into my pants and she brushed down the length of my dick, I was pretty sure it was right up there with the top ten best moments of my life. She stroked me softly, and I resisted the urge to close my wrist over hers and have her squeeze harder, stroke faster. I let her do what she wanted, and her exploration was slow and thorough.

At one point I did reach back and pull the condoms out, then shoved the jeans down so they fell toward my knees, but other than that I just kissed her, my hands stroking in her hair while she stroked me, my dick, my chest, my ass. I'm not going to lie, I liked that she said she didn't have a lot of experience. I liked the idea that as I maneuvered downward, over her breasts and across her stomach and pressed my finger inside her, that somehow my stamp on her would be greater than any other guy's. She responded by gripping me tighter, and I felt a hot rush of urgency.

"Come to the bed," I said, encouraging her forward and pushing her down on her back.

In a second I had her shorts and panties off. Before I climbed up alongside her, I got rid of the rest of my clothes, too, and fumbled for the condom. "Are you sure?" I asked her as I moved over her, teasing at her hot opening.

"Yes."

Good. I rubbed the pad of my thumb over her clitoris, then I pushed inside her. Her breath caught, and her nails dug into my arms. I stopped short, an agony of pleasure crashing over me. Holy fuck, she was tight and hot, and I was in desperate need of control. Holding on, I stilled my whole body except for the throb inside her and counted to five slowly. Then I started to move, enjoying the way she let her hips fall apart further and the way her fingers relaxed with each push, until she was holding me with a whispery touch, her sighs and moans of pleasure relaxed and beautiful. I wished I could see her expression, but it was too dark to see much more than the outline of her body, her face.

When I started getting too close, I pulled out and went down on her, feeling her body jerk at the first touch of my tongue.

"Phoenix," she said, and I had never heard my name like that. For the first time ever, I didn't despise it, the way she said it when she gripped my hair and had an orgasm, her thighs shuddering on either side of me, her sweet taste on my tongue.

When I moved back up and inside her, she was even more

relaxed, her body wide open to mine, and I didn't last long, exploding inside her with a hot shudder.

Collapsing beside her, I pulled Robin onto my chest and tried to breathe. With my right hand I peeled down the condom, left hand firmly wrapped around her. "Babe, you're amazing."

She didn't say anything, but I didn't mind. Too much pointless talking made me uncomfortable. But it seemed like everything Robin said was important. Her fingers spread over my chest, and the soft touch matched the pace of my breathing as it evened out.

I kissed the top of her head.

And long after she fell asleep, I lay there wide awake, naked.

Wondering if I had finally experienced the one high I couldn't resist.

Falling in love.

CHAPTER NINE

ROBIN

WHEN I WOKE UP, THERE WAS NO POUNDING HEAD, NO DRY mouth, no whisper of regret. Instead there was a warm, delicious satisfaction as I slowly became aware of being completely naked in bed with Phoenix. He was lightly snoring, his hair in his eye, arm still wrapped around me. Feeling a little giddy, I studied his face, his strong jaw, his long eyelashes.

I had been telling him the truth—I had made out with a lot of guys, but I didn't usually go home with them, except for Nathan, so I really didn't have massive amounts of sexual experience. But that, with Phoenix, had been awesome. It had felt like he was everything, in every inch of me, like our bodies truly were one.

Not to mention that I'd had an orgasm, which happened with a guy, like, never.

He must have sensed me watching him, because his eyes suddenly popped open, and he jerked forward. When he saw it was me, he settled back on the pillow and smiled. "Morning."

"Good morning." I shifted my leg over his and felt a shiver of pleasure, both at the way he felt, firm and rough, and the fact that I wasn't embarrassed to do it.

Phoenix rolled over so that he was on top of me. With a sigh, his eyes still sleepy, he kissed me. "Mm," he said. "Did you sleep good?"

"Yes," I answered truthfully. "You?"

"The best." He reached over and got a condom off the upside-down crate that served as my nightstand.

Then he was inside me again, and I sighed with pleasure, relaxed and lazy, still not fully awake. When I came, it was an even bigger surprise than the night before. Who comes during actual missionary position sex with zero foreplay first thing in the morning? Holy shit, it seemed I did, at least when Phoenix did that thing, where his thumb stroked over my clit and he moved in a way I couldn't explain, like stealth penis. A sneak attack, hitting the most perfect spot imaginable.

"Oh, God," I cried.

The look he gave me was so possessive and satisfied that when he gripped the headboard and came with gritted teeth, my eyes actually rolled back in my head as I had another little mini-orgasm.

When he stopped moving finally and I could think, speak, I swallowed hard and said, "Who has two thumbs and just came twice? This girl. Holy crap."

Phoenix laughed softly. "Glad to hear it." He kissed me again. "Best way to start the day."

"I concur." The moment was worth busting out extra vocab. And I was feeling more like myself than I had in a million years.

He stood up, pulling off the condom. In the morning light, I studied him. Nice. Very nice. "What does your tattoo mean?" I asked, rolling onto my side, propping my head with my hand, tugging the sheet over me. I wasn't comfortable just lying there totally naked when he wasn't actually touching me.

"Which one?" He scratched his chest, flipping his hair out of his eye. He didn't seem even remotely self-conscious about being naked, but then again, most guys weren't.

"The bleeding heart." I wanted to know who had broken his heart. Who I had to compete with, I guess. It was why I had asked him about Angel, which was not even remotely subtle, I know, like none of my actions had been, but I was going with my gut. And my gut said if I wanted to know something, I should ask the question.

But he just shrugged. "It doesn't mean anything. I just liked the artwork."

Taken by surprise, I just stared at him as he pulled on his shorts and said, "Be right back," and left the room. I could hear him go into the bathroom and shut the door.

It didn't mean anything? A life-size severed image over his own heart, dripping blood all the way down his rib cage and gut? That seemed a little hard to believe.

But maybe he didn't want to talk about it. It wasn't like I didn't have a secret of my own.

That deflated my lazy contentment, and I got up, pulling on shorts and a T-shirt. When Phoenix reappeared we went down to the kitchen and found Kylie sitting at the table eating oatmeal. I had class in ninety minutes, but she had a nine a.m. and looked on the verge of leaving, to my relief.

"Hey," she said, with a cheerful smile. "There's coffee left if you want it."

"Thanks." Guilt rose up in my mouth like bile. Just when I started to enjoy myself, to feel human again, it was back, and rightly so. The day I could look at Kylie and not feel a twinge of guilt was the day I officially sucked.

"Catch you later, you cute little lovebirds!" she sang out, dumping her dirty bowl in the sink and leaving it as she rushed from the kitchen, blowing kisses at us.

"She's a lot of a lot, isn't she?" Phoenix asked, opening up cupboards until he found the coffee mugs. He pulled two down. "So what time are you done with classes?"

"Three." I took the coffee he gave to me and took a sip.

"You doing anything? Want to hang out? They don't need me to work today."

I nodded. "Yes." I did. I wanted to spend every minute with him.

Every single second.

Every nanosecond.

Without thinking about it, I put down my coffee, snaked my arms around his neck, and kissed the shit out of him.

"I want to kidnap you," he murmured in my ear. "So that I never have to let you go."

"Please do," I told him.

"Classes just started yesterday," he whispered, mouth hot on my neck as he trailed kisses along my collarbone. "You can't skip."

"But I want to." I did.

"I'll pick you up at three thirty." He peeled the top of my T-shirt down and sucked the swell of my breast. "'Kay?"

"Okay." But I reached for the button on his shorts, thinking that it might be a much better idea to go back to bed.

Phoenix stepped away and shook his head. "Go to school. You're, what, half done with your degree? Don't screw it up now, not because of me."

I saw that he would feel guilty if I skipped, so I sighed and said, "Fine."

Phoenix laughed. "You're adorable when you're being a baby."

"I'm not being a baby!" Not much anyway.

He reached out and gently squeezed my bottom lip. "You're pouting."

I was. Damn it. But he just replaced his finger with his mouth and kissed me.

I went to class, but I didn't hear a word my professors said. Instead I daydreamed about Phoenix and me running off to New Orleans and living like hippies on my art and his tattoo work. We would have a dog and a tiny apartment in the French Quarter and I would never wear makeup again and he would always think I was beautiful.

There was nothing wrong with dreaming.

Except when I left campus at three I realized it was the first day for my Tuesday–Thursday classes, and I was already behind.

My schedule was heavy with business courses, and none of it seemed like anything I wanted to do. Ever.

But I didn't have a choice, did I? So I went to the coffee shop and started in on reading a textbook.

"I HAVE TO GO TO THE STORE," PHOENIX TOLD ME WHEN I picked him up at his cousins' house. "Do you mind going with me?"

"No. What do you need to buy?" I pulled down the street. I had been planning to go in the house and say hi to everyone, but Phoenix had been waiting on the front step and he'd gotten into the car immediately. I felt a little guilty, like I was blowing off Jessica, but then again, I didn't even know if she was home or not.

"Well, I went into prison with my clothes and five bucks and that's basically all I have to my name right now since my mom disappeared. I need to buy basic stuff like deodorant and some shirts. I can't keep borrowing my cousins' shit."

"Okay." I tried to imagine only owning the clothes I was wearing and couldn't. I had a whole bedroom full of stuff at my parents' house—clothes and mementos and old electronics. The thought of all of it disappearing freaked me out completely.

When we walked into the discount store, Phoenix said, "I have forty-five bucks, that's it. So I need to do some math. I'm getting paid every day under the table, but I had to pay Riley back for my phone, and I still owe them, like, another hundred bucks, so it's going to be tight for the next month."

Forty-five dollars? What the hell was he going to buy for forty-five dollars? But I got a cart and got my phone out of my purse. "We can use the calculator on my phone. By the way, I want to buy some art supplies after we're done here. The craft store has cheap canvases."

In recent years I had minimized my painting to school projects or pop art. I hadn't painted the way I had in high school in more than two years, but suddenly I wanted to really create, to take my brush and pour out my feelings in a genuine, dark oil. Maybe a self-portrait. Or maybe a lonely lighthouse. Something to express the emotions that had been overwhelming me, the ones I wanted to get rid of.

"Cool." Phoenix picked up the generic version of everything, from toothpaste to deodorant to sports drink, and put them in the cart. "What are we at?" he asked me.

I squinted at the screen on my phone. "Twenty-two dollars. But there will be tax."

"Okay. We're cool." He bought two T-shirts that were five bucks each and a pair of boxer briefs. "That's good enough for now."

Impressive.

What was even more impressive was that when we were near the checkout lane he decided to spend the last five bucks in his budget on a bouquet of flowers, not for me, but for his aunt's grave.

"I know they'll go brown in, like, two days, but I don't know, it seems like the right thing to do," he said, actually lifting the bouquet of cheerful daisies to his nose, which he wrinkled. "Well, they smell like shit, but seeing as she's dead, I guess it won't matter."

Really? Boys could be so sweet and silly at the same time. "I guess not. So I guess you're planning on going to the cemetery?"

"Yeah. I missed the funeral so I would like to do that. If you don't want to go with me, I understand. I can borrow Riley's car." He started to load his stuff onto the belt for the cashier.

"No, it's fine. If you don't mind me being there." Grief was a private thing, and I wasn't sure if I would be intruding or not. I wanted to add that he really shouldn't be driving, but I figured a guy who didn't have much of a mother wouldn't particularly appreciate a girl he had just started seeing to go all maternal-nag on him.

Phoenix cupped my cheek in the checkout line. "I don't mind you being there. In fact, I would like that very much. In fact, I like you very much."

It was official. I was falling in love with him. He was just so . . . intense, in a good way. And after the night before and that morning, it felt so natural to have him touch me. So tingly. So perfect. There was a familiarity, an intimacy with him that I had never experienced with any other guy.

He gave me that earnest look he had, the one that made me feel like I was the only human being on the planet, and I melted. I wanted him to kiss me and I started up on my toes when the cashier said, "I said, forty-three twenty-two."

Giving me a smile, Phoenix turned. "Sorry," he apologized to the cashier as he handed her his money.

My phone was buzzing in my pocket. I pulled it out absently, then quickly turned the screen toward my stomach when I saw it was Nathan. Shit. What the hell did he want? Casually I tilted my phone so I could read it and get rid of it.

You can't be serious about that guy.

I made a face as I deleted the message. Obviously he was talking about Phoenix, but the real question was, why did he give a shit?

My phone buzzed with another text.

He's a loser.

That annoyed me. It was none of Nathan's business who I was spending time with, and as far as I could tell, Phoenix was making the best of a crap start in life. Yes, he had been to prison, but it was for defending his own mother. He was completely drug- and alcohol-free, and I was pretty sure he always had been. So he wasn't in college, so what? Plenty of people couldn't afford to go to college or didn't want to.

Let me see you.

Seriously? Exasperated, I finally typed back a simple "no" while Phoenix collected his two bags and the flowers.

"You okay?" he asked as we walked out. "You look like someone just pissed you off."

The idea of lying to Phoenix made my stomach knot, but I didn't know how to tell him the truth without telling him the whole truth, which I couldn't do. I didn't want him to think I was a cheat or a bad friend. Which I was.

Ugh.

"I'm fine. It's just I don't really want to be back in classes. My school in-box is already filling up with syllabi and stuff from profs." That was true. It wasn't exactly a lie, but it wasn't the truth either. My stomach clenched harder.

"I don't even know what a syllabi is, but I'll take your word for it that it's no fun. School wasn't really my thing."

"No? You didn't like it?" I pounced on the opportunity to change the subject, deleting the second and third messages from Nathan with lightning fingers as we crossed the parking lot. It was still summer hot, and I could see the heat rising off the pavement.

"No, not really. I mean, I didn't mind the schoolwork, but we moved too much and my mom could never keep track of my records and stuff, so I was always confused about what was happening. And any sort of project that required supplies at home was impossible. I remember one time we were supposed to dress like a historical figure so I put my baseball socks on over my jeans and wore a winter scarf. I'm not sure what I was going for." We got into the car and Phoenix laughed. "It's funny now looking back. At the time, it wasn't really that amusing. I was the weird kid in my class, always. Me and this girl who used to eat her scabs. The other kids gave us space."

"She ate scabs?" That was a horrifying image. "And I'm sure you weren't as weird as you thought." Picturing a little Phoenix, keeping to himself, made my heart swell. "Everyone goes through an awkward phase. You should have seen me with braces."

But Phoenix shook his head as I started the car. "Uh-uh. I'm not buying that you were ever ugly."

I laughed. "Want to see my middle school yearbook?"

"Yes."

"No way." I may have come to terms with my vanity as a default positive since the beginning of the summer, but that didn't mean I wanted Phoenix to see me at my gawkiest.

"I'd show you a picture of me, but I don't have any," he said, and the amusement left his voice.

He didn't sound angry, not exactly, but when I glanced over I saw his fists were clenched, and he released them, one finger at a time. God, what would it be like, to have your memories locked only in your brain, nothing visible to remind you of them? No pictures, no report cards, no childhood toys, no baby clothes? It would be scary to me, like I was a vast nothing, history fluid as our minds tended to twist truth and the past.

"I'm sorry," I said, and I meant it more than those simple words could ever cover.

But he shrugged. "It's okay. There might be a picture or two at Riley and Tyler's house. Before Easton, Aunt Dawn was somewhat functioning." He turned his phone to me so I could see the directions to the cemetery. "Want me to turn the sound on for the GPS so you know where you're going?"

"Sure," I said absently. "So why did having Easton change things?"

"He has a different father, which is a bit obvious given that he is biracial. It was also obvious to my uncle, who is blond, who my aunt was still married to at the time. So when he realized she had cheated on him, he ran her over with his car. That's why he's in prison. He got fifteen years for attempted murder."

Jessica had mentioned something about Riley and Tyler's dad being in jail, but I hadn't gotten the full story. I made a face, horrified. "How did she survive that? My God, that's awful."

"It messed up her back and that is how she got started on the prescription pills. But tell me about your family. You don't talk much about yourself." His hand snaked out and took my right one for a second before letting it go.

I shrugged as I followed instructions to turn left. "I don't know. I told you about my family. They're just like . . . normal people. I haven't had a super-interesting life or anything."

"Normal doesn't mean you're not interesting. You don't need drama to be interesting."

Didn't you? I wondered again how I would define myself if I had to explain to someone in a dozen adjectives what made up me. Creative? A good speller? Punctual? I wasn't a good friend, not anymore. I wasn't fun. So what was I?

"I guess I just always figured I would do what my parents did . . . get a degree, a practical job, a house in the 'burbs. Their happiness comes from each other, from family, not from any personal ambitions or their careers. They worry about bills and medical care and the usual stuff." I looked at Phoenix, suddenly feeling like I might cry, with no idea why. "Is that happiness? Really?"

"If you ask my mother and the Beatles, happiness is a warm gun, aka heroin. But for the average person, I would say, yes, happiness is about the moment. Not the whole journey. It's 'Do I have what I need right now?' and if the answer is yes, then you should be happy."

"Yeah?" Following the urgent GPS voice, I pulled into the cemetery, suddenly aware of the irony of our conversation with the headstones rising all around us. When he put it like that, so simple, I realized that I was content. I did have everything I needed. Parents who loved me, a future income, a current job, friends for now, and a guy who looked at me like Phoenix was doing right then. "What if you make mistakes? How do you be happy knowing you've hurt people?"

"If you are even thinking about it, then you care enough to deserve forgiveness. We all fuck up, Robin."

Putting the car in park so we could figure out where his aunt's grave was, I turned to Phoenix, afraid to look at him, afraid he would see my shame.

But he took my chin and turned my face. "Hey. Want to tell me about it?"

I shook my head, mouth hot.

He studied me for a minute, and I fought the urge to look away.

"Okay," he said slowly. "But tell me this—are you happy when you're with me?"

Without hesitation, I nodded. "Yes, absolutely."

"Good. And are you happy when you paint?"

"Yes."

"Then let's do more of that. Because being with you makes me happy, too." Phoenix pulled one of the flowers from the bouquet out and snapped off the stem. He tucked it behind my ear, into my hair. "I'm alive, I've got my freedom, a job, two bucks in my pocket, and a beautiful woman who sees something in me. What else could I need?"

He actually meant it. I could see that. He was grateful.

And I was, too. For him.

CHAPTER TEN

PHOENIX

THE CEMETERY WAS TOO QUIET. I WANTED TO BLAST SOME Disturbed or go old-school Nirvana, blaring that crazy mother-fucker Kurt Cobain to shatter the silence and bizarre ritualistic quality of row after row of headstones.

Of course, I would probably get arrested if I actually did. The thought amused me. It probably wasn't a natural response to grief anyway, but then when did my family do anything normal? We were the opposite of Robin's family.

I stood in front of the grave of my aunt Dawn and stared at the grass, trying to comprehend that she was buried there. That we died and our bodies were lowered into the ground in a steel box and we stayed there for eternity. It was a head trip, and not a good one. There was no headstone for my aunt. No money for one. Which meant at some point no one would even remember she was here. I set the flowers down on their side. Other graves had a cool flower-holder thingy, but again, there was nothing at

Dawn's. I only knew it was hers because we had gone into the office and asked for her plot number at Robin's suggestion.

Robin was standing respectfully next to me, occasionally wiping at her eyes. I found it oddly satisfying that she was crying, which was fucked-up, but the thing was, I knew she was crying out of sadness for me. I'd never really had anyone care about me like that. I'd never really had anyone stand next to me in the figurative sense, and I had been telling her the God's honest truth—I was doing all right in the happiness department. Life wasn't necessarily easy or mess-free, but I felt damn lucky, which seemed like an odd emotion to be having at someone's grave. But that didn't mean I didn't feel bad that my aunt's life had gone down the way it had—I did. And I hoped that whatever was out there after death, she was finally at peace. Maybe rocking out to some Bon Jovi with big old eighties hair.

"Thanks for the cake you baked me for my seventh birthday," I said to the grass. "And for letting me stay with you that summer Mom got put in for possession."

Then because I felt too tall, too overpowering standing up, I squatted down and peeled the plastic wrapper off the flowers. "Sorry I missed the funeral. But just so you know, Easton and Jayden are fine. Riley and Tyler take good care of them."

Robin's phone buzzed in her pocket by my ear, and she jerked, then pulled it out and quickly swiped at her screen before shoving it back in.

"Sorry," she whispered.

"It's okay," I said, but it really wasn't. I couldn't help it. It was starting to frustrate me that Robin wouldn't tell me what was bothering her. We were doing this thing, a relationship, and

I thought she trusted me. But that was for working out later. Right now I needed to figure out how to say good-bye to someone who had always been a part of my life.

There had been times when I was sure my mother was going to die, when she had overdosed and flatlined. Twice I had been the one to call 911, once she had been with someone else, but death had seemed like a real possibility, a morbid inevitability. But now that it had happened to my aunt, it seemed unreal. How did a junkie do it? Gamble with their life every time they smoked meth, or stuck a needle in their arm, or snorted their pills? I guess, even when I had been the weird little kid with no father and an IEP from the guidance office for my supposed disorder, I never thought my life had that little value. Even if no one else cared about me, *I* did.

That was worth something.

But that was the disease of addiction—the user gave up their worth in exchange for the oblivion.

And now Dawn's oblivion was permanent.

"Some day, we'll get you a headstone," I told her. "You deserve that. But for now, I hope you enjoy the flowers."

Standing up, I realized maybe it was kind of freakish to talk to the ground out loud, but Robin didn't look like she thought I was certifiable.

"Ready?" I asked her.

"If you are, yes."

"I'm good," I told her, and I meant it.

That feeling lasted for two hours, then my mother shattered it.

We had picked up art supplies for Robin, and after eating some dinner at her place, we were kissing and I was seriously contemplating taking her into her room for a little action when my phone rang. No one ever called me, everyone texted, so the ring tone caught my attention.

It wasn't a number I recognized. We were on the couch, my phone on the table next to us, and I asked Robin, "Do you mind if I answer this?"

"Go ahead."

"Hello?"

"Hey, it's Mom."

Shit. My gut dropped to the floor. "Yeah?" I asked, tone neutral, even though my heart rate had just kicked up a dozen notches.

"Where you at?"

"Around." I wasn't telling her a damn thing until I knew what she wanted.

"I need a favor."

"No."

"You didn't even hear what it is," she said, sounding exasperated. "God, and to think of all I've done for you over the years. Could you be at least a little fucking grateful?"

That got me. I didn't yell, but I came close. "Mom, you moved when I was in jail and didn't bother to tell me! I don't know what you expect at this point."

"I had to leave quick and how was I supposed to get ahold of you? Your phone don't work in jail."

I sighed. Same old shit, different day. Always full of excuses. "Never mind. But what happened to all my stuff? My clothes and whatever?"

"I don't know. I told you, I had to leave in a hurry. Can I borrow a couple hundred bucks?"

"No. I've only been out for a week, I have two bucks in my pocket. But even if I had more, I wouldn't give it to you. I'm not paying for your fix."

"You're a little shit. I should have had an abortion, but your fucking father was too cheap to front me the cash. Guess you take after him."

Then she hung up.

No mention of the fact that I was in jail for protecting her. She obviously didn't think it was a big deal to have someone take a knife and carve her up like a steak. No mention of the fact that we hadn't spoken in five months.

I tossed my phone down on the cushion beside me and struggled to keep from exploding. It wasn't anything new, and she didn't hurt my feelings, not exactly. I knew that she lashed out to cut when she didn't get what she wanted. It was what she'd always done, and it was what an addict did when they were desperate for their drugs. But it still made me furious, that she could just pop up whenever she wanted and disrupt my life. She was like a bleach-blond tornado who tore through my trailer park a couple of times every season.

Robin put her hand on my knee. Her face was concerned. "Are you okay?"

I shook my head. "No. I need to do push-ups or punch a wall or something. I feel like my head is going to explode." I was flexing my fists compulsively, and my knee had started bouncing up and down in agitation. "I should be used to it, but it just pisses me off that she has the nerve to ask me for money for drugs. I don't think that keeping me in food and Levis gives her the right to guilt-trip me."

The anger pulsed inside me, and I debated whether to stand up and box it out or drop to the floor and push it out.

But before I could do anything, Robin's hand turned my face toward her. "Hey, look at me. You're entitled to feel angry. What she does is wrong. Don't act like it's a failing on your part to be mad at her."

I let out a quick breath. She was right, I knew she was right. But years of bottling shit up made me all too aware of when I couldn't keep it in anymore. "You don't understand . . . the anger I feel, it's like I'm a pop can that's been shook up, and if I don't pull the tab, I'm going to explode. It feels chemical."

"You're right, I don't understand. But I do know that the way your mother treats you is appalling and unfair, addiction or not. She doesn't deserve your loyalty, but part of the reason that I love you is that you will still give it to her, no matter what she does. I really admire that."

I froze, stunned by what she had just said, both by how vehement she had been that my mom sucked and the other part . . . the part that made my nostrils flare and my chest to tighten. "What do you mean, you love me?" She must mean generically speaking. Not love, as in *love* love. Just more like the way when you care for someone.

But she gave me a smile, and her fingers brushed over my chest and gripped my T-shirt. She looked up at me from under her long eyelashes, expression sheepish. "I know it's probably pathetically soon to say something like that, but this, what I feel, it's so strong and real, it *has* to be love. And if I love you, it only seems right that you know that, whether you think it's insane or not."

Girlfriends had told me them loved me before, but I never

believed them, because they didn't. And I figured that if I was so sure I knew when a girl didn't actually love me, I would be sure of it when she did love me. But for a second those words hung there, between us, while I tried to absorb what they meant. While I tried to remember this moment, to capture it and own it. "It might be a little insane that you love me, I'm not going to lie," I murmured, capturing her neck with my hand and pulling her mouth toward mine. "But what's not insane at all is that *I* love *you*. Because you're probably the sweetest, most amazing girl I've ever met. I don't deserve you."

"Yes, you do," she whispered. "You deserve everything you've ever wanted, Phoenix."

When she looked at me like that, her big brown eyes shining with emotion, expression wide open and honest, I could almost believe her.

"What I want is you." My hand was shaking, and this time it wasn't from anger, but from something else I couldn't really define in any words that made sense. I just knew that I had basically jumped off a fucking cliff and there was no net.

Because I was in love with Robin. Like real, hard-core, all-consuming, how-the-fucking-hell-did-this-happen love.

"Really?" she asked, and her vulnerable uncertainty nearly undid me.

My anger was completely gone, replaced by an urgent, possessive need to show her how truly and deeply I had fallen for her. "Yes, I love you. God, so much."

I kissed her. Hard. "Let's go to your room." Maybe sex wasn't the best way to express my feelings, but I didn't know the right words, and I felt caged, contained. Too much emotion.

But she didn't seem to think it was weird. Robin stood up and reached for my hand.

The second we were in her room, she tugged at my shirt, lifting it up to expose my chest. I finished the job, yanking it over my head. Then I pressed her against the door I'd closed behind us and lowered my mouth to hers. She tasted sweet and delicious and like mine, all mine. I crowded her with my body, kissing her hard and sliding my hands all over her. She had the most perfect curves, the most perfect lips, the most perfect response to my touches.

Emotion, passion, made my movements aggressive, sharp, my blood running thick and hot, thoughts scattered in all directions as I pulled up her dress so I could feel the warm heat of her skin.

"Can I?" I murmured, moving up her thigh.

"Yes," she whispered, head falling back to expose her neck to me.

That she didn't even question what I was asking for made me love her even more. This was it, the real thing, the end of the line for me, the moment that made everything else that came before it unimportant. Robin loved me, and that was all I needed to know.

Listening to her heavy breathing, her soft cries as I touched her, her knees falling apart, I fumbled in my jeans for a condom, knowing this had to happen, right here, right now, against this door.

"Oh, God," she said, eyes going wide with shock, when I lifted her hip to rest on mine and pushed inside her.

She didn't even know the half of it.

"This okay?" I asked, even as I moved. She was just so tight, so hot, I couldn't believe how amazing it felt, how perfect we were.

"Yes," she said, and her voice was breathy, eyes half closed. "It's good, so good."

That's what I was talking about. "Hold me," I said, "so you don't slip. Dig in hard, I like that."

Robin's fingernail scraped across my back, pressing into my flesh, and the sharpness matched the intensity of my emotion perfectly. I came inside her, gritting my teeth, enjoying the way she squeezed her inner muscles onto me in some instinctive chick voodoo that had me feeling like I'd do anything she wanted, now and forever.

Not wanting her to lose the momentum, I pulled out and dropped down in a squat so I could finish her, her hands in my hair, her shocked exclamation when my tongue touched her almost as satisfying as my orgasm. She couldn't see the smile I didn't prevent from spreading across my face as I slipped a finger inside her, tongue still working the swollen button in front of me. There was something about that sound she made, that little moan that was a whole octave higher than her natural voice, that drove me crazy. She was so damn sexy.

"Yeah, babe." But she didn't really need my encouragement. She was already there, yanking hard on my hair as she shuddered through her pleasure.

Leaning back on my heels, I wiped my mouth and stared up at her. "I want you to remember that forever," I told her. "Because I will."

CHAPTER ELEVEN

ROBIN

I SWALLOWED HARD, MY MOUTH HOT, THIGHS BURNING FROM strain, as I stared down at Phoenix. His eyes watched me from under that fall of dark hair, his gaze piercing and glassy and intense. I nodded in agreement, afraid to speak, scared that I actually might start crying. What was happening between us was so much, so passionate, so beyond anything I'd ever felt, it was overwhelming in the best possible way. It was like I couldn't contain it inside me, and my fingers shook, goose bumps rose over my body, my throat was tight.

We all wonder when we will fall in love, wonder how we'll know that our feelings are real, if someone is the right one for us.

Then it happens, and those questions seem laughable.

Because when it's real, you feel it in every inch of you, every cell, every vein, every nook and cranny. It moves, it rises with each breath, it's alive, and the world around you becomes sharper, crisper, in focus.

There is no question, only the answer.

Phoenix rose up, his body brushing against mine, and he smiled. "Hey," he whispered, kissing the lobe of my ear, his arms coming around me to gather me close.

"Hey." My legs felt unstable, but I felt wonderful, agitated in a good way, the air between us intimate and sweet with the smell of sex. I thought I would be embarrassed, but I wasn't. I just felt close to him, warm, safe.

"You're good for my temper," he said, kissing my neck before pulling back.

"Glad to help." It had almost broken my heart to see his stoic face when he had been speaking to his mother. I didn't even know everything that she had said, but it clearly hadn't been good because he had alternated between holding it together with clenched fists and a tight jaw, and bursts of exasperation. I wished I could help him more, but I knew it was his decision whether to cut her out of his life or not.

But I didn't want the moment between us to end either, so I shared my thought before I could chicken out and not say anything. "You know what I would like to do?" I asked, then continued before he could take a guess. "Take a bath."

His eyebrows shot up. "A bath?"

"Yes. Want to join me?" My level of the apartment had the roof pitch, which was part of the reason my room was so cozy, and the bathroom was the same, on the opposite side of the house. It had a tiny shower crammed into the corner, way too small for two people, even two people who wanted to be on top of each other, but the bathtub was original to the house, a claw-foot, cast-iron soaker, and I had been eyeballing it since I'd moved in.

"Uh, hell, yeah. I don't think I've taken a bath in twenty years." He looked bemused by the idea. "But I'm down with that."

"Awesome. And somehow I don't think you were showering when you were three months old."

"You don't know that," he said with a grin. "I was pretty independent."

Ten minutes I had the water running and lots of bubbles industriously foaming. I slipped off my dress and underwear and quickly got in, sinking down, not wanting to give him a lengthy view of me naked. It was stupid, I knew that, but I felt exposed just walking around with no clothes on. Yet I had been known to wear dresses that came up to here and went down to there, so my magic line of modesty was a bit ridiculous. It was what it was though, and Phoenix didn't comment on it.

He took his time stripping off his clothes and setting down two soft drinks, which he'd run down to the kitchen to get, on the toilet lid for us. It gave me time to study his body, remembering how it felt to have him press me hard against the bedroom door.

Phoenix stuck a foot in and winced. "Fuck, that's hot. I'm not sure about scalding water on my balls, babe. That sounds like a bad idea."

Relaxing back against the tub, I lifted a foot out of the bubbles and tickled his thigh with my toes. "Don't be a baby," I teased.

"What? I think sex makes you sassy." He made a face, but he sat down opposite from me, knees sticking out of the bubbles because his legs were too long. "Baby this." And he gripped my foot and lightly bit my toes.

"Hey!" I said, giggling, trying to jerk it back. "That tickles."

He smiled, a beautiful, relaxed smile as he lightly massaged my foot before putting it back in the water. He sank back, shifting so he avoided the faucet. "This feels pretty good, I have to admit. Even in August."

It did feel good. Like being in my room with him, it was just me and Phoenix in our own small space, away from the world. He gathered bubbles to his chest and held some in his hand, inspecting them, like he'd never had a bubble bath. Maybe he never had. I watched him, in awe of the way he displayed no fear, no true bitterness about his life. I knew that Tyler had said Phoenix had issues and he had said himself that he had problems processing his anger, but I wasn't sure anything I had seen was out the ordinary for someone who had grown up the way he had.

He froze in the middle of shaking bubbles off his palm. "What?" His voice softened. "When you look at me like that . . ."

"Like what?" I asked, even though I knew full well how I looked.

"Like you love me."

"It's because I do." I didn't think that I had ever actually been more sure of anything else in my life. It swelled inside me, and I felt it with each rise of my chest.

"I love you, too."

No guy had really said that to me before, not like that. Not straight out, *Yes, this is how I feel.* It seemed bizarre that out of all the girls he had probably met, Phoenix would want to be with me. I wasn't sure what I brought to the table. But I wasn't going to let any insecurity spoil the moment, because when I looked at him, there was no doubt in my mind that he did love me. For whatever reason, he did.

"I . . . ," I started to say, and then my throat closed up. I wanted to tell him the truth—that I was a horrible person who had blacked out and had sex with Nathan. That I didn't understand how I could do that. But the words wouldn't come out because I didn't want to see the love on his face change, evaporate.

Phoenix studied me intently. After a long pause, he suddenly moved, disturbing the water and sending bubbles floating into the air. "Scoot over," he said. "I'm coming to that side."

"What do you mean?" I asked, sitting forward and holding on to the tub so I didn't go floating away.

"Like this." He managed to get past me by standing up and resettling himself against the wall of the tub I had been leaning on. "Now get between my legs and lay back. It will be more comfortable."

I did, my face heating a little with both arousal and embarrassment that my butt was now firmly pressed against his nakedness, breasts rising out of the water. But Phoenix's arms wrapped around me felt wonderful as he kissed the top of my head, and I decided nothing outside of this room mattered.

Only me and him.

Happiness in the now, like he had said.

AS I MIXED PAINTS AND WORKED ON MY CANVAS, SKIPPING A pencil drawing first, Phoenix lay on the couch flat on his back, sketchbook over his head. I had no idea how he was drawing like that, but it seemed to work for him. Downstairs I could hear Rory and Tyler talking in the kitchen, but Kylie didn't seem to be home.

Tucking my hair behind my ear, I stared at my palette of blues and grays and black. I was painting a storm, with a tiny woman standing the foreground, being swept away. It was me, of course, and not in any way subtle in its metaphor, but I was taking pleasure in seeing it come to life. It was a quiet contentment I felt, being with Phoenix, rediscovering my art, staying away from alcohol.

It was like I was finally figuring out who the real Robin was, and I liked this new me, the one who didn't crave attention for the wrong reasons.

"Babe?" Phoenix called from the couch.

"Yeah?" I glanced up.

He was on his side craning his neck to look at me, his hair in his eye. "Look at me for a second."

"What?" I laughed. "Why?"

"I need to see your nose. I'm not getting it quite right."

My smile grew wider. So the perfect boyfriend became even more perfect. He was sketching me.

"Make sure you get my good side."

"All your sides are good."

The smile fell off my face, and I looked at him, feeling reflective.

Were all the real sides of me good? The ones that didn't come from a bottle of vodka? I thought maybe they were.

"Thank you," I whispered. "Can I see your sketch?"

"Nope. Give me a couple of days to work on it."

I hadn't seen any of his portrait work, but what it looked like didn't actually matter.

Just that he wanted to capture me.

The real me.

PHOENIX GOT UP WITH ME WHEN MY ALARM WENT OFF EVEN though he didn't have to be at work until three.

"I feel weird sleeping in with you gone," he said as he pulled on his jeans. "I don't know if it's okay with your roommates."

He had a point. I had just been avoiding discussing it with them. Which was not mature at all, or fair. So when we went down to the kitchen I was glad to see Rory and Kylie both there, Rory eating cereal, Kylie oatmeal.

"Hey," I said.

"Good morning," Kylie said, dressed in running clothes. "I'm going to Zumba before my class. Want to come with?"

My first instinct was to make up an excuse, but then I realized that wasn't going to solve the problem. "Um, okay, though you know I totally suck at it. I can only dance when I drink."

"Why is that?" Kylie asked. "It's like a universal phenomenon. Phoenix, can you dance?"

"No." He took the glass of orange juice I had poured for him. "But maybe I could bust a move drunk, I don't know. I've never been drunk, so who is to say?"

"You've never been drunk?" Kylie looked shocked. "Like ever?"

"Like ever." He leaned on the counter and put his glass to his lips.

"Wait, did you meet in AA?"

Rory put down her spoon. "Ky, if he's never been drunk, why would he need AA? And Robin hasn't been to AA. Have you?"

I shook my head. "No." I had brought up drinking, and I was already sorry I had. "I seem to be okay with just not drinking. I don't think I need a counselor or anything."

"When was the last time you drank?" Kylie asked.

Her tone was just curious, casual. She didn't seem to understand like Jessica and Rory did how sudden my decision had been.

"June."

"Wow. Like a summer detox?"

"Like a forever detox."

"I guess you two are good for each other then. It's totes awesome." Then she seemed to lose interest in the subject.

"We are good for each other," Phoenix said. "And I hope you don't mind that I've been around. I don't want to crowd you guys."

"It's fine," Rory said. "We all come and go with our boyfriends, as I'm sure you've noticed."

"But with the situation with Easton, I'll probably end up sleeping here a lot. If you want me to pay some rent or whatever, I can, once I'm a week or two into my job."

I was impressed with Phoenix's offer. It wasn't like he had much money, but that he was willing to put it out there, that it was only fair to pay rent, made me aware of how firm his moral grounds were. It also made me warm inside that he was going to be around almost all of the time.

"I'm okay with it the way it is, because I don't want to get into, like, logging in and out how many hours you, Nathan, and Tyler are here. Let's just promise to communicate if we're invading each other's space, okay?" Kylie said.

"I'm good with that," Rory said.

"Me too." I eyed the mostly empty fridge. I needed to go to the grocery store. "Do we have time to get a muffin before Zumba?"

"You're going to puke blueberry crumb up if you eat that, then Zumba."

"Then maybe I shouldn't go." For the first time in weeks, it felt like my appetite was back, and I didn't really want to give up the muffin fantasy I was suddenly having. "I'm super hungry."

"You should eat," Phoenix said. "If you lose any more weight you're going to disappear when you turn sideways."

"You have lost a ton of weight," Kylie said. "What diet are you on? I need to try it."

The Guilt Diet.

"I think it's from not drinking. There are a ton of calories in beer and all the juices I mixed vodka with. So much sugar."

"Well, I guess I'll just have to work out harder then." Kylie laughed. "I like beer too much to give it up. Does that make me a dude?"

"I don't think anyone is going to mistake you for a guy," I told her. "Seriously. But we should leave now so you're not late. But I'm skipping Zumba this time."

She hugged me. "You're so right. I missed you, by the way."

My throat closed up. "I missed you, too."

AFTER I LEFT PHOENIX AT THE BUS STATION AND KYLIE went on to Zumba, I headed toward the coffee shop to grab a bite before class, when I saw there was an activities fair set up in the student center. With the start of the new semester, every club in existence seemed to have a table with information set up, from table tennis to the Turkish cultural group to the Quidditch club. I wandered along the many rows, glancing at their colorful displays and wondering why I had never joined a single club at college. I had just never bothered.

There was a girl from one of my graphics classes behind a table and she gave me a friendly smile. "Hi," I said. "I think we have graphics together on Tuesday–Thursday. I'm Robin."

"Nice to meet you. I'm Helen-Marie. You should join the digital arts club if you're in the design program. We collaborate on projects and share ideas and basically have a lot of fun." She gave me another smile.

Helen-Marie held herself with an easy confidence I envied a little, her hair in intricate braids, her orange and gold jewelry a bright pop of color against her dark skin.

"Thanks," I said. "I think I will." I bent over to sign my school e-mail address onto her sign-up sheet. "I'm a commercial digital graphics major, but I love to get creative. It would be cool to hang out with some people who get that." I loved my friends, but maybe it was time to branch out a little, try to discover my own interests a little better.

"Cool, I'll e-mail you about the first event," she said.

With a wave, I moved on down the row and saw a sign for a group called Sober. Curious, I weaved through the moving crowd and approached the table. "Hi. So what is this all about?"

There was a guy there wearing hipster glasses and a funky hat. "We're just a group of students who aren't interested in drinking or doing drugs. We plan a lot of parties and events and stuff, and everyone is there sober. So it's for students who don't want Friday night to end with their face in the toilet." He smiled. "No judgment either way. It's just kind of cool for everyone to know what they're getting when they show up, you know?"

"That makes sense." I pursed my lips, thinking it through. It sounded . . . scary for some reason. Yet like it could maybe be a really fun thing for Phoenix and me as a couple. "My boyfriend isn't a student here but he doesn't drink either. Could he come to stuff with me?"

"Sure. As long as he's not a tool." Then he grinned. "Kidding, kidding. Sure you can bring him. I'm Christian, by the way."

"Robin." I smiled, feeling a strange sense of excitement. "Thanks."

By the time I made my way to class ten minutes later, I had also signed up for a group called ACT (Against Child Trafficking) because, well, how could I not sign up for that? The very thought of child prostitution was horrifying, and I figured I needed to do something for once that was important, or at least my little role in the big picture.

I had found passion with Phoenix.

Now I wanted to find passion within myself.

It was a start.

CHAPTER TWELVE

PHOENIX

"ANYBODY HOME?" I CALLED, YANKING OPEN THE SCREEN door to my cousins' house and heading in. I hadn't been there in almost a week and I wanted to pay Riley or Tyler the rest of the money I owed them for my cell phone.

Jessica was lying on the couch with a handheld mister in her hand directed straight at her face. "Hey," she said, sounding listless.

"Hey. If you're hot, why don't you go in the bedroom?" I asked. "I thought it has AC."

"It broke." The look she gave me was one of such pure agony, I was secretly just a little bit amused.

"Shit. That sucks." I imagine if I were still staying there I'd be bitching, too, but I was over at Robin's with central air. Jessica's expression was entertaining, but I felt some sympathy. "I'm here to pay Riley back so maybe he can buy a new window unit."

"He says it's impractical to buy one until next year, because it's only going to be hot for a few more weeks. I know he's right, but that doesn't make it suck any less to be sitting here sweating."

"True that. Where are the boys?"

"Easton and Jayden are in the backyard on the Slip'N Slide. Riley is taking a cold shower because I refuse to have sex when it's this hot. Tyler is working out in the basement because he is insane."

Now I did smile a little. Jessica had a gift for melodrama and she was funny, even I could admit it. "Okay then, thanks."

"Where's Robin?"

"She's at a club meeting."

"What kind of club?" Jessica frowned.

"Digital arts. I don't know what they do, honestly. She just joined it." I lifted my hand. "Catch you later. I need to talk to Tyler, then run." Robin and I had plans for the night, plans that made me want to punch the bag in the basement with Tyler.

He was actually on the ground doing push-ups, and when I jogged down the stairs, I dropped in line behind him and did forty myself.

Tyler went onto his side, breathing hard. "Slow down, fuck, you're killing me."

"You don't have to keep up," I told him, popping off another ten, loving the burn, the sweat that beaded on my forehead.

"I'm out. No thanks." He rolled on his side, hands on his knees. "What has you so twitchy?"

I finished and jumped up, bouncing on my heels, and headed straight for the bag, landing a punch. "Two things. First of all, I brought the rest of the money I owe you. I'm not tatting customers yet myself, but I'm doing okay at the shop, and hopefully in a few months I can afford my needle to start building a client list."

"That's cool. And thanks for paying us back so fast."

"Sure. Now the other thing . . . I guess I need to hear what you think." I was uncomfortable and I nailed a right hook harder. It felt like I was asking for support or involving them in my messy bullshit. But I did want to hear what his opinion was.

"Okay."

"So when I was in, I had a bit of a partnership with a few guys, and we all watched each other's backs. One time, this dude came at me with a fork from behind and I didn't see it. He was going right for the base of my skull and he could have killed me, but Davis took him down for me. So I owe this guy. And now he wants to collect." I was out of breath from boxing, but I didn't want to look at my cousin. All I wanted to do was hit the bag, over and over, until this problem resolved itself.

"Yeah? What does he want? Money? Offer him a deal . . . tattoo him for free or something."

If only he wanted money. "He wants me to run his drugs for him."

"What? Fuck that!" Tyler sounded furious.

"I know. You know I would never do that. Not in a million goddamn years. He wants me, though, because he knows I won't steal supply from him." Bam. My knuckles split open, and blood rolled down my fingers and the back of my hand. "But the problem is, I ran into him and Robin was with me. He knows what she looks like."

"Does he know where she lives?" Tyler's voice had gotten hard, and I knew why. Rory lived there, too.

"No." Left, right, left, right. I punched in a perfect mesmerizing rhythm, shoulders tight, sweat dripping in my eyes, blood chugging over my flesh, the sound hypnotic. I knew the second I broke rhythm because I did it on purpose. The bag nailed me in the chin with a burst of pain, my jaw jamming upward, knocking my teeth into my tongue. My vision went blurry for a split second.

I spit blood out of my mouth onto the bottom of my shirt, wiping the remnants with my forearm, and finally stepped back to look at Tyler. I stood with my hands on my hips, catching my breath.

"Dude," he said. "You okay?"

"Fine. So what do you think I should do?"

"How pissed is he going to be?"

"I don't know. I mean, you know a guy in there, doesn't mean he's the same out here." That's what scared me. He seemed like a nice enough guy, but he was a dealer. You had to have a certain disregard for other people to be in the business.

"That's true." Tyler looked like he wished to hell he didn't know that. "Why don't you feel him out, offer him something else you think he might want?"

"The problem is, I don't know what he would want. And if I ask him, I tip my hand."

"Just put him off for a day or two and we'll figure something out." Tyler stood up. "Now go get a towel, you're bleeding all over the place."

"Am I?" I glanced down at my hand, then wiped my bleeding chin. "I didn't notice."

Tyler scrutinized me. "You care about her a lot, don't you?"

That was a freaking understatement. "Yeah. I do. And if

anything happens to her because of me . . ." I couldn't stop myself from clenching my fists. "I'll never forgive myself."

"Nothing is going to happen to her. This guy is just trying to get something for nothing. He's not crazy enough to start real shit with you."

Tyler might be right, but I was worried. I couldn't help it. Being with Robin . . . it was the best thing to ever happen to me. She made me feel calm, happy. Important. I wanted to be the best thing for her, too, not the worst.

"It just feels like we can never leave it all behind, you know?" I said. "The drugs, the bullshit, it will always follow us."

"Heard from your mom?" he asked.

"No, just that one phone call." As usual, I had mixed feelings about that. "I don't want Robin to meet her. I know that's self-ish, but I don't."

"Look, I get where you're coming from." Tyler wiped his forehead with his arm. "I worry about dragging Rory into our family drama. I mean, she deserves better, right? But at the same time, I figure she is choosing to be with me, so I have to trust that. You have to trust that Robin wants to be with you."

Easier fucking said than done. "I don't think we were raised to trust."

"Nope." He grinned. "We weren't raised to talk about our feelings either and look at us . . . a couple of girls sharing."

"Do you want to be hit?" I asked him, but I wasn't really pissed. It was our default setting. When we got uncomfortable with our feelings, we joked around or got aggressive.

"You punch me, I will make you eat concrete."

I grinned. That could be entertaining, going a round with

Tyler. He might even give me a run for my money, but he couldn't beat me. I had more control and a little more crazy than he did. "No fucking chance."

"Dude." Tyler started laughing. "You have blood on your teeth. That is disgusting."

"Shit." I wiped at my mouth, trying to run my tongue over my teeth. "Is it gone? I'm supposed to be going to some party with the sober club that Robin joined." I was actually terrified. What the fuck did I have to say to a bunch of college students?

His eyebrows shot up. "The sober club? What the hell is that?"

"It's a bunch of students who don't drink getting together for stuff. Tonight is acoustic night at the coffee shop and I told her I would go. She's trying to make new friends." The thought made me frown. "Personally, I don't see the point. But it seems important to her."

"Why does she need new friends?"

We stared at each other, both suddenly uneasy. "That's a good question," I said. "And I don't know the answer."

But then Tyler shrugged. "I guess I can see wanting to be around people who don't drink. No temptation that way."

"Do you know something I don't know?" I asked him.

"It depends on what you know."

Really? "I know that something happened at that party. But I don't know what."

"I don't know either, man." He held out his hands. "I do know that maybe Nathan shouldn't have been the one to give her a ride home that night."

"What the hell does that mean?"

"Just that I saw them leave together. That's it. That's all it means."

But it clearly wasn't. He was trying to tell me something without telling me directly. I turned and punched the bag again. Hard.

"Go take a shower," he said. "Brush your teeth. Use Jayden's toothbrush, not mine. Go have fun with Robin."

I wasn't sure that I could, but I was damn going to try. I wasn't going to embarrass her.

THAT DIDN'T MEAN I WAS COMFORTABLE WHEN WE WALKED into that coffee shop, though. I had showered and brushed my teeth with paste on my finger, and I had asked Robin to bring me a clean shirt when she picked me up, so at least there wasn't still blood on me. But I still felt hugely awkward as I held the door open for her and followed her inside. It smelled like roasted beans and hipster.

"Wow, it's crowded," she said, and even she sounded slightly nervous.

Surveying the group, I tried not to judge, but man, the music coming from the corner of the room where they had shifted tables out of the way for a makeshift stage was pretentious and boring. The singer couldn't stay in key for more than two seconds, and I wasn't sure why having deep lyrics meant you could get away with having no vocal ability whatsoever. But whatever. Maybe the guy was fucking awesome off stage as a person.

Some guy waved to Robin and she sounded relieved. "Oh, that's Christian! Let's go say hi."

I wasn't going to be jealous. That was ridiculous. Robin loved me. She slept next to me every night and woke up next to me every morning. It didn't matter that this guy looked like he would be making six figures in five years.

Yet my fists clenched and unclenched, and I had to take a deep breath in, a deep breath out.

She was wearing a dress with a belt to show off her waist, and it was the first time I'd seen her put any sort of effort into her appearance. She had painted her fingernails and sprayed on perfume, which seemed to smack me in the face every time she moved. It didn't smell like her to me and I fought annoyance.

"Hey, Robin," the guy sitting down said. "Glad you could make it. This is Stefan, Blakeley, and Harper."

"This is my boyfriend, Phoenix," Robin said after greeting everyone.

"Is that your real name?" Harper asked me.

Was this chick serious? Because my name was weirder than any of theirs? "Yes."

"I like your tattoo," she said with a flirty smile, pointing to my sleeve. "Do you have any other ones?"

"Yes. My leg, my back, my chest."

Interest sparked further in her blue eyes. "Can I see them?"

"Harper, down, girl," Christian said. "Let them sit down. Ignore her, she has a tattoo fetish."

"Phoenix is a tattoo artist," Robin said as we sat down. She sounded proud of me, or at least that's how I chose to interpret it.

"Are you an art major?" Stefan asked. At least I thought it was Stefan. He and Blakeley had been introduced to me too fast, and I was kind of confused which one was which.

They were showing slight interest and being polite, so I couldn't complain. I just was well aware that we probably had, oh, nothing in common. "No. I'm not in school. I work full-time in a shop. Robin is a graphic design major, but she also paints."

Robin shrugged, her nose wrinkling up. "That's just for fun."

That surprised me, that she would diminish her art to a hobby. She had been painting almost every night while I was at work and I came back to her place to find the hallway to her bedroom propped with drying canvases. She seemed to be on a creative burst, and I thought it was awesome. "She's really talented," I told them.

"So is Phoenix," she said.

"Well, I can see why you two are together," Harper said with a roll of her eyes. "Mutual admiration."

Nice. But I tried not to roll my eyes back because wasn't that why most couples were together? "What are you studying?" I asked her.

"Alcohol and drug counseling."

"I'm premed," Stefan interjected before I could say anything. "People have no idea how much damage they do to their body when they drink and pop pills."

"I don't think they care," I told him, feeling Robin's hand snake over to intertwine with mine under the table.

"The liver damage, the destruction of brain cells . . . it makes no sense. Not to mention how asinine they all look stumbling out of clubs on a Friday night, drunken idiots looking to hook up."

Robin's grip tightened.

"Well, at least you aren't judgmental," I said casually, irritated as hell. What right did they have to discuss total strangers?

What fucking business was it of theirs? If I made the personal choice to be totally clean, that didn't mean I had the right to go around and point fingers at people who had a beer watching a ball game. I didn't go through Tyler and Riley's kitchen and toss out their beer and whiskey. Not every drinker was an addict.

"What, you think it's okay to get shitfaced?" he asked, looking at me with suspicion.

"I'm just saying, you need to live your life, but not someone else's."

"So you think my major is stupid then?" Harper asked. "Because I kind of thought I was going to be saving people's lives."

Not with that attitude. I held my tongue for Robin's sake. "Sure," I told Harper, not wanting to engage. "It's important. I wasn't saying otherwise."

The music swelled in the background, a grating, high-pitched whine that made me want to stab myself in the ears. I was losing control and ruining the night for Robin. Carefully, I relaxed the muscles in my shoulders and on down through my body.

"I'm sure in your line of work you see lots of interesting types," Christian said, with a smile that indicated he was trying to change the subject.

"What's that supposed to mean?" Robin asked, and I heard the shrill irritation in her voice.

So maybe I wasn't the only one having a bad reaction to this group.

"Do you have any tattoos?" I asked Harper.

But she shook her head. "No, I don't think it's very professional looking. Trashy, you know? But they're so yummy on guys."

Did she have any idea how rude she sounded? Obviously not.

Or maybe she knew full well how she sounded, she just didn't give a shit.

I turned to Robin. "You want me to get you a coffee or anything?" Please, spring me from this hell, was what I was really thinking.

"Sure, I'll have a latte."

"Anyone else need anything?" I was already standing up.

They all shook their heads no and I was able to escape. Regroup. Trying to ignore the fact that a latte cost five bucks—seriously?—I figured with me gone maybe the conversation could take a different direction and be more natural.

Except it didn't really work that way. When I got back with Robin's coffee, or whatever the hell it was called, Harper was blasting her former roommate, who wasn't there to defend herself. "I mean, it was like every weekend, a different guy after drinking herself to oblivion. How did she look herself in the mirror, you know?" Harper tossed her hair back. "But the final straw was when she slept with her best friend's boyfriend. I mean, really? Who does that?"

The blood had drained from Robin's face, and I knew without a doubt what exactly had gone down between her and Nathan.

Shit.

It was one thing to suspect, another to get confirmation. The thought of Nathan taking advantage of Robin . . . it made me sick. Furious. But those emotions had to wait. Right now I had to get her out of here.

"People make mistakes," I told Harper. "I'm sure you have too, despite your good intentions."

"Yeah, except I'm not a whore or a drunk."

"My mother is an addict," I told her. "And my aunt was an alcoholic before she died. But they are still human beings who deserve respect." With that, I stood up, Robin's drink still in my hand, and reached for her with the other one. "Maybe you should rethink your career choice, Harper. Otherwise, good luck." I gave them all a nod. "Wonderful meeting you." The sarcasm crept into my voice and I didn't even regret it.

Robin just gave a weak smile and waved. When we were at the front door, she mumbled, "God, I'm sorry. I guess this club didn't work out as well as the digital arts one did. I really liked the people I met there."

"These guys were assholes," I said, shoving open the door. "I'm sorry. I didn't mean to ruin the night or your chance to hang out with them."

"I don't want to hang out with them."

We had walked from her apartment, and as we started down the sidewalk, I burned with the need to ask her about Nathan. I didn't know what her response was going to be, but I needed to ask. It was picking at me, and I needed the truth. I needed to know she trusted me with the truth.

"Baby." I pulled her to a stop and took her cheeks in my hands. "What happened with Nathan?"

She jerked, her face still pale, eyes wide with fear. "What do you mean?" Her voice was uneven, breath hitched and nervous.

Making my voice as gentle as possible, I kissed her forehead and said, "I know something happened. I don't know what. But you can tell me. You can trust me."

She started crying and my heart sank. "I don't know what

happened. I mean, I *know* what happened, but the thing is, I don't remember it."

"You had sex with him?" I asked, wanting clarity. "It's okay, I won't get angry." I didn't think. I mean, I was angry, yeah, definitely. Mad at Nathan, mad that alcohol existed, mad that I hadn't been there to stop her from doing something she didn't really want to do, but I wasn't mad at her. And if I wanted her to trust me, love me, I had to stay calm, not let her see that anger and think it was in any way directed at her.

She bit her lip and looked away. Then she looked up at me and whispered, "Yes. I guess. He seems to think we did, but I blacked out. And I woke up at his place."

There were spots in front of my vision, I was so disgusted by a guy who would have sex with an almost unconscious girl, but I had learned how to hold it all back, to build the levee against the flood of anger. "So it was consensual, as far as you can tell? He didn't hurt you in any way?"

"He didn't hurt me, no. And I guess I was on board with it. Tyler saw us kissing in Nathan's car." She was crying harder now. "How could I do that? Why would I do that? It's horrible, awful!"

I wasn't sure I even wanted to think about it. Pulling her into my arms, I held her while she cried, trying to process exactly how I felt, swallowing hard. Did it thrill me that Nathan had tapped my girlfriend? Fuck no. Was I glad she'd told me? Yes. I was also just a little bit glad that she didn't remember it, which made me an asshole. But I couldn't help the reaction. I obviously didn't like that she'd blacked out, because that was scary shit, but I didn't want her to have had good sex with Nathan, even drunk. Which was selfish and stupid, so I shoved that thought aside and focused on her, what she needed, not me, what I needed.

That's what you do when you love someone.

You put them first, even when your insides were boiling like lava.

Now I knew why she was afraid to be around her friends, why she had stopped drinking, why she no longer wanted to party.

I figured while the catalyst was shit, the end result was a good thing, right?

"It's okay," I told her, kissing the top of her head. It wasn't, not exactly, but I'd get over it. It was more important she knew I had her back, that she could trust me enough to tell me the truth, no matter what. That there were no secrets between us, ever.

"You don't hate me?" She sobbed into my chest. "You don't think I'm a drunken whore like Harper and everyone else on the planet?"

The phrase "drunken whore" made my nostrils flare. No one had the right to call her that. No one. "No. I think you made a mistake that you've regretted ever since, and you made changes to make sure it doesn't happen again. I think that makes you mature."

She pulled back and looked up at me, her gaze searching. "Really? You're not going to break up with me?"

"Of course not. Jesus." The thought was unimaginable. Every day was Robin, and Robin was every day. "I'm glad you told me. That's an awful secret to keep inside, baby. Let me share your pain." I wasn't sure how to explain it to her, but I tried. "I'm like that bird, you know . . . I can hold up the sky for you, Robin."

"Thank you," she whispered, eyes shining. She went up on her tiptoes and kissed me. "You are the most amazing man I've ever known."

That made me feel a little self-conscious. "You're still young," I told her.

She gave a watery laugh. "No, I'm serious."

I laughed, too, relieved that she seemed okay. Relieved that I seemed okay. "So am I." I took her hand and started walking again.

"You're really not mad? I mean, what I did to Kylie . . ."

That was a complicated question because it was a complicated situation. Would I want it to have never happened? Hell, yeah. But I didn't want her to feel any upset from me at all, so I glanced at her, reminding myself she could never be the source of my anger.

Keeping my tone neutral, I asked, "If you were sober, would you have done that?"

"No. Absolutely not."

"So it was the alcohol, which you're not touching anymore. I can live with that. Lesson learned, right?"

"Oh, God, yes." Her voice was emphatic. "I don't even know who that person was. It's so damn scary to realize that you basically go to a place that isn't even in line with who you are inside . . . I mean, it's one thing if alcohol loosens you up, makes you go for something you secretly wanted, or you get flirty or aggressive or whatever, but this was like against everything I possibly believe in. It makes no sense. It's like it wasn't even me, and that is terrifying."

The night was warm but breezy, and I held her hand tightly as we went back to all the shops on Clifton, most of them closed for the night. Only the pizza parlor was still open, the tables all full of customers. I stroked her fingers and thought about what she'd said. It was why I had never touched booze or drugs. "I would be terrified, too. But you know, I've seen it over and over with my mom and my aunt. You become, I don't know, the id to the ego, or whatever that theory was. It's like drugs and alcohol push you into a pure selfishness."

"Or recklessness." Robin shuddered. "Thanks for what you said in there. I appreciate it. And not every social drinker has a problem. I just know I don't know when to stop and that *is* a problem."

"I'm proud of you for stepping away from what you know is bad for you." She was the first person close to me who really had.

"It's been so awful . . . I want to tell Kylie, because I feel so horrible, but I know it will just hurt her."

"I don't think you should tell her. What's the point?" I tossed my hair out of my eyes. "But I'm not going to lie. I want to punch Nathan in his pretty face."

"I don't want you to do that," she said quietly. "I want to move on."

My throat tightened. If that's what she wanted, that's what I would do. Hell, I would do anything she asked, because when she looked at me, I saw love . . . for the first time in my life, I

saw pure, sweet love. Not sneering, not wheedling, not irritation, not guilt or exasperation, but just love from someone who
didn't even have to love me.

She just did.

I nodded. "I do, too. You don't throw my conviction in my
face, and I will never throw this in yours. We're moving forward. Together."

"Together," she whispered.

CHAPTER THIRTEEN

ROBIN

PULLING THE TATTOO SHOP DOOR OPEN, I DROPPED my keys into my cross-body bag and glanced around for Phoenix. His text had been vague and suspicious, a request that I meet him at work to see something important. I was a little nervous, because I suspected he had gotten that cobra tattoo done and I wasn't sure there was anywhere on his body I really wanted to see that every day. Then again, while I wasn't up on tattoo pricing, I also knew he was dead broke still and a piece like that had to be at least a few hundred bucks for the outline, and more for the shading.

I was also nervous because I had his surprise birthday party planned for when he got off work, and I still needed to pick up the cake, prep the food, and wrap the gifts I'd gotten him. I wanted his birthday to be perfect.

In the week since I'd told him about Nathan, we had only gotten closer, because I wasn't holding anything back at all. He spent every night with me, but I still had plenty of time to study when he was at work, and he was totally fine with me going to the ACT and digital arts clubs. I had met Helen-Marie for coffee a couple of times between classes and I really liked her. Phoenix was spending time with Jayden and Easton when Tyler and Riley were working and he was enjoying doing that. They looked up to him, and he needed that purpose, whether or not he knew it.

Phoenix had spent too much of his life alone and I didn't want another birthday to go by where he was solo at Dairy Queen. I didn't have anything big planned, just the usual group at our apartment, which fortunately did not include Nathan because he was working, but I wanted Phoenix to see how much he mattered to me. How he mattered just in general.

This was the first time I'd been to the shop and I felt a little naked with my bare skin next to all the heavily inked artists and customers waiting in the lobby. It was mostly a big, open room with lots of tattoo art displayed on all the walls, cubicles to one side where the artists worked. The buzz of the needles filled the room, along with heavy metal music. Phoenix fit here, I could see that. A year ago, I would have felt uncomfortable walking in, and I would have attempted to dress the part to fit in, but now it didn't bother me that I wasn't rock star enough for this crowd. Being comfortable with who I was, in my own skin, was an awesome feeling.

What I found when I didn't think about my clothes, about dressing to impress, was that I gravitated toward patterns and texture, comfortable clothes with something funky about them. I guess it was the artist in me, but I was definitely morphing into Boho Girl, and it felt right. It felt like me.

"Can I help you?" a guy with a shaved head and ear gauges asked me.

"I'm looking for Phoenix. Is he available right now?"

"You're Robin, aren't you?" he asked.

I nodded.

"Hey, I'm Bob." He stuck his hand out over the counter. "Nice to meet you."

"You too." So this was the owner, the one who hadn't cared that Phoenix was fresh out of jail. I wanted to hug him, but restrained myself.

"I could tell it was you. He's in the third room on the right there. Go ahead on over. It looks fucking unreal. Almost as beautiful as the real thing," he said with a wink.

That confused me a little. How beautiful was a cobra? But then again, art was art, and it all brought its own particular beauty.

Phoenix was lying on his side on a table, arms over his head, another guy bent over him with the needle. "Hey, baby, perfect timing. He's just about finished."

"Doesn't that hurt?" I asked, the sound making my teeth rattle and my stomach turn just a little. It looked like the guy was working on Phoenix's flank, below his ribs, the paper towel in his hand smeared with black ink and blood. Ugh.

"It's not that bad." Phoenix smiled at me, that smile that made my heart squeeze.

"There you go." The artist sat back on his chair and surveyed his work. He spritzed it down and wiped it again. "Looks badass." Then he finally turned around and looked at me. "Hey, Robin. I'm Paul."

"Hi. Nice to meet you." I gave him a big smile. It made me girly happy that Phoenix had obviously been talking about me at work, given that both Paul and Bob knew who I was.

But then Phoenix stood up, his hands behind his head, skin red and raised from the needle, and he turned to look in the mirror. There wasn't a snake inked on his skin. There was me.

I gasped. "Phoenix . . ."

"You like it?" he asked, turning left and right to admire it in the mirror. "It looks amazing. Paul, you rock."

It was my portrait. It was me, not smiling, but looking out solemnly, head tilted, hair tousled like I was outdoors, eyes peering up from under my lashes.

"Dude, that was a killer sketch of her," Paul said. "You really captured her." He peeled his gloves off and told me, "I'm not big on tattooing someone else's sketch, but in this case it made sense for Phoenix to do the drawing, and he can't ink his own side, so I said I'd do it. Glad I did. You look fantastic."

I did. I looked . . . pretty. And I was on Phoenix's body. Forever. Tears filled my eyes. I had thought that he had abandoned the sketch he had started of me because he had never shown it to me. I had asked once, but he'd said it wasn't finished. But now here it was, and it was beautiful.

It wasn't a massive tattoo. It fit well in the spot, and it wasn't the kind of portrait tattoo that is basically someone's round head slapped onto them with a circle enclosing it. The way my hair was done, windblown and loose, the edges of the tattoo looked natural as they spread out. I was wearing a necklace that I didn't own, that didn't exist. It was a thin chain with a tiny bluebird charm.

"What do you think?" Phoenix asked when I still didn't say anything, my lip starting to tremble.

I just nodded. Then finally I managed to force out, "You are really talented, Phoenix. It looks fantastic."

"Good subject matter." The corner of his mouth turned up. "I thought about a kitten but decided on this instead."

Giving a watery laugh, I bent forward to study it closer, amazed. "No one has ever sketched me before." Let alone put me on their flesh permanently. The fact that he didn't seem concerned that we would ever break up made me even more in love with him. This was more forever than even marriage.

He couldn't have given me a better gift, especially after telling him about Nathan.

"It's my birthday present to myself," he told me.

I reached out, like I could touch it, intrigued by all the individual lines raised on his skin, at the intricate shading that had gone on to make my hair, my eyes, all with a needle. As an artist, I was fascinated. As his girlfriend, I was stunned.

"Now you'll always be with me," he said.

"Seriously, dude?" Paul asked, busy cleaning up his equipment, still on his rolling stool. "I'm gagging."

"Fuck you. We're having a moment."

We were. I stood back up and kissed him quickly, before whispering in his ear, "I love you. Thank you."

"For what?" he asked, his eyes dark with desire and emotion.

"For this. For you. For everything." That wasn't exactly what I wanted to say, because I was struggling with words.

Paul wasn't. "Let's get a picture, then I need to bandage it."

As Paul used Phoenix's phone to take a few shots, and I did, too, with my own phone, I suddenly knew what I wanted. Phoenix had been wanting to practice his own tattoo skills but hadn't been able to. Now was his chance.

"Phoenix, I want that little bluebird on me." I wanted a visual reminder of him on my body, just like I was on his. "Can you do it?"

"What?" he asked, looking startled. "Are you sure? Where?"

My first thought was over my heart, but then I would never be able to see it. "Here." I pointed to the inside of my wrist. "Tiny, like the charm on the necklace. Quarter size."

He nodded. "Okay. If it's okay with Paul. Can I borrow your equipment?"

"Sure, Birthday Boy. Since you won't let any of us buy you a beer or a shot." Paul shook his head at me in mock sorrow. "Whoever heard of anyone turning down a free drink on his twenty-first birthday?"

"She doesn't drink either," Phoenix told him, as Paul covered his tattoo up with white gauze.

It felt a little conceited, but I was sorry to see my portrait covered up. I couldn't stop staring at it in awe, and I looked down at the image captured on my phone.

"Then I guess you two are perfect for each other," Paul said.

"Damn straight," was Phoenix's opinion. He patted the table. "Have a seat, babe. I'll draw up the bird."

"Does it hurt?"

"Not the drawing," Paul told me with a grin.

Paul was about thirty, with tattoos all over his arms and his neck. He was wearing a Slayer T-shirt and cargo shorts. It seemed to be the uniform of choice in the shop, which made me feel more confident about the gifts I had bought for Phoenix for his birthday. I had basically bought out the classic rock T-shirt section at Hot Topic, knowing he had been existing for weeks with only two shirts, one pair of shorts, and one pair of jeans. He wore the same shoes every day, so I had consulted with Tyler and bought him a pair of black Converse high-tops.

"Shut up," Phoenix said. Then to me, "Yes, it hurts. Do you want Paul to do it instead so I can hold your hand? The good thing is it's so small it will take less than ten minutes."

Could I be brave for ten minutes? "I'll be fine, then. I want you to do it."

"I can hold your hand," Paul offered with a grin.

Phoenix pulled his shirt back on and gave his coworker a glare.

"Kidding." Paul made a funny face at me. "He doesn't have much of a sense of humor, but I guess you already know that."

There was some truth to that, but I wasn't with Phoenix to have someone cracking jokes for me all day long. His sense of humor was quieter, like mine. "I have better things to do than laugh when I'm with him," I told Paul.

Phoenix grinned. Paul let out a bark of laughter.

Feeling pleased, I sat down on the table, letting my feet swing loosely as they moved around me, doing their thing. Paul was pulling out ink and a fresh needle. "Do you want color?" he asked.

The one on Phoenix was just in black, but I wanted an actual bluebird. "Blue, please."

Phoenix held up a drawing for me. It was a tiny, chubby, absolutely adorable bluebird. He let it hover over the back of my wrist. "Like this?"

"That's perfect." I touched his thigh, tucking my hand into his pocket, just wanting contact. It seemed like I could never touch him enough.

"Don't do that when I'm tattooing you, babe," he said with a sexy smile. "You're damn close to what I would consider a major distraction."

My nipples went hard, and I sucked in a breath. My thoughts hadn't been going in that direction but now they most definitely were.

"Oh no." He pulled my hand out of his pocket and set it on my thigh. "Don't look at me like that. I still have to work for another three hours."

"Yeah, don't look at him like that," Paul said, standing up. "I'm single and you're making me jealous."

"No, she's not setting you up with any of her friends," Phoenix said before I could respond.

"Did I ask?"

"I think all my friends have boyfriends." Even Helen-Marie and the two other girls I had clicked with in the digital arts club were dating guys.

"I really was kidding," Paul said. "No worries." He pointed at Phoenix. "Don't fuck this tat up. I'm going to grab a bite to eat."

"Thanks for the vote of confidence." Phoenix gave me a searching look. "Do you really want me to do this?"

"You can, right?" I was sure he could, but I didn't want to force him to do something he wasn't comfortable with.

"Sure. This is an easy piece. But I can't say I love the idea of hurting you."

"As long as this is the only time," I said with a smile. "Or the only way, I should say."

"It is. It will be." He touched my chin with the latex glove he had pulled on. "Do you want to watch or close your eyes?"

"I want to watch."

He laid the image onto my skin and rubbed, then pulled it off. The black outline of the bird was there, looking adorable. "He's so cute."

"Don't say like me," Phoenix said. "Because I won't believe you. Okay, first touch. Take a deep breath and let it out. Relax."

He bent over me, and the buzzing increased. I couldn't help it, I let out a hiss at the first contact.

Holy shit. That hurt. It felt, well, like a needle being dragged through my flesh.

"You okay?"

"Yes?" I didn't say that with a huge amount of conviction, but then I looked down and watched the black line tracing over the outline of the bird and I saw that he had already done one wing and the bottom. It clearly wasn't going to take too long, so I could deal.

He wiped away the splatters. "I'll go as fast as I can while still making it look good. Though it is distracting to be doing you . . . I'm not usually attracted to my clients."

"Don't make me laugh. I don't want to move my arm. And you can be doing me later. It is your birthday, after all. You totally get birthday sex."

He glanced up at me. "And today would be different from any other day, how? We have a lot of sex, babe, for which I'm very grateful."

Hopefully no one in the shop was listening to this conversation. "But today you can put in any special requests you might have."

"Oh, yeah? Anything goes? Or are there, you know, boundaries?" He wiped my arm and rolled a foot away on the chair, cleaning the needle to get the blue ink.

"No boundaries."

His eyebrows shot up, disappearing under his hair. "Now that's fucking hot."

"No boundaries, unless you want a threesome or something. I'm not doing that." I wasn't sharing him.

Phoenix made a face that had me relieved. "Fuck no. Why would I want that? You're everything I need and want. Though I would not say no to a striptease and a lap dance combo, that's for sure."

All of a sudden I was feeling a hot rush of blood in my face, and I didn't think it was from the pain. The thought of doing what he wanted made me super excited, but a little nervous, too. "I'm not a very good dancer."

Phoenix glanced up at me. "Baby, that is not the point. Naked enthusiasm is all that's required."

"Oh. I can do *that*."

He made a sound in the back of his throat. I watched the blue appearing on my skin, the sensation a sharp scraping, but I was thinking about sitting on Phoenix's lap. It was a pleasant distraction. Did I have the guts to strip in front of him? It was his birthday. I had offered for his choice. And I was getting a tattoo, which proved I had some form of bravery in me, no matter how small.

I pictured the look on his face.

I could totally do this.

He wiped my wrist again and said, "All done. If I could, I'd kiss it better, but you'll have to settle for me kissing you other places."

My skin was stinging and red, but there was a perfect little bluebird on my wrist. My thoughts were torn from the image of him kissing me here and, uh, there by the sheer adorableness of the tattoo. "Oh, he's awesome!"

"Is it a he?" Phoenix asked in amusement as he sprayed my wrist, then sat back and peeled off his gloves.

"Of course." I held my wrist up and turned it around and around to admire it. "It's supposed to have your energy and you are very masculine, in case you haven't noticed. So weird that this wasn't here ten minutes ago and now it will be forever. Sort of like how a month ago we didn't know the other existed and now I can't imagine life without you."

Phoenix stood up and moved between my legs to kiss me. "There is no life without you," he said.

CHAPTER FOURTEEN

PHOENIX

TEN O'CLOCK AND NOTHING. NO PHONE CALL, NO TEXT, nothing.

It was stupid, I knew that, to think that my mother would remember it was my birthday, let alone an important one like my twenty-first. Hell, she probably didn't even know what day of the week it was. She probably didn't even remember the exact date of my birthday.

Not hearing from her was no shocker.

Yet it still hurt.

Frustrated, I finished sweeping up the shop and waved to the guys, two still doing tattoos. Bob was letting me leave early since it was my birthday and I had Robin waiting at her place for me. It was only a fifteen-minute walk and I'd be with someone who did love me.

So why did I give a shit about the woman who didn't love me?

Because I was a pussy, apparently.

Feeling my mood darkening, I tried to shake it off, touching my side where my new tattoo stung. I decided to take the bandage off before I left and I peeled my shirt off and removed it, yanking hard on the edges, enjoying the sting as the tape tore at my skin. Not many people understood that I didn't mind the pain from the needle during a tattoo. I kind of liked it. It made me feel sharp, alive.

Tossing the bandage, I ducked into Paul's open cubicle to check out his work below my ribs. The skin was shiny and red and swollen, but damn, it was a fucking amazing tattoo. Robin stared back at me in the mirror, her eyes big and raw. It was a sketch I'd started the first day we'd spent together, at the park, while she had leaned on her arm and stared out across the grass to the fountain, lost in her thoughts. Then she had turned and glanced at me, and I had seen something even then that had told me there was a connection between us.

It had grown stronger and stronger and now she was with me all the time, literally and figuratively.

The placing of the tattoo was the opposite side from my bleeding heart tattoo, because I didn't want them to be in the same line of view at the same time. Two different meanings. Two different women.

"You done admiring yourself?" Paul asked, bent over a girl's rib cage.

It looked like she was getting a dream catcher tattoo, which seemed to be in the top five tattoos for girls eighteen to twenty-three. It rivaled flowers, stars, and hearts for first place. I wondered what nightmares pretty young girls had that they seemed to think they needed to tattoo on their bodies as a way to cap-

ture them. Or maybe they wanted to hold on to good dreams.
Funny how I always went to nightmares.

"Not yet," I told Paul. "Not to brag or anything, but this is a
sick tattoo. I love it."

"How is that not bragging?"

That made me smile, yanking me a little out of my brooding
mood.

"Let me see," the girl said.

I moved over so she could see my side by turning her head. She
was petite and pretty, probably popular at college. She looked col-
legiate, with her hot pink shorts and her delicate gold jewelry.

"Oh." Her mouth formed an O, and her eyes went wide.
"That's beautiful. Is that your girlfriend?"

That was enough to make me feel a stupid swell of male
pride. I couldn't help it. "Yeah, it is. Thanks."

"God, she is so lucky you would do something like that." She
gave an odd little laugh that was tinged with sadness. "Not a lot
of guys would do that."

The sound made me ashamed of my first reaction to her.
What, like average suburban college girls didn't go through rough
shit? Robin was proof of that. So sure, I'd had a less than ideal
childhood, but fuck, we all hurt.

"I've been told I have a little crazy in me," I said. "Most guys
just bring flowers, and I've never done that."

"Some guys don't do either."

"Then they're pricks," Paul said, shading a feather.

She smiled. "True."

"It looks good," I said, gesturing to her tattoo. "Paul does
good work, you'll be happy with it."

"Thanks. Has your girlfriend seen that yet?"

"Yeah, she came up right as Paul was finishing it up." Tossing my shirt over my shoulder, I said, "But I'm out of here. See you tomorrow, bro." I held my fist up for Paul and he paused in his work to tap me with his elbow, keeping his gloved hands clear.

"Happy birthday, jerk-off," he said.

I grinned. "Thanks."

"It's your birthday?" the girl asked.

"Yes. Twenty-first."

"Oh, wow, happy birthday then."

"Thanks." I waved to Paul and everyone else on my way out, pushing the door open to the warm night air. There were ashtrays on either side of the entrance and I wrinkled my nose at the stale smoke, moving away quickly.

Pulling my shirt back on, I headed down the street toward Robin's, checking my phone again.

Nothing.

CLIMBING THE STAIRS TO ROBIN'S APARTMENT, I WAS looking forward to sliding into bed next to her and just holding her in the dark. The lap dance, if she was really serious about it, could wait until tomorrow. Exhaustion seemed to have settled into my bones and I wanted a glass of milk and sleep.

Maybe I was on edge. God knew I was always suspicious. But when I pushed the door open, which wasn't locked, I knew instantly something was wrong. The hallway that opened to the kitchen was dark, and there were shadows on the stairs leading up to the living room. I sensed immediately someone was in the house, waiting in the dark. I could hear breathing, the slight rustle of clothes as they crouched. Tensing, I stood still, letting my eyes adjust to the lack of light. Debating whether I should go to the kitchen for a knife first, or if turning my back on whoever it was would be stupid, I calculated distance between me and the stairs.

Chances were Rory and Kylie were either down the hall or with their boyfriends. Which meant Robin was upstairs by herself and the intruder was between me and her. So I forgot about getting a knife and moved fast. Head down, I connected with a body, and there was a grunt of shock. Masculine, solid, strong, was my instant assessment. Using the element of surprise, I yanked and twisted, kicking his knees out from under him, so he tumbled to the floor with a hard thump and a curse. I landed on his chest, and I was pulling my fist back to knock him unconscious when I heard multiple voices and a girl's shriek.

What the fuck?

The lights came on suddenly, blinding me momentarily.

Then I realized I was about to punch my cousin. I was on top of Riley and he was staring up at me, amusement on his face.

"Get off me!" he said, shoving at my chest. "And happy birthday, asshole."

"What?" I fell back onto my heels and looked around, confused. Robin, my cousins, Jessica, Rory, and Kylie were all on the stairs and Robin was holding a sign she had painted that said HAPPY BIRTHDAY, PHOENIX.

"I don't get it," I said stupidly, because I didn't get it. My heart rate was slowing back to normal. "Dude, I thought you were an intruder," I told Riley. "I was about to beat the shit out of you."

"I figured as much. But it was supposed to be a surprise birthday party."

"Surprise!" Jayden yelled, raising his fists up and shaking them.

Easton was trying to climb the banister to the second floor and he said, "It's your birthday, *bitch*."

That made me laugh, breaking the tension I'd been feeling.

"Easton!" Tyler reprimanded.

Robin's eyes were wide. "Sorry, Phoenix, I didn't think . . . I just thought it would be fun to surprise you."

She looked so upset I felt bad. I stood up and leaned around Easton to give her a quick kiss. "Oh, you definitely surprised me. Thanks, babe." I reached my hand out to Riley to help him up.

"At least we know we're safe if the house is ever broken in to," Kylie said cheerfully. "I mean, you were basically about to rearrange Riley's face. How awesome is that?"

"Super awesome," Riley agreed, then rolled his eyes.

"I could hear breathing," I told him. "No one should be breathing in the dark."

"I have a cold," Jayden said. "Sorry."

"Nah, it's cool, U," I said, giving him a fist bump. "Thanks for coming. No one has ever given me a surprise party before. I wasn't expecting it."

Jayden gave me a look like I was the one who needed the short bus. "That's why it's a *surprise*."

He had me there. "Good point, man. I stand corrected."

Hell, I'd never had a birthday party at all, let alone a surprise birthday party. For my twentieth, I had taken Angel to Olive Garden, but she had embarrassed me by getting pissed at the waiter when he wouldn't let her order a jack and coke. Then the bill had come, and I'd felt sick that I had spent fifty bucks on a dinner that I hadn't even enjoyed. My nineteenth birthday I had spent in line for unemployment after I got laid off from my factory job. My sixteenth birthday had sucked because I had realized I couldn't get a driver's license because my mother couldn't find my birth certificate.

This year, I'd already thought I was a thousand times ahead of the last half dozen or so birthdays.

But this?

Fucking awesome.

"We have cake upstairs," Robin said, still clutching her sign. "Maybe we should go up."

Jessica nudged Riley. "Phoenix really got the jump on you."

"He did not," my cousin protested. "Another thirty seconds I would have had him on his back."

I doubted it, but I wouldn't want to go a round with Riley if he were really pissed or if he was protecting his family. He could be feral. I guess that was one thing Tyler, Riley and I all had in common besides blood.

"Thanks for doing this," I told Robin, taking her hand as we went upstairs. "This was really sweet."

"I'm sorry," she said with a sheepish shrug. "It was stupid to be in the dark like that. I should have known better."

"You know what? I'm glad you don't think the way I do. I'm always assuming the worst and you're not. That's a good thing."

But it was clearly bothering her. She was quiet as we went into the living room, and I frowned. Was this too much of a clear reminder that I was a criminal? I couldn't help it. I had grown up with dangerous drug dealers and Mom's loser boyfriends in and out of my house. I was always looking over my shoulder and that wasn't going to change, probably ever.

There was also no denying that I was damn uncomfortable getting presents. It was a foreign concept, and as Robin put out a tray of appetizers and Kylie tossed around cans of pop, I looked at the presents being set on the couch next to me in awe. "All these are for me, seriously?"

"Open them!" Easton demanded.

I picked the smallest one first because it seemed less intimidating. It was a SpongeBob gift bag and it looked like a drunk monkey had stuffed the tissue paper into it.

"That's from Jayden and me," Easton said.

"Thanks, man," I said. "And a gift bag and everything. We're getting to be legit, aren't we?"

"There's a girl in the house now," Riley said with a shrug. "Jess thinks that crap is necessary."

Jessica smacked his arm.

"I picked it out," Jayden said, already cramming a handful of cheese off the tray into his mouth. I didn't envy Riley and Tyler having to keep him in food. The guy could pack it away.

Which was evident in the gift he'd given me. It was five king-size candy bars. "Damn, thanks, guys. I'll have my sugar fix, that's for sure."

Easton was reaching out like he was going to steal one of them back and Tyler swatted at his hand. "Knock it off."

I grinned at Easton. "Dude, there's cake, you know. Chill. And thanks." I looked at Jayden. "Both of you."

"You're welcome," Jayden said, with a regal nod that cracked me up.

Next was a sketchpad from Rory and Tyler and a charcoals case from Riley and Jessica. Yeah. That was a fucking lump in my throat. My cousins looked as awkward about the whole gift giving as I felt, with Tyler making a point to mention that everything was Rory's idea.

"So if it's stupid, don't blame me," he added.

God, we were all such brats when it came to emotion. Why were any of them insane enough to be with us?

Rory frowned at Tyler. "Really?" she asked him.

"That didn't sound right, did it?" he asked.

"No. It didn't."

He shrugged. "I'm sorry. But this . . ." He gestured to the food, the paper party plates that declared "Happy Birthday!" and the cake that had been airbrushed with a cobra on it. "We aren't used to it. We don't know how to act."

"My plan wasn't to make you uncomfortable," Robin said, looking upset.

"You're not," I assured her. "It's just that no one has ever done this for me. For any of us. I'm . . . what's the word?"

"Touched?" Kylie suggested.

I winced. That sounded so . . . tender. But it was the truth and Robin deserved to hear that. "Yes. Touched."

Jessica burst out laughing. "You sound agonized. It's ridiculous. But Phoenix, we understand. Everyone has baggage, just in a different brand. Now let's eat cake. You can open your gifts from Robin when you guys are alone because I have a feeling that's going to make all of us uncomfortable."

"Good idea," Riley said.

"Cake!" was Easton's opinion.

Robin said, "I forgot a knife." She moved toward the stairs and I followed her.

"Hey." I took her hand. "This is the sweetest thing anyone has ever done for me."

There were tears in her eyes and I felt like shit.

"I should have asked you. I'm sorry. But I just thought you'd like it."

"I *do* like it." I pulled her to a stop and into my arms. "Robin. Why do you do that? Why do you always think that what you do isn't enough, or important, or whatever? This is *perfect*. The best birthday I've ever had."

"Really?"

"Really." How could she think otherwise? I kissed her softly, loving the way her lips felt beneath mine. "Mm. Who needs cake?"

"Easton will implode if we don't cut it," she said with a smile.

"True." I pulled a knife out of the drawer.

She went in the freezer. "One more thing."

She pulled out a box with a bow on it. Dilly Bars from Dairy Queen. "Holy shit, how did you know I love those?"

"Because when we first met you said you'd probably spend your birthday eating one by yourself, enjoying your freedom."

"I did?" I asked, stunned that she remembered that. I didn't even remember saying it. But she was right. That was exactly how I had imagined spending my birthday. I had a lot more than that, all because of her. "Babe. You're the best. I love you, do you know that?"

"I love you, too."

My phone buzzed in my pocket. I pulled it out as we walked back upstairs. And smiled when I saw the text.

Happy Birthday Turd. Mom

So she had remembered after all. It meant a lot, maybe more than it should. I showed the screen to Robin. "My mom remembered my birthday. And "Turd" was her nickname for me when I was a kid. Cute, huh?" I answered with a "thanks."

"She loves you," Robin said simply. "Even if she isn't always good at showing it."

"I know." I did. Expecting more was asking too much.

Upstairs Jessica was on the couch and laughing as Riley pinned her down. It looked like he had cake smeared on his mouth. "I cut the cake," she said, wheezing as he bounced her up and down on the cushion. "Sorry, Phoenix. I should have waited." Riley gave her a cake kiss and she screamed and turned her head.

But I was actually relieved. It took the pressure off a whole candles/cake-cutting thing where everyone would be looking at me. A corner of the cake was already missing and Easton was swiping his finger across the wax paper and eating globs of frosting left behind. "No problem." I took the knife from Robin and cut a chunk out and held it up with a grin. "Come here, babe."

I expected Robin to dart away, but she surprised me by moving so fast I didn't react. She lifted my arm and slammed the cake right into my face. It was creamy and crumbly, and I jerked back as Robin grinned at me.

"Is that what you mean?" she asked.

Which of course everyone found hilarious.

"Badass, huh?" Tyler snorted. "You can hear breathing in a dark room but you can't beat your girl in arm wrestling?"

"Suck my dick." I wiped my face. "Hey, by the way, look what I did today." Fingers covered in frosting, I lifted my shirt up and showed them my new tattoo. "Pretty awesome, huh?"

"Dude." Tyler nodded in approval. "That is killer. You draw that?"

"Yep."

"OMG!" Kylie screamed. "Robin, that's you!"

Robin laughed. "I know. It would be pretty awkward if it was someone else."

I snorted. "Cute."

Riley shook his head. "You've screwed us all, man. Now they're all going to expect portraits."

"I'm not tattooing your girlfriend's face on my body," I told him, expression deadpan.

Riley laughed and gave me a slap on the back. Hard. "When did you become such a comedian?"

"That's Robin?" Jayden asked, bending over to take a closer look. "I thought it was Selena Gomez."

Jessica shot pop out of her nose and started choking as she laughed.

"Christ, you're killing me," I said, holding my side. Damn, laughing made my tight skin pull even harder.

But there was no way *not* to laugh.

"I do not look like Selena Gomez!" Robin said, giggling.

"It's a compliment," Rory told her. "She's very pretty."

"*Muy caliente.*" Robin grinned. "And that, my friends, is sadly the bulk of my Spanish. Oh, and *feliz cumpleaños.*"

"*Gracias*," I said. "But I think you're way hotter."

"Don't tell me you know Spanish."

"A little. I took it in high school."

Robin laughed. "You're probably better at it than I am. It's my personal failing."

Cutting another piece of cake, I bit it. "*Cosita*, we all have plenty of those." I held the cake square in the air like it was a glass. "Here's to another birthday above ground."

"Cheers," Robin said with her Diet Coke.

CHAPTER FIFTEEN

ROBIN

WHEN I WAS A KID, BIRTHDAY PARTIES FOLLOWED THE SAME pattern—lots of food, lots of people, lots of inexpensive presents, a massive cake, and running around the yard like we were filming a remake of *Lord of the Flies*. There was a lack of parental supervision and an excess of sugar. They were perfect afternoons, and the only thing that changed from year to year was the decoration on the cake. My mother didn't go in for big themes or extravagant luaus or bowling parties or water parks. She thought spending hundreds of dollars on a kid's party was beyond their budget and created unreasonable expectations for the next year.

I never missed having a bounce house or pony rides. Birthdays were about the joy of running wild and tearing off wrapping paper and the added bonus of accidentally nailing my brother with the piñata stick. It worked for me.

Which was why I was relieved when Jessica broke the ice at

Phoenix's party by swiping some of his cake. He had been so painfully uncomfortable opening his gifts that I had known I had messed up. I should have warned him about the party. He wasn't the kind of guy you sprung a surprise on, as was obvious when he attacked Riley thinking he was a burglar.

Whoops.

But once he had relaxed, I thought he'd had fun, and now we were alone in my room, sitting on the bed, and he was opening the other presents I'd gotten him, the shirts and the shoes.

With his back against the wall, he held everything up and studied it, and he looked genuinely pleased. "I don't know how to say thank you," he said. "This is . . . everything was . . ."

"I know." I squeezed his hand. "You're welcome."

"How is your tattoo feeling?" he asked, turning my wrist.

"It's fine. It stings a little, but it's so small, it feels like a bee sting, that's all. Everyone thought it was cute. The real question is, how is yours?"

"It's fine." Phoenix slouched, the new shoes propped next to his feet, a Rolling Stones T-shirt lying on his chest. He puckered his lips at me, asking for a kiss.

He was so damn cute, how could I resist that?

But I did. "I have one more surprise." I stood up.

"God, are you sure that's a good idea?" he asked with a laugh. "I might wind up assaulting someone else."

"If you assault anyone other than me in the next half an hour I'm going to be very upset," I said, and then before I lost my nerve, I peeled my dress off over my head and let it drop to the floor.

His jaw dropped, and he made a strangled sound in the back of his throat. "Holy fuck . . ."

That was a good response, one that made me feel slightly less self-conscious about standing in front of him in a completely see-through bra and thong. They basically didn't even need to exist, that's how much coverage there was. It was pretty much just red netting, the kind they wrap mints in at weddings. I had also gotten a bikini wax for the first time in six months, and I felt sexy. Slightly unsure what to do with my hands, but sexy at the same time. No vodka required.

Phoenix set his gifts on the nightstand and sat up straighter. "What happens next?"

"Naked enthusiasm." I tapped my phone on the nightstand, and it started playing music off the sexy-times playlist I had created. "Why don't you sit on the edge of the bed in front of me?"

Phoenix crawled across the bed without further encouragement, his jeans sliding down his hips, hair in his eyes. The muscles of his shoulders rippled, and I sucked in a breath, no longer self-conscious. I was just hot for him. Very, very hot for him. When he was facing me, legs spread, palms flat on the bed, his gaze smoldering and sexy, I started to move, dancing slowly. Not like I did in a club, not with a manic bouncy energy, but just a slow, sensual swaying, lifting my hands into my hair to pull it back off my face.

Turning, I watched him over my shoulder, personally aroused and proud of myself, feeling together, happy, whole. I owed him that, for thinking I was beautiful when I was broken, hair dirty, clothes haphazard. Ironic how people would look at him and assume dysfunction, when I was the one who had needed him.

His lips parted, and his eyes dropped down to my ass. "Am I allowed to touch?"

"No." Slowly, I finished the rotation and climbed onto his

lap, where I gyrated, making sure he got plenty of cleavage in his face. But I wasn't quite as confident in that position that I wouldn't fall on the floor, so instead I shoved him onto his back to gain better leverage.

"I think I'm about to become a man," he murmured.

That made me smile as I spread my hips and kissed my way down his chest, flicking my tongue over his nipples. He was plenty of man long before he met me. Sitting back up, I slowly undid my bra and peeled it off, tossing it to the side. I had him pinned as I straddled him, and I pushed my hair back again, enjoying the feel of power over him. His nostrils were flaring and his eyes were heavy with lust.

My original thought had been to go down on him, but given the position I was in and how inconsequential the thong was, I decided to go with what was right for the moment. Shifting the scrap of fabric to the side and rising up a little, I realigned our bodies so that I sank down onto him, clamping his thighs with mine, free hand gripping his chest. Phoenix gave a low moan, his eyes rolling back. I felt a moment of pure feminine satisfaction that I had done that.

As I started to move, I asked, "Is that the kind of lap dance you had in mind?"

"Even better." Phoenix held onto my hips and pumped up into me. "And all I have to say is happy fucking birthday to me."

I would have laughed except I was too busy having an orgasm.

Maybe his party had been a success after all.

"GIRLS' NIGHT!" KYLIE SHOUTED AS SHE RAN UP THE STAIRS a week later, shaking a bottle of vodka in the air. "Let's go, bitches!"

She was wearing short shorts and wedges and a stretchy top that stopped just below her bra. Jessica was similarly dressed, though she wasn't showing as much skin. Rory was sitting on the couch in a floral dress with her leg crossed, foot bouncing up and down. I was wearing a sundress and cowboy boots because that felt right, comfortable to me. Going out to a club was a huge step for me. I had no intention of drinking, no desire to, nor did I want to sex it up. I just wanted to go and dance and have fun with my friends.

"Who is in for a shot before we go?" She had Dixie cups in her other hand, her gold bracelets rattling as she spread the cups on the coffee table. "Robin, I didn't bring a cup for you because I didn't think you'd want one."

"I don't. Thanks."

"Don't worry, I already did your shot." She winked at me.

I couldn't help but laugh. That was so Kylie. "But you know what, I'm going to do a shot of Diet Coke with you guys." I went down the hall to the bathroom and got another cup and poured some of my soft drink into it as Kylie poured out the shots. I didn't want to be totally left out. It was stupid, like why did it matter? But I still wanted to have that camaraderie, that connection.

So I raised my cup along with theirs and drank it like it was alcohol. It certainly burned a lot less going down. And I didn't have that same reckless, fist-pumping, let's-get-fucked-up feeling surging through me.

We all set our cups back down.

"Whose phone is blowing up?" Jessica bent over and glanced at the screen.

I realized it was my phone. "Oh, it's probably Phoenix. He's getting off work right now."

"It's Nathan," Jessica said with a puzzled laugh. "Why is Nathan texting you?"

And just like that my face went hot and my entire world came shattering down around me.

"What?" I asked, with a weird little laugh that didn't sound normal. I knew it didn't sound normal. Neither was my grab for my phone. "Why would Nathan text me?"

But the phone was already in Jessica's hand and Kylie took it from her, giving a confused laugh. "Did he text you by accident? God, are those guys trashed already? It's not even ten yet!"

My heart was racing and hot bile rose in my mouth. "Kylie. Let me have my phone," I said, desperate for her not to read whatever Nathan would have written. It couldn't be good. It wouldn't do anything but hurt her.

Now Rory was leaning forward on the couch, looking confused, and Kylie was narrowing her eyes at me. "Why?"

"Let me have the phone," Jessica said, her voice urgent.

She knew. I could tell that she knew. Or at least suspected that it would be bad. Very, very bad.

"No." Kylie turned her back on us and read the text out loud, "'When are you going to break up with that loser?' What the fuck does that mean? Why would he care if you're dating Phoenix?"

"Oh!" I said, like I had just realized something. "It must be my *cousin* Nathan. My family isn't super thrilled with me dating Phoenix." Lie. Total lie.

"You have a cousin named Nathan?" Rory asked.

"Yes." No.

"I didn't realize that your family was upset about Phoenix," Jessica said. "Dude, I can so relate."

My family didn't even know Phoenix had been to prison. They just knew he was a tattoo artist, nothing more. I was giving it another month or two before I brought him to Sunday dinner.

But none of that mattered because Kylie knew I was lying.

She turned around and stared at me, shock on her face, her thumb still on the screen where she had clearly been scrolling back through the texts.

It had been careless to not delete them. But maybe at the same time, I wanted proof that Nathan had been contacting me and I never answered, or told him to stop. Especially in the weeks after it had happened. Or maybe I wanted her to know that he wasn't a nice guy at all, if this ever came out.

But whatever the reason, now those awful texts were the very thing that made my terrible secret no longer a secret.

"Kylie," I whispered, shaking my head, not knowing what to say, what to do. There was a buzzing sound in my ears, and the tears were already there, blurring my vision, blurring the horrible sight of her staring at me looking like I had stabbed her repeatedly.

"You fucked my boyfriend?" she demanded. "You *fucked* my boyfriend? How could you do that, Robin?"

"What?" Rory gasped. "She wouldn't do that. You wouldn't do that." She looked to me for confirmation, but I couldn't deny it. "Oh no," she said weakly.

Kylie made a sound of disgust and looked at the phone again. "May 31. Text from Nathan reads, 'Last night was effing amazing. Let's do that again.' June 3. Text from Nathan. 'Is it weird that I think your pussy tastes better than chocolate?'"

Oh, God. I shook my head, stomach churning. "Stop. Don't read any more of those." I felt like I couldn't breathe, like I was going to faint.

"Don't?" Her finger came up, and she was crying now, heaving sobs. "Fuck you! How could you do that to me? I thought we were best friends. Oh, my God . . ." She dissolved into tears.

I was crying, too. "I didn't mean to! I don't even remember it, Kylie, I swear to you. I totally blacked out and when I realized . . . God, I was just sick. You have to believe it, I would never, ever hurt you."

"Well, you have!" she shrieked. "Drunk is no excuse. None." Then suddenly she was texting on my phone, crying and tapping and sniffling.

Oh, shit. "Kylie, don't . . ." That was so not a good idea. She was texting Nathan on my phone. I reached for it in a panic.

But she just put her hand out and glared at me. "Don't even, Robin, I am so serious right now. I will cut you." Her voice was venomous.

"Just give me the phone," I pleaded, reaching for it again.

But Kylie shoved me, and I stumbled.

"Okay, let's just calm down," Rory said, eyes wide as she came around the coffee table. "Kylie, maybe we should go outside and talk about this."

"I want to see if that fucking asshole answers." Kylie wiped her nose with her finger, her perfect French manicure neat and tidy against her streaking mascara and leaking nose.

I closed my eyes briefly, knowing that she was not going to see what she wanted to. That she was only going to add to her hurt.

"Oh, look, he answered," she said, waving the phone and giving a watery laugh. "What was that, about a minute? Can't remember the last time he answered me that fast. But then again, my pussy doesn't taste like chocolate. And I can't remember the last time he wanted to fuck me hard, which was what he suggested to you in one of these twenty-seven text messages. Yes, twenty-seven!" She took a breath, then her lips moved as she silently read.

"What did you write to him?" Jessica asked nervously.

Did it matter? It wasn't going to change anything. My hands were shaking, and I was sobbing myself, not even sure what to say to defend myself. There were no words to make this better and I hated myself all over again.

Kylie didn't answer. She just suddenly lunged at me with a shriek, her nails catching me across the face before I could react. The sharp pain and the flailing arms caused me to scream, too, and I threw my hands up to block any further blows.

But she was already retreating, her face crumpling as the anger turned to distress. She threw my phone at me, and it bounced off my chest painfully and crashed to the floor.

"Kylie, let me explain," I begged.

She just shook her head and waved her hands back and forth. "Shut up. Just shut up." Digging in her pocket she pulled out her phone and dialed a number. When the person on the other end answered, she screamed, "How could you? I'm breaking up with you and I never want to see your fucking face ever again!"

When she hung up, she stumbled toward the stairs and tripped in her shoes. Yanking them off, she took off down the stairs, crying.

"I'll go after her!" Rory said frantically, grabbing her purse.

"I should go," I said, starting toward the stairs.

"No." Jessica put her hand in front of me. "It won't help. Let her process."

"But . . . ," I said weakly. I knew she was right. I was the last person Kylie wanted to see. "Oh, God." I crumpled over, hiding my face in my hands, sobbing.

"What the hell happened?" Jessica asked, sounding stunned. "Why would you have sex with Nathan? That's so not you. You don't even hook up with the majority of guys you make out with, so explain to me why."

Shaking my head, I sat down on the floor and crossed my legs, not bothering to wipe my face. It didn't matter. Nothing mattered except I had severed an artery in my best friend and she hated me and would forever.

"Remember that party at the Shit Shack where Riley threw that guy's face into the booze can?" I said, voice shaky.

Jessica frowned. "Yeah. You were hanging with that Aaron guy."

"He ditched me. And we were super drunk, remember? You were upset, and we drank a crapload of vodka." I fingered my bracelet, spinning it around and around. "I was really, really drunk."

"So was I. I fell out of my shoes and puked after yelling at Riley for not wanting to have sex with me. Because you know, nothing is hotter than a drunk girl falling all over the place." She rolled her eyes. "Did Aaron do something? He seemed like a nice guy, but you never know. I mean, if he did something and then Nathan was helping you . . ."

The words were stuck in my throat. But I forced them out. "No. He just went off with some other chick after I made out with him and then, I guess, Nathan took me home. The last thing I remember is going to the keg for another drink. And then I woke up the next day in Nathan's bed. Everything else is just . . . nothingness."

"I knew something happened at that party." Jessica shook her head slowly. "God, I should have stayed. I knew I should have stayed. And the next day you didn't answer my text until, like, dinnertime and it just seemed like something was wrong. Then you basically withdrew all summer."

Miserable, I nodded. "I completely blacked out, but we obviously did . . . and I just feel so awful. I mean, why would I do that? Who the hell does that to her friend? I *hate* myself for that night. That's why I quit drinking. I don't trust myself, because I didn't think that even shitfaced I would do that."

Jessica bit her lip. "I don't know why you would do that either. I mean, we've all done stupid shit drunk, but I've never blacked out, so I don't know. I don't know what I could do that loaded."

"It was the worst moment of my life waking up and realizing what I had done." I shuddered.

"So this is why you wanted to move out. Why you stopped drinking and stopped washing your hair. God." Jessica's voice was soft, and I couldn't tell if she felt sympathy or if she was just absolutely disgusted by me.

"Yes."

"So what was all that with the texts?" she asked. "I mean, you woke up and freaked out and took off, right?"

I nodded.

"And you told Nathan it was a mistake?"

"Yes." My eyes were puffy and stinging, cheek throbbing from Kylie's nails, and I welcomed the discomfort. I deserved way worse than a nail raking. "But Nathan doesn't feel bad about it. He texted me all summer, trying to hook up with me. I told him to stop, like, multiple times. I thought he had for a while until I started dating Phoenix. For some reason that bothers him and he started again."

"So what Kylie read was a bunch of sexts from Nathan?"

Nodding, I picked my phone off the floor and handed it to her. Maybe if she knew the whole truth she could be there for Kylie in a way I couldn't. "Look. I didn't encourage him in any way. I just wanted him, it, to go away."

Jessica scrolled through, twin spots of red appearing on her cheeks. "That asshole. Jesus, poor Kylie . . . God, how could he do this?"

I knew what she seeing. There were two dozen texts saying things like, "Want to see you, taste you. Mmm." "Had so much fun. Ur a little freak and I love that." "Bored and horny. U busy?"

My responses were pretty clear. "Not interested. Stop texting." "It was a mistake, not happening again."

"What did he write tonight?"

"She texted him that she was thinking about that night and he wrote, and I quote, "'Best blow job of my life. Name time and place and lets make it happen again.'"

I actually gagged. For a second I thought I might throw up, just right there on the living room floor, all in my own lap. But I took a few huge gulps of air and fought back the nausea and the panic. "He's an asshole. Kylie deserves better than this."

"Hell, yeah, she does. I wonder if he is texting and hooking up with other girls."

It wasn't a thought I'd ever had before, but it didn't seem like a stretch that he probably was. It seemed to come far too easily for him, with absolutely zero guilt. "I don't know. I hope not, for her sake. And maybe I should go get STD testing." That thought hadn't occurred to me before either. I had just figured I was a drunk mistake that he discovered he enjoyed, not that Nathan was a serial cheater.

"I think that's a good idea."

I lost it again, choking on a sob. "If I could take this back, I would. God, I would give anything to undo this. Poor Kylie."

Jessica looked grim. "Well, now she knows that he's a dick. She was going to find out sooner or later, whether it was you or someone else."

"Well, I wish it was someone else if it had to happen at all. Knowing it was me makes it extra awful."

"I'm texting Rory. We need to make sure Kylie doesn't do something stupid." Jessica went for her phone. "Shit, she already texted me. She's going to find Nathan to confront him. Rory is with her but she wants backup."

"I can't go, can I?" I asked, already knowing the answer.

"No. That's not a good idea. Does Phoenix know? You need to give him a heads-up or you might be losing a boyfriend tonight."

Again I couldn't tell if she was sympathetic or if she was just thinking out loud. Sniffling, I nodded. "Phoenix knows. I told him what happened."

Jess looked surprised. "You told him? But you didn't tell me?" Her tone was hurt. "I asked you point-blank what happened at that party and you told me nothing. This was a whole lot more than nothing."

"How could I tell you?" I asked, agonized. "Then I would have just put you in the worst position ever. If you kept the secret and Kylie found out, then she might hate you for that. If you told her then she would be devastated. I couldn't do that to you, force you to keep my secret. It was my horrible mistake and I thought if I just kept a lid on it, eventually it wouldn't matter anymore."

"I see your point, but truthfully, Robin, I don't even know what to think." Jessica grabbed her purse and headed for the stairs. "Maybe you and Phoenix should stay here tonight and I'll take Kylie to my place. She needs time."

"Yeah. Sure. Of course."

Then she left and I was alone.

Sitting on the floor, face itchy and wet with tears, nose running, throat scratchy, heartbreaking, I yanked off my cowboy boots. I thought about texting Phoenix to come over but knew that was selfish. He never got to hang out with his cousins and he was tonight. I didn't want to ruin that. But the room was so silent, no fridge upstairs to hum, no windows open to traffic, no clock to tick. It was just me and my thoughts, going around and around, thoughts of Kylie never speaking to me again. Thoughts of Jessica and Rory never speaking to me again. Thoughts of Kylie, her heart breaking, the pain she was feeling. So sure that her boyfriend loved her, only to find out he clearly didn't.

When my boyfriend had cheated on me, it had hurt like hell and that had been high school, that had been a two-month relationship, and by cheat I meant he kissed another girl at a party.

Not this. Not betrayal on this level after a year of dating. Kylie and Nathan basically lived together.

And yet, he had done this.

And I had done that.

My eyes fell on the vodka bottle, left on the coffee table. I turned away, texting Jessica and Rory.

Neither answered.

Instead I got a text from Nathan that said, "Fucking cunt. Why did u tell her?"

Closing my eyes, I felt new tears prick at the back of my lids, and I listened to the silence grow louder and louder, my ears ringing.

When I opened my eyes the vodka was still there, shiny and large and within reach of my hand.

If I drank it, I would feel better. The pain, the shame, would ease up. But then tomorrow I would feel worse.

But if I drank it, I would feel better now. And tomorrow I would feel even worse.

But if I drank it, I would feel better now . . .

I reached for the bottle.

CHAPTER SIXTEEN

PHOENIX

"WHY DO THEY CALL IT 'GIRLS' NIGHT?'" NATHAN ASKED. "Why does it have to have a title? We don't call it 'Guys' Night' when we hang out."

Truth was, I didn't give a shit what anyone called any of it. All I knew was that I had been planning on hanging out with my cousins while Robin was with her roommates. I hadn't bargained on spending a night in the company of Nathan, who I couldn't fucking stand. I was glad that Robin was feeling comfortable hanging out with her friends, and I had encouraged her to have fun, go dancing or whatever.

But I think it was safe to say she was having a hell of a lot more fun than I was.

We were at Zeke's, a neighborhood bar, and Tyler and Riley knew the owner/bartender. I didn't mind being in a bar. There was a pool table and a jukebox and a TV, plus the point was to talk to each other, right? At least as much as dudes do.

What I did mind was Nathan, aka Dickhead, running his mouth the entire time. He was a bragger, and he flirted with every woman who walked in the door, most of who were well past the point of cougar status. They were like . . . I don't know . . . meerkats? Though maybe the label shouldn't apply at all, since they weren't the ones in pursuit, Nathan was, making a point of waving and smiling to every woman on every stool as he strolled to the pool table with Tyler.

"I don't know how long I can hang with this," I told Riley.

"What, being in a bar?"

"Douche lord over there," I said, jerking my thumb toward Nathan. "I know he's one of Tyler's best friends, but he rubs me the wrong way."

"He's not my favorite either. I think they're friends still because they've been friends since middle school. Nathan has gotten a bit big for his britches since he went to college. At least Tyler stopped letting that loser Grant troll around. I couldn't stand that waste of space."

"Grant?" I had a vague memory of a skinny kid who wouldn't look anyone in the eye. "Is he the one who slashed the teacher's tires and got arrested with the knife still in his hand?"

"That's the one."

"Tyler needs better friends." I sipped my root beer from the bottle.

"Yeah, well, slim pickings in the neighborhood."

"True that." It wasn't like I'd kept in touch with anyone from school. "The guys at the shop are cool. Normal."

Riley laughed and threw back his whiskey. "What the hell is that?"

"I think maybe for the first time ever you and I are basically living it," I said. "No drama. Feels awesome, doesn't it?" Nothing but work and Robin and family . . . peace and quiet. We'd been together a month and were going stronger than ever. Good stuff.

"It sure does." Riley gave me a grin. "Got some good news today, too. At Jessica's insistence, and okay, as a result of Jessica doing all the paperwork, the bank let me refinance at a lower interest rate. They rolled the back-owed money into a new loan, but the payments are still the same. With me, Jess, and Tyler all working, we can afford it, so we get to keep the house."

"Wow, that's awesome. Seriously." I was impressed with how Riley had managed to create a life for himself and his brothers. I reached out and gave him a fist bump.

"God knows it's not exactly where I want to live, but there is no way we could have that space for as little money if we rent anywhere else. And I don't have to switch Easton's school or upset his life anymore than it already has been. And in ten years, I'll own that dump clear and free." He raised his glass and grinned. "It makes a man proud."

"It should. You done good, man."

I was about to say more, but suddenly there was a loud crash. We whirled around and saw Nathan throwing a pole stick across the bar, a look of fury on his face. Both Riley and I jumped up as we saw Tyler holding his hand out and murmuring to Nathan.

"What's going on?" Riley asked. "It's just a game, man."

"This isn't over pool," Nathan said through gritted teeth. "Kylie just broke up with me."

"What?"

I hung back, on edge, arms crossed.

"In a five-second phone conversation." He raked his hands through his hair, pacing back and forth before rounding and pointing a finger at me. "It's that bitch Robin's fault!"

Oh, hell, no. He was not going to fucking go there with me. I dropped my arms and took a step toward him. "Excuse me?" I asked, my voice steely cold.

Zeke appeared between us and gave Riley an apologetic look. "Dude, you need to take him out," he said, tilting his head toward Nathan. "You know you're always welcome, but he broke the pool stick and that ain't cool."

"Sure, no problem, I understand." Riley gave Tyler a long look. "Get him out of here. Phoenix and I will stay."

"He's not going anywhere until he apologizes for calling my girlfriend a bitch," I said, knowing that I should just let it drop. But I couldn't. If Kylie had broken up with Nathan, and Nathan was accusing Robin of being to blame, then that meant Kylie knew what had gone down. Which meant being the slimeball that he was, Nathan was trying to throw Robin under the bus. Fuck that.

Thinking about Robin, how much she had suffered, how devastated she would be right now, made me really upset. Pissed.

"Dude, don't," Riley said. "Come on, just leave it alone."

Tyler had Nathan by the arm and was trying to wrest him toward the door, but Nathan was fighting him. "I'm not apologizing!" he yelled at me. "That selfish little bitch did it on purpose! She fucking set me up and now Kylie knows about me and Robin."

"Shut up," Tyler said, pushing him harder. "This isn't cool."

I moved closer to Nathan, even when Riley darted and tried to block me. "What is he talking about?" he asked.

"Say it, Nathan," I said, egging him on, and knowing full well I was egging him on. But the fury was coursing through me like an electrical surge, and I wanted just one more insult so I could put my fist into his sneering dickhead face. Did he have any idea how much Robin had agonized over what had happened? How worried she was about hurting her friend? Obviously not. He was just concerned with saving his own sorry ass. "Go on, blame a girl for you being a tool. Let me hear your pussy explanation for why you can't take responsibility for your own actions."

"Hey, Robin was there when I fucked her. I kept it a secret. She could have kept her mouth shut." Nathan sneered. "But maybe she's so used to having a cock in it, she doesn't know how."

And that was my fist in his face.

There was no conscious thought. Just a reaction, a lightning-quick move, my head a haze of burning hot anger, adrenaline lending me enough power to drop him to the floor with one hit. Nathan went down hard, and the sound was satisfying, but not nearly enough to clear the cloud of anger distorting my thoughts. I kicked him on the foot. "Get up!"

Riley tried to grab my arm, but I shook him off. He and Tyler were both speaking but I didn't hear what they were saying. My entire focus was on the piece of shit scrambling to his feet, wiping at his mouth, which was bleeding. The sight of that red smear excited me, made me pleased. I wanted more of it. I wanted his face distorted and swollen, eyes shut, a bloody pulp. He thought he was so fucking sexy, wait until I was done with him. Wait until he understood what happened when someone called my girlfriend a whore.

He was moving too slow for me, so I punched him again

without waiting for him to fully stand. He grunted and fell backward with the impact, right into the door. Zeke opened it, and Nathan spilled out onto the sidewalk. Bouncing on the balls of my feet, I followed.

"I'm calling the cops," Zeke said, shaking his bald head at us.

I didn't care. I didn't give two shits. By the time they got there Nathan would look like raw ground beef.

But Riley came at me from the side with a football move, plowing me down the sidewalk about three feet like I was a tackle dummy and screaming, "Knock it off! You don't want to do this, man."

"Let me go! Yes, I do!" I scrambled, going down low to dart out of his reach. "Don't make me hit you, Riley."

"You want to go back to jail? You'll get three years this time!"

I knew that logically, but anger was propelling me. Wild, uncontrollable anger, but by the time I escaped Riley's grip, Tyler had dragged Nathan to his feet and was shoving him in the back of his car on the street. Riley pulled the back of my shirt. I swatted at him.

"Fucking stop it!" I yelled. "Fine. I'll let him go." I knew where he lived. Taking a deep breath, I paced back and forth on the sidewalk. "Shit. Shit. Shit."

"Walk, asshole," Riley shoved me in the direction of home. "I don't think Zeke actually called the cops, but just in case."

I raked my hands through my hair. "Did you hear what he said about her?" I asked, my voice hoarse and raw. God. The pain I knew she must be feeling, it was my pain. I pulled out my phone and tried to call her, but there was no answer. It went right to voice mail, so her phone was probably turned off.

"That was pretty shitty," Riley admitted. "I am not saying I blame you. If someone had said that about Jess I would have lost it."

"Can you try calling Jessica?" I asked. "Robin isn't answering. If Kylie knows she and Nathan hooked up, then she must be furious with Robin, too. I'm worried about her."

"You knew, didn't you?"

Nodding, I walked faster. "Yeah. She told me a few weeks ago. She was drunk, blacked out, woke up with Nathan back at the beginning of the summer. It's why she quit drinking. It's been eating her alive, the guilt over Kylie."

"Damn." Riley shook his head. "What a fucking mess." He put his phone to his ear. "Hey, babe, what's going on there? Shit hit the fan here."

Trying Robin again, I cursed. Of course it was still turned off.

"So where are you girls? Uh-huh. And Robin? What time was that? Okay. Yeah, I love you, I'll call you back. Bye."

Riley looked at me. "Rory and Kylie and Jess are all at my place. They left Robin back at the apartment."

"But then why isn't she answering?"

"I don't know. She's probably upset. She's probably taking a shower or something."

It didn't make sense. Robin would reach out to me when she was upset, I was sure of it. So what was she doing, alone? The thought terrified me.

"I need a car."

We were cutting down his street, and I suddenly realized as we came up to the house that Nathan's car was in front of the house.

"No. No, Phoenix, don't." Riley already knew where my thoughts were going. "That's grand theft auto."

"Then I'll borrow your car," I said, bending over and picking up a good size rock off the tree lawn. I smashed it into Nathan's window with a beautiful crash, sending glass shattering all over me and the grass.

"Ah, fuck, seriously?"

"Look away if you don't want to be a part of it," I told him as I leaned in through busted glass and popped the trunk.

Going around the back of the car I lifted the trunk and found what I was looking for—a tire iron. Then I took it to Nathan's car, feeling the pulse and vibration up through my arms as the metal and fiberglass clashed together with each ferocious blow. Steadily making my way around the car, I hit it over and over, sweating and furious, the jarring contact rattling my teeth, the crunch of glass beneath my shoes feverishly satisfying. Vaguely in the background I was aware of the front door to the house opening and voices, but it didn't matter. I saw my reflection in the passenger window, but I pictured Nathan's sneer as I hit so hard the iron left my grip and went sailing straight through to the backseat.

Panting, I turned and walked away, spitting on the ground by the back tire, trying to rid my mouth of the foul taste that coated my tongue, the back of my throat.

There was a whole crowd staring at me in shock. Jessica, Rory, Kylie, Jayden, Easton. Riley was shaking his head.

"That's what I think of a guy who cheats on his girlfriend," I said to my audience. "That's what I think of a guy who has sex with a girl who is so drunk she doesn't even know where she is or who she's with."

Wiping the sweat off my forehead, I walked past them to the house, my new tattoo burning and itching as the healing skin pulled. "I need your keys!" I yelled to Riley over my shoulder.

But then I stopped and turned around. I locked eyes with Kylie. "I'm sorry." Not for the car, but for the hurt she was feeling.

She just stared at me in shock, face swollen from crying. After a second, she nodded, and I thought she understood.

RORY DROVE ME TO ROBIN'S. SHE HAD SAID SHE NEEDED TO pack a bag for herself and Kylie and that she personally wanted to check on Robin. She also told me quite clearly that she didn't think that I was in a frame of mind conducive to driving. And that was exactly how she said it. Conducive.

No, I was not feeling conducive to driving, whatever the hell that meant.

I felt calmer but not totally rational.

I was too damn worried about Robin.

"Riley said no one in the neighborhood will call the cops because it's not their car. They won't get involved. So don't worry about that," she said.

"I wasn't."

Rory looked insanely small driving Riley's ancient Mustang, her auburn hair back in a ponytail, her dress something that in my mind was more suitable for a little kid at Easter or your grandmother's couch, but I could see what Tyler saw in her. She was very matter-of-fact and not one for any sort of drama. I'd never once heard her raise her voice.

Robin didn't shout either. She saved her passion for her art and for our bed.

Knowing it was pointless, I called Robin again. No answer.

"How is Kylie?" I asked.

"She is in shock. I mean, it was a double blow. Well, actually I suppose you could say a triple blow. Not only was it her friend and her boyfriend, but Nathan obviously did not regret it considering how many texts he sent after the fact, and their content."

I cleared my throat, my jaw clenched, knuckles sore where I had hit him. "I don't want to hear about the content. Sorry."

Something about my voice had her glancing over at me nervously. "Sorry, that was thoughtless."

"Have you heard from Tyler?"

"He has Nathan at the house. He is being belligerent. He wants to come over and talk to Kylie, but Tyler told him she doesn't want to see him."

I gave a laugh of disbelief, rubbing my face. "What a freakin' mess. God, why isn't Robin answering?"

"She's upset, ashamed." Rory pulled into a spot in front of the house. "I wish she had told us."

"She couldn't." I got out of the car, anxiously waiting for Rory to get out of the car. Something was wrong. I knew it. I could feel it. Goose bumps rose on my skin. "Rory, hurry. Please."

I started running. I don't know why. I just did, pounding up the stairs to the landing to their apartment. I didn't wait for

Rory or her key. I just hit the door with my shoulder, hard, sending it flying back against the wall, wood splintering as I tore the
lock from the hinge.

"Phoenix! What's wrong?" Rory was behind me, coming up
the stairs.

But that's when I saw her, and I shouted, "Call 911!" I fell to
the floor where Robin was, grabbing for her crumpled body.
"Oh, God, oh, God, Robin, baby, Robin, wake up."

Tears came to my eyes as I held her, trying to process what I
was seeing. She was waxy white, and there was vomit all down
the front of her dress. Her body was limp, unresponsive, legs bent
at a weird angle. There was a mostly empty vodka bottle on its
side on the floor next to her. All the breath seemed to suck out of
my body like a vacuum had been brought to my lips. I couldn't
speak, couldn't think, couldn't move.

"Turn her on her side!" Rory ordered me in a sharp and com-
manding voice I didn't normally associate with her.

"What?" I stared blankly up at her through watery eyes. "I
don't think she's breathing," I told Rory, and then a raw,
anguished sob ripped out of my chest.

The phone was at Rory's ear, and she told the operator, "Yes,
blood alcohol poisoning. She's been sober for about three months
and now it looks like she drank at least a third of a bottle of
vodka in less than ninety minutes." Rory was breathing hard and
talking fast as she shoved past me to push on Robin's back. "Help
me roll her, Phoenix, come on. We have to clear her airway in case
she vomits again."

"Is she alive?" I asked, even when I didn't want to know
the answer.

"Yes. Her breathing is shallow, but she'll be okay as long as she doesn't asphyxiate on her vomit."

"Jesus." That snapped me out of my stupor. She was alive. Robin was alive, and that was all that mattered. I rolled her onto her side. Her body was so cold, her face so clammy, her eyes not closed completely, but only the whites were visible, the absence of her irises disturbing. I was in agony seeing her like this, and I didn't understand how this could happen. "Why would she do this?"

"Yes, thank you," Rory was saying to the operator. "I hear the sirens now. I'm going down to let them in."

As the pounding of Rory running down the stairs receded, I held Robin's hand and brushed her hair back off her forehead. Bending over, I tried not to cry, and drew in a shuddering breath. I hadn't cried since I was six years old. That I had tears in my eyes now shocked me, but God, if Robin was gone . . . I would be gone. Done. The light in my life would go out. My hands were shaking and I kissed her temple.

"Hang in there, you're going to be fine," I murmured, my voice hoarse and unsteady. "It's going to be okay. I promise."

Then the paramedics were there, jabbing an IV into her arm and taking her vitals as they loaded her onto a stretcher.

"How much did she drink?"

"Is she on any other recreational drugs? Prescription drugs?"

"Has she been suicidal?"

I couldn't answer, and I heard Rory's voice from a distance, like I was caught in the eye of a storm and everyone else was whirling around in the tornado, motion and sound and reality out there in the funnel cloud, while I stood frozen in the center, helpless.

It was like the night my mother had overdosed. The sights, the sounds, my terror.

But I wasn't alone. I wasn't eleven years old.

And Robin needed me.

I dragged myself back into the present, muscle by muscle, just the way I did when I needed to control my anger. When they lifted the stretcher, I stood, a firm grip on Robin's hand. She was cold, limp, her lips a horrifying bluish white.

"What's her name?" the brawny guy setting a bag of fluid onto her lap asked.

"It's Robin," I said.

"You her boyfriend?"

"Yes." My chest tightened.

"Are you sober? Can you follow us to the hospital?"

"I don't drink," I told him, my voice choked and harsh. "I've never been anything but sober."

He studied me and nodded. "Okay, good. She's going to be okay, man, don't worry."

"Yeah. Okay. Thanks." I had to believe him.

Because if she wasn't okay I had no idea how I would survive. None whatsoever.

CHAPTER SEVENTEEN

ROBIN

I WAS DREAMING THAT MY GRANDMOTHER WAS SITTING AT the head of the table, shaking her finger at me and calling me a gringo whore, and I was crying because it wasn't true . . . was it? Maybe it was. I turned, like someone behind me knew the answer to that question, and I saw Phoenix lying on a tattoo table. He was getting a 3-D tattoo, the letters popping up off of his flesh into the air, a marquis sign that blinked over and over. VODKA.

Why was he getting a vodka tattoo?

He turned to look at me, and the tattoo on his chest started to bleed for real, the blood rolling down his rib cage and onto the floor, and his hand went limp, and his eyes stared straight through me.

"Where am I?" I asked him, my words silent in the empty room, the light from his tattoo blinding.

But he didn't answer.

When my eyes opened, I still didn't know where I was.

Jerking awake, I glanced around the room frantically. There was beeping behind my ear and glowing lights to my right and I squinted. That was a countertop. And I was in a hospital bed. I tried to sit up and realized I had an IV in my arm.

Phoenix was in a chair next to the fluorescent tube light on the underside of the wall cabinets. "Hey," he said, and his voice sounded strained, hoarse.

"What's going on?" I asked, trying to prop myself up but feeling nauseated. My head was pounding, and I couldn't form a coherent thought. The confusion moved through my head like an aggressive fog. "Is this the ER?" The curtain behind Phoenix didn't mask the sound of nurses and other people moving on the other side, a sense of hustle to their movements. "What happened?"

"You have blood alcohol poisoning," he told me. "But you're going to be okay."

Then I remembered. The text from Nathan. Kylie's horrible reaction. Being left alone, in the silence. With the vodka bottle. Drinking the first shot. Then another. And another.

Phoenix looked exhausted, dark circles under his eyes, his back bent, elbows on his thighs holding him up.

"How did I end up here?" It wasn't like I hadn't done multiple shots before, but blood alcohol poisoning sounded serious. Like almost died kind of serious. I swallowed hard and shifted my head slightly. There was a trailer effect, like I was leaving pieces of my skull behind at one-inch intervals as I turned. I didn't remember anything beyond checking my phone as I downed the vodka.

"Rory and I found you passed out, covered in vomit. There

was an empty bottle next to you and your lips were blue, your heart rate way slower than normal."

With each word he spoke, I was more and more shocked. "What? Oh my God. I didn't think . . . I didn't mean."

Fear gripped me in an icy hold. "I'm going to be sick."

Phoenix was up on his feet as I scrambled to sit all the way up, leaning over the metal bedrail. He shoved a pan off the counter under my mouth just in time to catch a spray of vomit. "Oh, God," I groaned, as my stomach heaved.

His free hand stroked the back of my head. "It's okay. You're okay, baby. Just puke it out."

My eyes were filled with water, and I tried to wipe the snot away from my nose, but I fell forward. "Why do I have an IV?"

"They're flushing your system with fluids and giving you glucose."

"Oh." I hugged the rail, my shoulders shaking. "I'm sorry," I said, because it seemed like the right thing to say.

"Why would you do this?" he asked, and his voice cracked. "I know you were upset, but when I saw you like that . . . holy shit, it was one of the worst moments of my life."

"I didn't mean to." How could I explain to him the pain of knowing how badly I had hurt Kylie? How seeing her rage at me had sliced every wound that had started to heal wide open? "I was alone and no one was answering their phone. It was sitting there and I wasn't going to, but then I just wanted to dull the anxiety a little. Only when I did a shot, nothing happened. The room was so quiet and I felt so anxious . . . I took another shot. Then I started to feel a little rush, and it was such a relief that I had one more and I tried to paint and then I don't know . . ."

I didn't know.

It was just like before, only this time I had risked never waking up.

I started to cry, and Phoenix set the pan down and pulled me against his chest. "Baby. Shh."

His arms felt good, strong, and I breathed in his scent. "You might have saved my life."

His fingers gripped me tighter, but he didn't respond.

"Kylie knows, and she hates me," I said.

"She'll get over it. Just give her some time." He rubbed my back. "Now I'm going to go get the doctor and tell him you're awake, so hang tight, okay? I'll send Rory in."

For a second I gripped him tighter, not wanting to let go, but then I fell back against the pillows and nodded. My body felt shaky and weak.

When Rory came in a minute later, I tried to smile, but I was too embarrassed to say anything, do anything. "Hey," was all I managed.

"Hey," she said, her face concerned, hair slipping out of its ponytail. "I'm so freaking glad to see you awake and talking. You really scared me, Robin."

"Thanks for taking care of me." I picked at the tape on my IV. It was pulling my skin. "I wasn't trying to pass out, I just want you to know that. I just didn't want to hurt so much. Seeing Kylie's face . . . I just wanted that image to go away."

"I know." Rory took my hand in both of hers and squeezed

my fingers. "We shouldn't have left you alone with a bottle of vodka. That was stupid."

But I shrugged. My problem wasn't anyone else's. "It's not your job to babysit me. And everyone left in an unexpected hurry. Did Kylie confront Nathan? Is she okay?" I couldn't get the picture of her screaming and crying out of my head.

"No, she's not exactly okay, but truthfully, I think she is way more hurt by Nathan than by you. I mean, those texts were brutal. He was just blatant in his desire to cheat." Rory looked behind her at the curtain separating us from the staff area of the ER. "Listen, just so you know everything that went down, Phoenix hit Nathan. He would have probably put him in the hospital if Tyler hadn't dragged Nathan away. Then he took a tire iron to Nathan's car. He smashed literally every window and light and left dents and scrapes all over it. We all saw him doing it and it was actually kind of scary, I'm not going to lie. It was like he wasn't in control of himself."

I remembered him telling me that he only beat the shit out of people who deserved it, and I knew he hated Nathan on principle, but I didn't entirely get the rage. Maybe my brain was still too foggy. "He knew about Nathan. I told him a few weeks ago. So I have no idea why he would go ballistic like that. He didn't get in trouble, did he?" That was my main concern, if anyone had called the cops. Phoenix would go back to jail, no question about it.

"No. It's okay. But my God, what a night. I think we need to stop doing Girls' Night." She gave me a smile. "Too much drama."

"It wasn't Girls' Night. It was me. All of it."

"No, it wasn't all you. Don't take Nathan's guilt on to yourself."

"I don't want to talk about it right now," I said, because I didn't. Guilt had become so familiar to me, it was odd and scary to have my secret shame out there in the open, for my friends to discuss and question.

I already knew what I had to do—what I had been planning originally, before I had met Phoenix and let Tyler convince me that I needed to pretend nothing had happened. I needed to move out. There was no place in that apartment for me while Kylie was trying to recover.

"You didn't call my parents, did you?" I asked, the thought sending me into a panic. My mother would be shocked, my father would be so disappointed. My grandmother, well, she would be disgusted. "What time is it anyway?"

"It's six a.m., and no, I didn't call your parents. We left your phone at the apartment by accident, and it was the middle of the night and it looked like you were going to be okay, so I didn't go back for it. Should we have?"

I shook my head. "God, no. This would destroy them."

Phoenix came back around the curtain with a nurse then, and Rory stepped back to let her check my vitals.

After she went through a whole round of questions, she said, "The doctor needs to stop in, but you can leave at any time if you'd like to go home. We'll go over the instruction list for home care, and I have some information for you to take home about the dangers of binge drinking and resources available to you."

There was no judgment in her voice. She was smiling and rubbing my arm. It actually made me feel worse. If she were bitchy about it, I could get defensive. But there was nothing there but the kind concern of a total stranger.

"Thanks," I said, as she gently pulled the tape back on my IV. She had short, spiky red hair and hot pink scrubs.

"I have kids who are in their late twenties. College has too many keg parties. Hopefully this was a lesson learned for you."

"Yeah," I said, because I was supposed to. And it was a lesson. But then so had waking up naked with Nathan, and yet I'd done it again. That scared me to the point that I felt numb. I wanted to ignore all of it, I wanted to lie on my couch for a week straight, eating cereal and watching TV, painting every canvas I could get my hands on with shades of deep, bruised purple.

"It won't happen again," Phoenix said, and something about his tone had me glancing toward him. That sounded weird. Like he planned to put an ankle bracelet on me or something.

"You can change back into your clothes." She put a bandage where the needle had punctured my wrist. "Be back in a flash with the doctor."

Rory reached for the clothes they had obviously removed from me at some point. I was still wearing my bra and panties, so I sat up and tried to slip out of the arms of the gown without flashing both Phoenix and Rory.

"Oh, God, this dress is still wet," Rory said, blanching a little.

I was so exhausted, I didn't care. I just wanted to get home and sleep. Except that it stunk. "Gross." But I pulled it on anyway, because I didn't really have a choice, and hey, it was my own puke. I supposed I deserved it. The gown fell away as the dress slid down into place, damp and smelly.

Phoenix, who had been standing there silently, his body completely still, suddenly started and yanked the curtain back with more power than was needed. "I'll go pull the car around. Rory, let me have the keys."

It was totally obvious that he wasn't processing any of this any better than I was.

Ten minutes later I was climbing into the back of Riley's car on shaky legs, sighing as I sunk down, my eyes closing. The physical discomforts—the pounding head, the dry mouth, the tremor—gave me a focus on something other than my thoughts.

But one kept coming to the forefront anyway—that I didn't want to risk death. That if guilt drove me to that place, then I was going to have to figure out how to let go of the guilt.

To forgive myself.

Ultimately, I couldn't control if Kylie or my other friends did or not. But I could control my own feelings. And I could control my actions.

But first I wanted to sleep, for days and days, until my head no longer felt so heavy and my thoughts so sluggish.

Phoenix helped me up the stairs to the apartment and into the living room, his firm arm around me, taking the bulk of my weight as I leaned heavily on him. The two flights of stairs wiped me out, and I said, "I can't walk to my room. I need to rest on the couch."

Nausea was crawling up my throat, and I was out of breath. As I sank down I saw Rory scrambling to grab the empty vodka bottle. She slipped it into her ever-present messenger bag.

"Are you okay?" she asked. "Can I get you anything? I should take Riley's car back soon, but I can run to the store if there's anything special you want, like Gatorade or Popsicles or soup?"

I was about to speak, but Phoenix beat me to it. "I can get

her whatever she needs. You should get the car back to Riley. Thanks for everything, Rory."

"Yeah, thank you." I wanted a hug but wasn't sure if I could ask for one.

"Sure. I'll talk to you soon." She looked at Phoenix. "Take care of her."

He nodded.

Once we were alone, I curled up on the couch and tugged at the hem of the dress, trying to pull it up without much luck. I wanted the smell away from me. It wasn't helping my squirrely stomach. Suddenly Phoenix's hands were pulling it up over my hips and past my ribs. He wasn't being particularly gentle and I protested. "I got it."

"Let me help," he said gruffly, sliding a hand behind me and forcing me up into a sitting position.

My head spun from the motion, and my face went hot. "Phoenix, stop."

But the dress was already over my head, and I sank back. I closed my eyes briefly, then I looked up at him. "That's a little rough," I complained. "I don't feel good."

"Whose fault is that?" he asked, and the anger in his voice shocked me.

Using the lower half of my dress to cover myself, suddenly cold and feeling way too exposed in just my underwear, I stared at him. He wasn't making eye contact with me. "Tell me how you really feel," I said, annoyed and exhausted.

I didn't really mean it as an invitation. I meant it as a warning that he was being a jerk, but he sat on the coffee table across from me, his knees touching the edge of the sofa.

"You know what, I will, Robin. I'm not doing this again. I'm not. I can't."

"Do what?" I asked, not liking the sound of that at all.

"This." He pointed up and down my body. "You almost died, and you don't seem particularly upset about that fact. But I can't be constantly afraid that this will happen again. I can't live with another addict."

His words were like a slap. "I'm not an addict," I said, recoiling. "And I know what I did was stupid. I have no intention of ever doing it again."

"You said that two days ago, too."

That gaze was accusatory, and I shrank back, ashamed, but at the same time angry. How the hell did he consider this being supportive? Hadn't he told me he would always be there for me? "Last night was one of the worst nights of my life. I've lost at least one really good friend and caused her a ton of pain. I will probably have to move, and I don't really know how Jess and Rory feel about me. It was a terrible way to deal with it, I admit that, but it was an unusually terrible night."

"So what, every time you have a crisis, you're going to reach for the bottle?"

Ouch. That hurt. That just hurt. Even though I knew he came from a background of broken promises and addiction, damn it, it still hurt. It was insulting. It felt like he was lashing out at me, and so I lashed back, still physically ill and needing a kiss, not condemnation.

So I said, "Like you reach for the tire iron? Yeah, I heard about what you did to Nathan's car. And that you started to beat the shit out of him but were stopped. Am I going to have to worry that you'll lose your shit and wind up back in jail? What if you kill someone next time?"

It was so the wrong thing to say.

He exploded, leaping off the table and flipping it onto its side. "Oh, so this is my fault? Is that what you're saying? My crazy draws out the worst in people?"

That was not what I meant at all, and it felt like he was purposefully misunderstanding me. "Calm down."

"Don't tell me to fucking calm down." His hands raked through his hair back and forth with a rapid urgency. He paced across the room, his fists clenching and unclenching. "And you know what? I wish I had killed that asshole who was raping my mother. I wanted to. Another five minutes and I would have. And I wouldn't have been sorry. Is that what you wanted to hear? You want to hear that I'm fucked in the head? Well, I am. There you go."

Completely unsure what to say to him, I just stared at him in disbelief, my heart beating so fast I felt short of breath. I didn't even know this side of him, and it was a little scary. "No one is saying there's anything wrong with you."

"My mother did. She always did. And I know there is. But I can control it. But not when I see the girl I love unconscious on the fucking floor!" He made a sound of pure frustration and kicked the side of the table he'd turned.

I was too tired to do this. I smelled like stale vomit and hospital antiseptic, and my hand still shook when I held it out. I didn't want to do this. "Maybe we're not good for each other," I murmured, weary. "You said that when we started dating, and maybe you were right."

Because all I was hearing was that I reminded him too much of his mother and that he couldn't deal with that. Well, I couldn't deal with being put in the same category as her. It felt like in that case, love was altogether too close to hate.

"What is that supposed to mean?" he asked, looking wounded.

"It means I want you to drive me home, to my parents' house. I'm going to tell them I have the flu and I'm going to stay there for a few days. You can drive my car back here. I'll get a ride when I'm ready to come back."

"You're leaving me?" he asked, sounding bewildered.

"You just got done telling me I stress you out, so this will be a good break for both of us." There was a lump in my throat, and I didn't think it was really going to be any sort of good for me, but I couldn't stay there. Not with Kylie exiled to Tyler and Riley's and Phoenix looking at me like I disgusted him.

"I don't want you to go."

Ignoring him, I stood up, shooing away his arm when he tried to help me. It was about an hour too damn late to be suddenly considerate. I was pissed and hurt and I wanted to be alone. Honest to God, truly alone.

Maybe I could finish what I had started this summer, figuring out who I was, in a safe place.

Without a word, I went into my room and started packing a bag, my head still spinning, but adrenaline pushing me through. I stepped into giant pajama pants and pulled on a tank top.

He stood in the doorway. "Robin. Baby. Are you breaking up with me?"

"No." Exasperated and light-headed, I sat down on my bed. "Unless you want me too." So passive-aggressive, but I needed a freakin' bone here. I was tired of being the bad person. Worn down from the guilt. I needed him to say he loved me no matter what.

"Of course not. Unless you want *me* to."

This was stupid. "Just get my keys. They're in my purse. And seriously, Phoenix, do not tell my parents what happened. It will scare them."

He snorted.

"What?" Enough with the attitude.

"Nothing." He put his hands out, which further irritated me. "It's just that you don't seem particularly worried about the fact that you scared the shit out of *me*."

"This isn't about you!" I screamed. "This is about me! Me! About my feelings! For once, just once, it's fucking about me!"

I'm not even sure where that came from. But it just felt like the scream I'd been holding in all summer came roaring out.

And it kind of felt good to get it out, to hear my voice, strong and loud again.

Phoenix just reached out and yanked my bag out of my hand to carry it for me, and turned and stalked off.

"Thanks," I said, and yes, that was sarcasm.

CHAPTER EIGHTEEN

PHOENIX

IT TOOK EVERYTHING I HAD NOT TO JUST DEPOSIT ROBIN IN her car and go running down the street in a hard sprint to expel all the anger and frustration from my body. Did she have any clue how close to dying she had come? I had expected tears, apologies, sad Robin, but aside from looking like she needed a nap, she didn't look upset. In fact, she acted like she had done nothing different the night before than any other night.

Well, maybe it was easy for her to pretend like it hadn't happened since she didn't even remember it, but for me? Not so fucking easy.

And she had screamed at me. And said "fuck," which she almost never said.

Leaning against the window, she had her eyes closed, which was basically a "don't talk to me," which didn't help me from being pissed off.

Because getting pissed was what I did when I was scared and

damn it, she had terrified me. I had thought she was dead for a second there. And then just when I was starting to catch my breath, she turned her back on me and acted like she wanted to break up with me.

So yeah, I was in a bad place, and when I'm in a bad place, I lash out.

Jesus. Just like my mother.

That was not a good thought to be having.

But how could Robin be mad at me? How the fuck would she feel if she'd had to watch EMTs rushing her to the hospital? Watch the doctor examine her while she mumbled weird shit incoherently . . . It had been awful, and I couldn't help it if I wasn't able to just be, like, all casual over her almost drinking herself to death.

"Where are we going?" I asked her. "What is your parents' address?"

"Take 75 north to 275 west," she said, voice tired. "Mt. Healthy exit."

"Okay. Do you want anything?" I asked as I started driving. "We can stop at the store."

"No."

Silence.

"I want a coffee so I'm going through the drive-thru."

Silence.

That was worse than her shrieking at me. "Baby, talk to me."

"I'm tired," was all she said.

"I know." I felt like a dick for yelling at her earlier, for not leaving it alone until she at least had some time to recover. But hell, was I really the best person to take care of her for the next day or two? What did I know about being nurturing or whatever? Nothing. Maybe her being with her mom was the best thing for her right now, and when she was feeling better, we could talk. We could work all this out and be back to where we should be.

I couldn't imagine going through this again, but I also couldn't imagine not being with Robin. Both hurt. It all just hurt so much that there was a tight knot in my gut and a pain in my chest and I wanted to punch a wall until those loosened up and I was breathless and my fists were bloody. Until the pain was concentrated in sore muscles, burning lungs, and bleeding, broken skin. Not in my heart.

"Do you want me to pack up some clothes for you later and bring them out to you?"

"No, it's fine."

Her voice was calm, passive.

It made me crazy. Desperate. I wanted to get some kind of reaction from her. I wanted to both take care of her and shake her.

Twenty minutes of silence stretched out as I drove and she pretended to sleep. I knew she wasn't actually dozing because her foot went up and down in a rhythm that she never seemed to notice but generally made me want to put my hand on her knee to stop it. It was like an agitated bounce that made me tense, because it meant she was tense.

By the time we got off the exit and she gave me terse directions to her parents' house, a seventies split-level with overgrown bushes, I was on the verge of explosion.

Unfortunately, right then the garage door went up and I saw movement. Her parents and a tiny woman I took to be her grandmother came out onto the driveway, looking surprised. Robin opened her door and got out, so I did the same.

"Robin, are you okay?" her mother asked, barely even glancing at me.

"I have the flu," she said, and the lie didn't sound convincing to my ears, but her mother seemed to buy it. "I was sick all night and I just wanted to come home." She burst into tears. "I don't feel good."

"Oh, sweetie." Her mother pulled her into a hug. "We were just going to church, but I'll stay home with you. Daddy can take Nona."

Those tears were what I had been waiting for. The fact that she saved them for her mother didn't sit well with me. I stood there, feeling unwanted and unneeded, tossing the keys around my finger.

Her grandmother was staring at me, and I was aware of her dark eyes assessing my tattoos, my hair, my clothes.

"Is this your *chillo*, Robin?"

"Nona!" Her father shot his mother a glare. Then he stuck his hand out to me. "I'm Juan, Robin's father. Thanks for bringing her home."

"I'm Phoenix. Nice to meet you." I didn't know what a *chillo* was, but apparently no one was supposed to ask that.

"Well, for heaven's sake, let's go in the house," her mother said. "I'm Julia, by the way. And this is Nona."

Nona glared at me.

Juan and Julia. Robin's mother had delicate features and hair that might have been dark brown, but that she now dyed a deep red. Her father had black hair shot with silver, and they were both of average height and average build. They were attractive and looked like they belonged together, exchanging glances that showed they knew what the other was thinking or feeling at any given moment. The fact that they were sixty only added to the contrast between their stability and my mother's hot mess of a life.

"Do you need me to move the car so you can leave?" I asked her father.

"We're not going," Nona declared. "I'll watch mass on TV. Take Robin in the house, Julia."

Her father gave me an amused look. "I guess we're not going. This was a waste of a dress shirt."

I tried to smile back, but I couldn't quite make it happen. I wasn't sure if I was supposed to leave or go in the house with them, and I felt uncomfortable. This whole normal family thing was something I both envied and hated. I didn't know how to do this.

But Nona came up to me and wrapped her arm around mine. "Help me into the house."

That didn't leave me many options but to walk with her back through the garage.

"Is Phoenix your real name?"

Again with the name. Thanks, Mom. "Yes."

"Was your mother a hippie?"

If hippie could be defined as drug user, then yes. "No, not necessarily. She just wanted my name to be unusual."

"She succeeded."

"Don't mind her," Robin's mother said as she led Robin into the house. "Nona thinks because she's old that gives her the right to say whatever she is thinking."

"It does," Nona told me. "I'll be a hundred years old this year, you know."

"Wow," I said, surprised. She had thin skin and even thinner hair, but she didn't look that old. "That's amazing."

"She is not," Robin's father said, sounding annoyed. "She's trying to impress you."

"How do you know?" she asked. "A woman's age is a secret."

"You told me you were twenty-seven when I was born."

"Maybe I lied."

He rolled his eyes.

I liked Nona. She was jacked up, and I understood that better than nice and normal.

But once inside, she went into the kitchen with Robin's mother to watch, and I'm guessing to criticize, the making of tea for Robin while her father retreated upstairs, probably to change out of the dress shirt. Robin lay on the couch, an afghan spread over her by her mother. I hovered in front of her like a jackass, wanting to pace but forcing myself to stand still.

"Your family is nice."

"Yeah, they are." Her hair was snarled and limp, and the skin under her eyes was bruised. As she folded her hands under her cheek, they trembled a little.

It killed me to see her looking like that.

"What is a *chillo*?"

"A lover."

"Oh." What a retro word. But it said so much more than boyfriend. It seemed weighed down with passion and intensity, and I realized I kind of liked that. What we had shared, it was beyond just crushing on each other, and it was part of the reason I was standing there agonized.

My phone buzzed in my pocket, and I was annoyed to see it was Davis, wanting to meet up with me.

Seeing Robin here, in this normal house, made me wonder if

she was right—if we weren't good for each other. How could she ever tell her parents I was a convicted felon? How could I ever fit in to her life? And how could I ever be the support she needed when the thought of her drinking just pissed me off?

She was definitely right about one thing—we both needed space. I couldn't stand here waiting for a scrap of attention, a sign of any sort of emotional attachment.

It was fucking pathetic, and I wasn't doing it.

"I guess I'll head back," I said. "Unless you need anything."

"I'm okay." She finally looked at me. Really, truly looked at me. "I'll call you in a few days."

In a few days? She was dismissing me? Telling me to go away? Fuck that.

"You can't just snap your fingers and make me disappear," I said. "We need to talk about stuff, not ignore it."

"You said you would never throw it in my face, but you did." Tears welled in her eyes.

"I said I'd never throw what you did with Nathan in your face, but I have a right to be upset about the drinking." I was using a low voice, conscious of her family nearby. "And you threw my anger in my face, too, so I'd say we're even."

"It's not a contest. Just give me a few days, please, just some space."

"You can't hide every time something bad happens. You can't shut down." Didn't she see that's what she did? She retreated and withdrew.

A tear trailed down her cheek. "And you can't hurt me every time you're scared. You promised to hold up the sky for me, Phoenix."

That cut me as deeply as a bowie knife. Most of my life I'd been a failure in one way or another. I sucked at school. I sucked at friendship. I sucked at being a good son.

But I had wanted more than anything to be a good boyfriend to Robin. To have the outside action match the love I felt on the inside.

To hear that I had fucked that up, too, well, I couldn't handle it.

"That's not fucking fair," I told her. "I've always had your back. This wasn't something little. I found you unconscious! I'm not trying to hurt you, I'm trying to get you to see how messed up last night was."

"I am very much aware of how messed up I am. Thanks for reminding me."

"Now you're purposefully misunderstanding me."

"Just leave. Please."

Damn. That was rough. It must have showed on my face because she winced. "I'm sorry, that didn't sound right. I didn't mean to be hurtful."

But I shook my head. It was too ingrained in me to be strong, to hide my feelings. I had spent a lifetime pretending my mother didn't hurt me. I wasn't about to admit that Robin had and could. "Don't flatter yourself," I said. "You can't hurt me."

Without saying another word, because I knew I would lose it, say something really ugly, I turned and left.

It wasn't until I got out onto the main road heading for the highway that I allowed myself to shout in the empty car in pure frustration.

"Damn it!" I pounded the steering wheel and wondered

why the hell I had to meet Robin if I wasn't going to get to be with her.

Because the right thing to do would be to walk out of her life for good and let her become the person she was supposed to be, a graphic designer with an accountant husband and a house in the suburbs. Not saddled with a loser who had a record and no money.

But when I got back to her place to drop her car off and walk home, I went inside for some sick, masochistic reason. I headed straight toward the oil paintings she had been working on. Flipping through them one at a time, I saw the dark emotions she had clearly been pushing out through her art.

I lay on the bed—*our* bed—and stared at the ceiling, remembering the way she had looked at me on my birthday and the first time we'd had sex, her eyes all soft and warm.

Then I stole a picture of us smiling for the camera that she had printed and tucked into the mirror on the door and I left.

FOUR DAYS. FOUR WHOLE DAYS WENT BY AND I DIDN'T HEAR a single word from her.

I didn't text or call her either, but I was just doing what she asked me to do. Giving her space.

Space sucked.

It sucked hard.

I was going crazy, the days endless, the nights worse. I slept on my cousins' couch, or pretended to sleep. Mostly I lay there, thoughts turning in a whirlpool in my mind, wondering what I was supposed to do. Wondering whose idea of a joke this bullshit was. Hadn't I been handed enough crap in life? Now I had to love someone only to have her fade out of my life?

No. It was just bull-fucking-shit.

"You could call her," Tyler said to me Thursday night as I sat watching TV with Jayden, and he saw me check my phone for the seven hundredth time.

"Mind your own business."

Tyler made a face at me. "Fine. Be miserable."

Rory and Jessica were in the kitchen, and I had purposely avoided asking them about Robin. I didn't even know if either of them had talked to her. It felt too much like begging to ask them about her.

"I will, thanks." I was. I was dying to know how Robin was. If she had told her parents the truth. If she was physically feeling better. If she were missing classes. If she hated my face.

My hands were swollen and bruised, scabbing over, from all the boxing I had been doing in the basement. I had been tempted to go over Nathan's car a second time, but I had resisted. He had shown up to get it on Monday but he hadn't come into the house and he hadn't said anything about the condition to Tyler. I figured he was waiting for the right time to get even with me. Whatever. He was an idiot if he didn't realize I would enjoy it. I didn't even feel bad that I had put Tyler in an awkward position. His friend was an asshole, end of story.

"She's coming back tomorrow. Rory told me."

Then I should probably stop sneaking over to her apartment and stealing random shit and lying on her bed. It was weird, and I knew it was weird, but it made me feel close to her. In one moment of weakness I had even left a card for her on her dresser, and now it was too late to get it back. I mean, seriously, a greet-ing card? I had never bought one in my entire life and, first of all, was shocked to see they cost like three bucks, but secondly, it was absolutely cheesedick of me. Lame.

It was also too late to give back the painting I'd lifted, the one of the lighthouse, its spotlight cutting across a choppy sea. Or the perfume that she always wore that I didn't even like. I had them stashed in Jayden and Easton's room because they would ask the least questions. Though I did have a sneaking suspicion Jayden had used the perfume himself because he was smelling a little floral.

"Glad to hear it," I said evenly. "She must be feeling better. How is Kylie?"

Tyler shook his head. "Kylie is a hot mess. Nathan is blowing up her phone with apologies."

I snorted.

"He knows he fucked up and he's hurting," Tyler said. "You know he's going to come after you to take out some of that anger."

I shrugged. "I can out-anger him any day of the week."

"I know. That's what scares me."

The front door opened, and I glanced over to see my mother walk in the door. Shit. Now? This was when she chose to finally make an appearance? Worst timing ever.

"Hey, Phoenix, I need to talk to you," she said.

Of course she did. I was definitely not in the mood for a little mother-son chat. "Hey, Mom, so nice to see you for the first time in six months. I'm good, thanks for asking."

She frowned. "Don't be a smart-ass."

Notorious for wearing clothes that were two sizes too small and twenty years too young for her, she was wearing denim acid-washed shorts and a tank that made it very obvious she did not have a bra on. Jesus Christ. I wanted to sigh. In fact, I think I actually did.

"Hi, Aunt Jackie," Easton said from where he was rolling around on the floor for no apparent reason.

"Hey, brat," she said, tickling his ribs with her toes.

Yep, she was barefoot.

"How did you know I'd be here?" I asked, not moving from the couch.

"Where else would you be? You ain't got a pot to pee in, and I know you don't want to live with that twat girlfriend of yours."

That made me sit up straighter. "Do not call Robin a twat," I said. "Seriously, Mom, don't go there with me."

"Robin?" She looked surprised. "Who the hell is Robin? I was talking about that slut Angel."

"Oh." I relaxed back. "We broke up while I was inside. But don't say that about her either. It's not nice."

"It's not nice," she mimicked, making a face. "God, you're such a pussy."

That did it. I just said, very, very calmly, "Get out. Get out of this house. Right. Now."

But she scoffed. "You can't throw me out of Dawn's house."

"*I* can," Tyler said. "Now show a little respect or you can leave. You haven't seen Phoenix even once since he got out and you walk in here calling him names? It's bullshit, Jackie."

Wow. Cousin was sticking up for me. I was surprised to realize how much I needed that, someone to be on my side.

"God, why is everyone being so sensitive?" she complained, pulling out a cigarette and a lighter.

"You can't smoke in the house," Tyler told her.

"What?" For a second I thought she was going to argue, but she just gave a huff of exasperation and stormed to the kitchen, presumably to go out the back door.

I jumped up to follow, well aware that Jessica and Rory were in the kitchen and did not deserve to have to deal with her. She had stopped short in the doorway. "Who the hell are you?" she asked them, even though I knew they had both been at my aunt's funeral. She clearly didn't remember meeting them.

"Mom, this is Jessica and Rory, Riley's and Tyler's girlfriends. This is my mom, Jackie." I was more than a little mortified having to do introductions because I knew whatever my mother said, it would not be nice or classy.

And she didn't disappoint as they murmured greetings, both pasting on a smile. "Damn. My nephews have expensive tastes." She glanced at me. "How about you? Where is your girlfriend, this Robin you were so defensive about? She got money?"

I could see the predatory gleam in her eyes. "No. She's at her parents." I held the back door open. "Come outside so you can have a cigarette. I'll sit with you."

She rolled her eyes. "Lucky me."

But I didn't say anything. I just held the door open for her until she passed through. I saw the pity on Rory's and Jessica's faces and I felt the familiar sense of shame that I always did when people felt sorry for me.

The sun was high, hitting me right in the eyes as I sat on the top of the picnic table and my mom sat next to me. When her hand shook as she tried to light her cigarette, I took the lighter and held it for her.

She blew out some smoke with a sigh. "Thanks." Lifting her hands to gather her heavy and bleached hair up into a ponytail, I caught sight of the scars on her stomach.

I took the edge of her shirt and lifted it further to see for myself what that asshole had done to her. The lines were white slashes on her flesh, as he had tried to write "Iggy" but was mostly unsuccessful. I made a sound in the back of my throat. "Did they heal okay?"

"What?" She glanced down. "Oh, yeah, it was fine. Looks like shit but whatever. My stripper days are over anyway."

I actually laughed. "Well, there you go, Mom, always looking on the bright side."

She grinned, and I saw she had lost a tooth slightly to the right of her front teeth. "I missed you, Phoenix," she said. "I know you don't believe me, but I did."

I wasn't sure what to say to that, so I didn't say anything.

"You serious about this girl?" she asked, taking a drag. "What's she look like?"

I lifted my shirt to show her my tattoo. "Like this."

She gave a low whistle. "Damn, I guess you are serious. She's pretty."

"I know. But we may have broken up."

"What? Why?"

"She got super drunk and I got super pissed."

I expected her to tell me I was stupid and what was the harm with a little drinking, but she didn't. She just nodded. "You know I have to tell you something."

Oh, God. I braced myself for something horrible. "Do I want to know this?"

"Sure. It's nothing bad. I just wanted to tell you that I lied to you about your father. He wasn't just some guy I went out with a few times. I was in love with him. The only man I've ever loved."

"Really?" She had always told me that my dad was a loser but he'd been awesome in bed. Which is, of course, what every guy wants to hear his mother say. Not.

"Really." She picked at a scab on her knee, her fingernail polish chipped, a shocking pink color. "But he couldn't deal with me drinking and using. He turned his back on me when I needed him the most. Not that I'm saying he could have stopped me from doing what I was doing, but I needed to know he believed in me, you know?"

There was a lump in my throat that threatened to cut off my airway. She was trying to tell me that I needed to be supportive of Robin. My first instinct was to feel defensive and to resent that she would have the nerve to offer me advice. But I knew for her to be serious about something instead of joking around or being bitchy, she must really think it was important. And I knew, deep down, that she was right. Robin's problems were mine, too, no matter how much I wanted to walk away, because I loved her. And I should try to help her, not run scared. Was I perfect? Obviously not. So I damn well couldn't expect her to be.

"I don't blame him for leaving. He had to do what was right for him, but I can't say that I've ever really gotten over it. I fucked up by picking the drugs over him, but he just walked away and damn, that was painful, sending me straight for more drugs. So I always just chose shitty guys because I know they're shitty. No chance for me to be hurt when they leave."

I nodded. "You do choose shitty men."

She laughed and nudged me with her knee. "Shut up. But

maybe that's why I wasn't the best mother either. I didn't want to love you too much. But I couldn't help myself. I did anyway. You came out of the happiest time in my life."

Now I really didn't know what to say. "I love you, too." I did. How could I not? She was my mother.

"You were a cute baby, you know. Born with all that dark hair. Big old eyes. You'd be so quiet and calm and then bam! You'd just start screaming."

Apparently not much had changed.

"So you ever talk to my father after he left?" There was something nice to be said about knowing they had cared about each other, that I wasn't just the result of a blind grope in a dark room.

"No. I saw him once at a biker bar. He was always into bikes. But I freaked out and ran away before he saw me." She shrugged. "It sucks to spend your life loving someone and not being with them. Don't do that. If you love her, fight for it, you know?"

"Yeah." I did. She was right. It wouldn't be easy, but what was? I *loved* Robin.

"Now stop making me all sentimental," she said. "Say something dickish so I feel normal again."

I reached out and flicked her cigarette with my finger and thumb, sending it sailing into the yard. "Quit smoking." I grinned as she sputtered. "How was that?"

"Turd."

But when I wrapped my arm around her in a semi-hug, she actually leaned into my touch.

And for the first time in a decade, I felt like she was a mom, not just the woman who had given birth to me.

Bonus.

CHAPTER NINETEEN

ROBIN

I STOOD IN THE SHOWER AS LONG AS I COULD STAND, THE water pouring over my face in a hot stream, washing away my tears and the tangy ripe odor of sweat and liquor and vomit. If only I could wash away my guilt and my confusion.

It seemed no matter what I did, I felt guilty. I worried about hurting everyone, my friends, my parents. Phoenix.

And invariably, what I did was hurt all of them, and me too.

Phoenix's face had been terrible. I knew then, right when he said that I couldn't hurt him, that I had. That I had hurt him like his mother had, that she was the inspiration behind his bleeding tattoo, and now I had added to that pain.

But I couldn't deal with my own pain and guilt, and I definitely couldn't deal with his anger. Not right now.

Leaning against the shower wall for support, my legs still rubbery, I dozed in and out of sleep, dreaming, or maybe daydreaming, I wasn't entirely sure.

But in my head, I climbed aboard the rowboat I had painted, and rowed myself to the empty lighthouse in the midst of the stormy sea, and I stood on the rocks, waves crashing into me. It was cold and damp and lonely on my perch, the lights of land across the water winking at me in welcome. But I couldn't cross back. I didn't have the strength to row back from where I had come. So it was just me.

The knock on the bathroom door startled me, and I jerked awake, alert. "Yeah?"

"Are you okay?" my mother called.

No. "Yes."

"Can I come in?" she asked.

"In a sec." Turning off the water, I shivered, goose bumps rising on my flesh. My mother had brought me an old terry cloth robe to wear, and after a cursory drying off, I wrapped myself in it. "Okay."

She opened the door and gave me a smile. "I bet that wore you out."

"It did." Our house had been built in the seventies, and the hall bathroom had never been remodeled. It was still full of dark wood and lots of gold accents, and there was a little cutout for a vanity chair, which had been the same brass stool my entire life. I sank down onto it now, my lungs straining, the air too humid to breathe properly, hands still trembling. I was starting to worry that was a permanent thing, that weird little jitter to my fingers.

My mother came behind me and took the towel off the floor and dried my hair for me, her touch gentle. It felt so good to have her take care of me, like I was a little girl again, comforting me after my brothers had picked on me mercilessly. She picked up a brush and started to go through my hair, detangling the snarls that had been made as I had done who knew what in my incoherent state.

Suddenly, watching her in the mirror in front of me, the full impact of what had happened hit me and I started crying again. I could have died. Never, ever, in any way, had I ever been suicidal. I didn't want to die. At all. Ever, frankly. I sure in the hell didn't want to die now. But I could have, and it would have been my fault, and I would have caused my parents massive pain.

Phoenix had every right to be angry with me.

I was angry with myself.

"Robin. What's going on?" my mother asked quietly. "Does this have anything to do with Phoenix? I have to admit, he wasn't what I was expecting. He's not the usual type of boy you date."

"No, he's not," I said, voice tight with my tears. "Mom, I have to tell you something, and it's not good."

Keeping secrets hadn't done anything good for me, and I realized that even if it meant my parents would be profoundly disappointed in me, I needed to be honest with them. I couldn't do this by myself. Facing the truth was going to be hard, but hiding from it was worse.

"Yes? You know you can tell me anything. Are you pregnant?" she asked gently.

Ironically, something that would have given me a heart attack back in high school now seemed like the least horrible thing to have happening. Being pregnant would be way less frightening than being an alcoholic.

Still watching her in the mirror, her fingers smoothing over my now fully brushed hair, I told her, "No. I'm not pregnant. I don't have the flu. I ended up in the ER last night with blood alcohol poisoning."

Her fingers stilled. "Oh my God, baby. And you're okay, the doctors said you're okay?"

I nodded. "I'm fine. Phoenix and Rory called 911."

She made the sign of the cross. "Thank you, Jesus."

"I didn't mean to," I said. "It was an accident. I was upset and I drank more than I should have."

Her face had lost color, and I could see her searching for the right thing to say. "Do you drink more than you should often?"

I shook my head. "I did. But not any more. Phoenix doesn't drink at all, and he's really mad at me. I scared him. I scared myself."

Her arms came down around me, and she gave me a hard hug, her lips brushing over my hair.

And I cried, because I had disappointed everyone who mattered to me. Most of all I had disappointed myself.

I WANTED TO TEXT PHOENIX. A HUNDRED TIMES I STARTED, and a hundred times I deleted what I was writing.

The truth was, he deserved more than a text message apology. I needed to say it in person. I needed to look him in the eye and tell him that I understood why he reacted the way he had and that I was sorry I had scared him.

For three days I slept and sat out on the back deck in the sun and thought. About me, about my future, about who I was. I cooked with my mother and I sketched and I did research on my mom's laptop, looking at the options my parents presented me for alcohol counseling. There was one program where you went every day for three hours for a week, then once a week for three months. I thought I could do that, actually wanted to do that. I didn't think I was going to repeat the vodka disaster, but why not make sure? Phoenix was right—I needed to know how to handle a crisis without escaping into alcohol.

I looked at rental apartments, and I looked at art programs. I didn't want to be a graphic designer. I didn't want to sit in a cubicle and click my mouse in design software. I wanted to be outside, painting in the park.

With Phoenix.

Alone with the trees ruffling their leaves, the first hint of fall in the air as I heard the high school marching band practicing two blocks away, I ran my finger over my bluebird tattoo.

Then I sent three texts to three different people. All three said the same thing.

Can I see you today?

KYLIE WAS THE ONLY ONE IN THE APARTMENT WHEN MY MOM dropped me off, giving me three hugs before she would let me leave the car. In the kitchen, Kylie leaned against the counter in a defensive posture, her expression stony.

"Hey," I said, softly. "Thanks for meeting me. I just wanted to say in person that I'm sorry. Really, truly sorry."

"I honestly don't have anything to say, Robin. I don't even know what to say."

"I know. I don't really know what to say either, other than that if I been sober, I never would have done what I did. It's no excuse, but I care about you and I never, ever wanted to hurt you." There was no apology in the world that was going to fix what I had done, but I needed to at least offer it.

She nodded. "Okay, thanks for saying that. But I can't promise that I will forgive you. I just need time." There were suddenly tears in her eyes. "I'm not in a good place."

"I know," I whispered, tears coming to my eyes as well. "Me either. If you want to stay here in the apartment, I can move back to my parents. Just let me know."

Kylie bit her lip. "Remember our first semester at college? We were all so excited for the freedom, and we were all so sure we had everything figured out . . . now I know we don't know anything. Nothing makes sense. I want to be stupidly naive again."

I totally understood where she was coming from.

But the truth was, I didn't want to go backward. Only forward.

"Well, just learn from me . . . alcohol is not the answer."

"I just can't believe how much I misjudged Nathan. You could see the texts he's sent me. He's so *cruel*."

No clue what to say, I just did what made sense to me, not caring if she rejected my gesture or not. I just wanted her to know I cared that she was hurting, so I reached out and hugged her.

Kylie hugged me back.

IN MY ROOM, I FOUND AN ENVELOPE WITH PHOENIX'S BOLD and stylistic handwriting on it. *Robin*.

Inside was a card with a couple in their eighties laughing on a park bench, holding hands. He had labeled them. *You. Me.*

The greeting card had been left blank on the inside, but Phoenix had written his own simple message. *I miss you. I love you.*

Clutching the card to my chest, I lay on my bed, tears rolling down my cheeks to fall on the comforter.

My pillow smelled like him.

NATHAN OPENED THE DOOR AND GAVE ME A COCKY LOOK. "Unless you're here to suck my dick, I have nothing to say to you."

I stood in the doorway and took a certain amount of pleasure in the black eye he was sporting. Compliments of Phoenix, I had to assume.

"Sorry, no," I said. "But I'm sure there are plenty of girls with low self-esteem who you can take advantage of."

He snorted. "What do you want, Robin? I thought we had fun and then you go and tell Kylie and your boyfriend trashes my car. You are not my favorite person right now."

"I never meant to tell Kylie. I never wanted to hurt her. She found your texts on my phone." I had expected his anger, and I was prepared for it. I had just wanted to face him one last time and tell him exactly what I thought of him and his dickheadedness. "We made a mistake but you made it worse. You don't deserve Kylie."

"Yeah, well, you do deserve Phoenix. Go off and be losers together."

Oh, he was a fine one to talk. But it didn't really bother me. It was what I expected. "I will, thanks." I gave him a sweet smile. "But stop texting Kylie hateful things or I will do to your balls what Phoenix did to your car."

That seemed to catch him off guard. "Excuse me?"

"You heard me. You can say whatever you want to me, call me any nasty name you can think of, but leave Kylie the hell alone. Now." I threw the plastic grocery bag in my hand on the floor at his feet, enjoying how appalled he looked. "And here's the last of your crap from Kylie. She says to tell you to go to hell."

I turned and walked away, calling over my shoulder, "And I'd like to add, fuck off."

Damn, that felt good. Instead of hiding out, I was standing tall. Saying exactly what I felt. Defending a friend who I had hurt tremendously.

Nathan just slammed the door shut without a word.

That's right. I was done with him.

Just one last stop to make.

THE MINUTE I PULLED INTO THE DRIVEWAY AND SAW DAVIS on the front step, I should have backed out immediately. But I didn't have the finely tuned sense of self-preservation that Phoenix and his cousins had. Totally the opposite. My first thought actually was that maybe Davis knew where Phoenix was, because he hadn't answered my text.

But when he stood up and greeted me with a smile that was nothing like the casual friendliness he'd shown in the park, I felt a tremor of fear. "Where's Phoenix?" he asked.

I shook my head. "I don't know."

"Bullshit. Come in the house and let's talk about it." He opened the front door, making me wonder if Tyler and Riley had really left it unlocked or if he had picked the lock.

There was no way I was going in the house with him. "Sorry, I have to get to work. I'll let Phoenix know you're looking for him." Maybe if I were polite, friendly, if I acted like I didn't know anything was wrong, I could just retreat and call Jessica and let her know not to go home without Riley.

But Davis grabbed my wrist so hard I gasped. "Get in the fucking house," he said, and I saw in his other hand he had a knife.

Oh my God. I started to sweat, my fingers shaking. I couldn't think, had no idea what to do. I should kick him or hit him or scream. But I knew that none of the neighbors would come to my aid and he was twice my size. I was fragile, I knew that.

He couldn't really want to hurt me. He probably wanted money, or drugs, or both.

Which proved again how naive I was.

He dragged me into the house and shut the door, and when I looked at the cold anger in his eyes, I realized that he could kill me. He could kill me without thinking twice about it, and I felt the fear that Phoenix must have felt when he saw me unconscious. I finally understood what that had done to him, because for the first time, I wasn't looking backward at a close call, I was staring into the face of my mortality, and it was terrifying.

"What do you want?" I asked, amazed that I found the courage to speak.

He had placed himself between me and the door, but I took a few steps toward the kitchen, keeping my eyes on him. I was wearing a sundress and I wasn't sure how fast I could run in it, but I was going to try to make a break for the back door. It would be better than going down without a fight.

He grinned. "Don't worry, I don't want you. You're too bony

for my taste, so as much as I might enjoy sharing a woman with Sullivan, it ain't going to be you."

Ridiculous to be proud of the fact that he didn't hurt my feelings, but I was. His opinion of me didn't matter in the slightest, and I was hugely relieved that he had no intention of raping me.

"I'm not sorry to hear that," I told him.

He laughed. "Look, I just need someone to pick up a package for me, that's all. You've got a car, and no one will notice you because a lot of students live in the building. Just go and ring the doorbell and take the package, and hand them the cash I give you."

So he wanted me to pick up his drugs for him.

"Then you'll consider you and Phoenix even?"

He nodded. "Totally. I can't go myself. The neighbors know who I am, and someone might call the cops."

Which meant that they might call the cops on me. "What if I get caught?"

"Rat me out." He shrugged. "You're not going to get caught. Put on your backpack or whatever and act normal. Look, there's a thousand bucks riding on this. Do this and I'll disappear, I guarantee it."

This was so illegal. This was the end of my life as I knew it if I got busted. But I knew it was safer for me to do it than Phoenix. Not to mention his personal feelings about drugs. It would go against everything in him to run drugs for Davis, and most likely what would happen was they would wind up in a fistfight. And while Phoenix certainly had rage and a fair amount of skill, Davis was huge. I doubted that Phoenix would come out of it unscathed.

So I had to do it.

I was never brave.

For once I needed to be brave.

If I expected Phoenix to have my back, I had to have his, right?

But this was illegal. So wrong. Phoenix wouldn't want me to do this. "What if I say no?"

He shook his head slowly. "You don't want to say no, trust me."

My heart was racing, and I felt sick to my stomach, but I knew this was too risky. Either way it was risky, so it was better to take the legal risky route. "Yes," I told him. "Yes, I do."

He took a step forward, the knife in his hand, and I was pulling out my phone, dialing 911 already when the front door opened.

It was Tyler, Phoenix, Riley, and Rory. It took the guys all of three seconds to assess the situation.

"Go," Tyler said to Rory, shoving her back out the front door while shielding her with his body. "Lock the car until Robin comes out, then go."

I was already bolting toward the kitchen, knowing full well Davis would reach for me, which he did. But I was fast, or maybe too scrawny, because only his fingertips touched my arm. Or maybe Phoenix or Riley pulled him backward. I didn't turn around to look, I just ran.

But I did hear Phoenix say to him, "If you ever come near my girlfriend I will fucking kill you with my bare hands, you know I will."

A shiver slipped up my spine. Once I was in the driveway, I finally let out the breath I was holding and got in the car with Rory. "Who was that?" she asked, looking scared.

"Drug dealer. Drive around the block. Do you think we should call the cops?"

"I don't think the guys would like that. Easton, you know, the custody. Did he have a gun?"

"Not that I saw." Rory cruised down the street, but she was already using voice command to call Tyler. He didn't answer.

Suddenly feeling like I was going to throw up, I stuck my head between my legs. "I don't think I handled that very well," I told her, my words muffled from the fabric of my dress.

"I think you handled it better than I would have. I would have peed my pants." Her phone rang, and she answered it. "Are you all okay?" Relief crossed her face. "Okay, good. We'll be back in a minute."

She hung up. "Everything is okay. They're all fine and Davis left. He knew he was outnumbered. Phoenix wants you to meet him at the park in half an hour."

I EXPECTED IT TO BE AWKWARD WHEN I SAW PHOENIX. I HAD been shut down physically and emotionally when he left my parents', and we hadn't exactly had the best conversation. I also knew he would be feeling guilty about Davis.

But when I pulled into the parking lot at the park, he was sitting on a bench already waiting for me, hair in his eyes, arm tossed carelessly over the back. His eyes were closed, like he was enjoying the sun, and any nerves I had evaporated.

God, I loved him. I looked at him, and it just made my heart ache.

When I stepped out of the car, he was already standing, and he came toward me, steady, his hands in the front pockets of his jeans. He was wearing one of the band shirts I had given him for his birthday.

Without saying a word to me, he just cupped my face with his hands and kissed me. It was a deep, intense kiss, his tongue sliding across my bottom lip, his breath hot and sweet. His fingers were rough and callused on my skin, but his touch was gentle, worshipful, his kiss everything I could have hoped for and more.

"I'm sorry," I whispered into his mouth.

"I'm sorry," he said in echo. "I shouldn't have left like that. I was an asshole."

"I shouldn't have screamed at you. You're right, I was shutting down." I snaked my arms around his waist and leaned into the familiar feel of him, taking in his masculine scent, the warmth of his shirt from the sun, the muscles in his thighs against me.

"Come here," he said, pulling me to the bench, and onto his lap. "God, when I saw you with Davis . . . I'm sorry. I never thought that he would find you."

"I know, it's not your fault." I perched there, fingers clenching his T-shirt, kissing him again, and sucking lightly on his lower lip, relieved that he didn't seem furious with me. I started crying, I couldn't help it. "I love you."

"I love you, too.

"Thank you for the card."

He smiled. "You make me sappy."

"I like sappy."

His thumb rubbed over my hand and his expression grew

serious. "Robin, you know that I've always been someone who lived in the now, who dealt with the now. But for the first time ever, you made me believe in a future. You made me want a future. You made me believe in you and me. And when I saw Davis with you . . . I thought, how can I drag you into my shit like that? I can't ever walk away from the past. It's always going to be with me."

"I know that."

He nodded. "And I also realized that it's not up to me to protect you or save you from being with me. That you're smart and you know what you want and I trust that."

That meant more to me than anything else could have. "I know that what I want is you. I believe in you and me, too. And when I was there in the house with Davis, I realized what it must have been like for you to find me passed out, and I never want to hurt you like that again."

He didn't say anything. He just kissed me, a deep, tender kiss that made my whole body tingle.

"Phoenix, what happened to your hands?" I had looked down and realized his knuckles were bruised and scabbed, and his hands were actually swollen. "Is that from your fight with Nathan? It looks too old for what happened today."

But he shook his head. "No. I have to tell you that you were right—I can't react to every crisis with anger. That's my problem that I have to deal with. When I was a kid I was diagnosed as having intermittent explosive disorder. It means I lose my shit uncontrollably. I always think I can control it, which is dumb considering the very definition means I lose it. So I have no right to criticize you for slipping and drinking. I went off on that car, and I would have preferred to go off on Nathan."

It wasn't surprising to me. I knew his anger was different, deeper. "I start alcohol counseling next week, just so you know. What scares me is how I sat there with that bottle and knew that it would make feel better, short term, but worse long term. Yet I couldn't resist it. Not really."

"My rage is alive . . . it's like it's moving cell by cell through my body. I should probably take the medication." He gave me a small smile, brushing my hair back. "If you can deal with your stuff, I can deal with my stuff, and we'll deal together. Fair?"

"Fair." I nuzzled my lips over the side of his face.

"So what do we do now?" he asked.

"'There is no remedy for love, but to love more.' That's Thoreau," I murmured.

Phoenix kissed the corners of my mouth. "'The future for me is already a thing of the past. You were my first love and you will be my last.' That's Bob Dylan."

I smiled.

CHAPTER TWENTY

PHOENIX

MY MOM WAS ACTUALLY CRYING. "SERIOUSLY?" I ASKED, rolling my eyes. But secretly I was pleased that she cared.

"Shut up," she said, sounding annoyed, wiping at her eyes. "I'm entitled to fucking cry when my only kid moves a thousand miles away."

We were standing in the driveway at Tyler and Riley's, a dusting of snow on the ground, the dead Christmas tree that Jessica had decorated the month before now on the lawn, waiting for garbage removal. Robin's car was packed with all her belongings. I had a duffel bag of my stuff on the front step, waiting to be crammed into whatever space was left.

My whole family was next to my mom, bundled up against the cold, saying good-bye. I was excited about me and Robin heading south, but I realized I was going to miss these motherfuckers, every one of them. My cousins had given me a place to stay and legit friendship, and my mom and I had been working on being nicer to each other. She had even finally told me my father's name, but I hadn't pursued getting in touch with him.

I rubbed Easton's head. "I'm going to miss you, dude."

"Can I come visit?"

"Sure, you can," Riley said. "When I win the lottery."

"We're going to have a lot of cool stuff when we win the lottery," Jayden said. "Because you always say that."

I laughed. And how could I not miss that guy and his unintentional humor? I gave him a fist bump. "Keep sending me those stupid pictures of dogs being shamed. They make me laugh, cuz."

"I will," he promised.

Riley and Tyler both gave me a one-armed hug. Jessica, who still didn't seem to particularly like me, managed to give me a hug and a smile, probably because she was glad to see the last of me for a while.

Rory's hug was more genuine. "Take care of Robin," she told me.

"Not a problem," I assured her.

Robin was in the house, using the bathroom before we left. We had already said good-bye to her family, who had been amazingly accepting of me over the last few months. I think the tattoos were overlooked by the fact that I was sober. They liked that I offered no temptation to Robin to drink. Which she hadn't. And I was taking my little bottle of prescription meds to Louisiana with me, working through my issues with taking any sort of pills, knowing it did help me feel less tight inside.

But truthfully, I hadn't had a whole lot to be angry about.

Robin came out, zipping up her winter coat, a smile lighting up her face when she caught my eye.

"Ready?"

Yep. She still made my mouth hot and my lips turn up in a stupid grin I couldn't contain.

"I can drive first," I told her. "Now that it's, uh, actually legal for me to drive." I had gone and finally ordered documentation online and had taken the test to get my license. I had also given Davis three hundred bucks to put a deposit down on an apartment and had cleared my debt to him. I had been worried that moving would violate my parole, but I'd been given the go-ahead.

Robin had spent the fall semester with a whole new schedule, dropping out of all of her business classes before it was too late and quickly trading them out for art classes. The one that she had taken on a whim, glassblowing, had turned out to be something she had completely fallen in love with. Which was why we were moving to New Orleans. She had transferred to Tulane to study at their glassblowing program, which was supposed to be one of the best in the country. I had gotten a job at a tattoo shop by answering an online ad, and we had a studio apartment waiting for us.

"See you all in May!" Robin said, giving out hugs. She even hugged my mom, who looked like she'd swallowed a bug.

I had never left the Cincinnati area. Not in my whole twenty-one years.

As I crossed the bridge into Kentucky, Robin singing a song off the radio in the passenger seat, I focused on the road stretching out in front of me.

Hell to the yeah.

Reaching over, I snaked my fingers through hers.

Yep. The future for me was already a thing of the past.

Keep reading for an excerpt from
the next book in the True Believers series

SHATTER

Available now from Berkley

KYLIE

TWO HOURS LATER MY HEAD WAS SPINNING, BUT I AT LEAST had a game plan for further studying. Darwin/Jonathon had shown me that the class was divided into elements, mixtures, compounds, gases, and measurements. He subdivided each of those for me into additional categories and talked me through every definition and gave example formulas, which I almost maybe understood if I squinted and thought really hard.

I had three days before my exam, so if I spent every waking moment between now and then reading the notes over and over and over again, I might pass. Maybe.

But I was getting a little loopy. While he was in the bathroom I was going through some online study sites and I found a bunch of chemistry jokes. I couldn't help it. I copied one and e-mailed it to him.

He was looking at his phone as he came out. "Did you just e-mail me while I was in the restroom?"

He really was cute. It just wasn't right. His jeans fit the way they were supposed to and I found it interesting that he only needed a T-shirt in November. His tattoo was a complex sleeve of numbers and diagrams.

I nodded. "Yes, I did. Jonathon." I was still testing his dual personality names.

He gave a low, husky laugh as he settled back into his chair while reading his screen. "Really, Kylie?"

My head was propped with my palm and I smiled, feeling comfortable with him. He smelled good. Like coffee and clean skin.

"What did one ion say to the other?" he read back to me, even though I knew what it said since I'd sent it. "I've got my ion you."

I laughed. I couldn't help it. It was stupid, and even I understood it.

To his credit, he laughed with me. "See? Chemistry is *fun*."

"Oh, yeah. It's a laugh riot. Hey, what do you do with a dead chemist?" I asked him, glad to rest my brain for a minute. I was a little afraid it was smoking from overheating.

"You barium."

No way. He'd heard this one before. "Damn it! How did you know the answer?"

He tapped his temple. "Me use my head."

"Well, *Darwin*." I let the nickname roll off my tongue. I still wasn't sure which one suited him better. "I guess I should let you get back to your regularly scheduled life. Thanks for all your help."

"You're welcome." He efficiently packed up all his stuff. "You'll do fine on this exam as long as you don't panic."

Easy for him to say. "So what all is in your tattoo?" I asked, reaching out and running my finger along his arm, over the maze of numbers.

He looked startled that I had touched him and I realized that probably wasn't appropriate. But I came from a touchy-feely family and I had always been someone who reached out and made contact without any thought about it. I hugged my friends, I put my hands on arms when I spoke to people, I squeezed knees. If I liked you—and it was rare I met someone I truly didn't like—I touched. The me before the RAN incident wouldn't have even thought twice about it, but now I suddenly felt like I needed to apologize or something. Like he would think I was hitting on him.

But he just started pointing out parts of his sleeve. "The periodic table of the elements. Avogadro's number. The molecular graphic for propane."

After that, I couldn't follow any more. "But won't professors think you're cheating? If you have stuff on your arm?"

The smile he gave me was patronizing. I don't think he meant it to be, but his answer told me how clearly stupid my question was. "When you're studying reaction kinetics and advanced nucleic biochemistry, you don't need to cheat on basic chem."

"Oh." I felt heat in my cheeks. Most of the time, I was perfectly happy with who I was. But then there were other times, like then, where I just didn't want to be the dumb blonde. Just once, I wanted to be taken seriously, instead of having everyone think I was cute, but ten IQ points off from needing the short bus. "Duh."

"In between are dates representing people and events that are important to me. My birthday. My mom's birthday. The first time I—" He looked up and gave me a grin. "Well, you get the idea."

So genius or not, he was still like any other guy. Needing to brag. "Are you seriously telling me you inked the date you lost your virginity on your arm?"

"I never said that."

But he did wink at me, and I thought he was actually growing even cuter the longer I sat with him. "Honestly, it should look like a total mess, but the artist did a really good job. It's very cool."

"Thank you." He pushed his chair back. "You ready to head out?"

"Sure." I stood up and pulled my coat off the chair.

"Do you have any tattoos?" he asked.

"No. I do have a piercing, though."

"Belly button?"

"No." Let him interpret that however he wanted to.

His eyebrows shot up. "Are you telling *me* you have your love button pierced?"

I laughed. "Love button? And I never said that." I winked back at him after echoing his words.

"Oh my God," he said, standing up and picking up his messenger bag. "You're dangerous."

I wished. "To be dangerous you have to be evil or supersmart, and I'm not either."

"Those aren't the only ways to pose a threat."

Suddenly I was afraid to hear what he might say. So to distract myself, I looked at my phone, and was immediately sorry I had. I had a text from Nathan.

I love you.

My smile evaporated and I shoved my phone in my pocket. I didn't want to see that. He kept coming at me like that, trying to apologize, begging me to take him back. But how do you trust someone who not only hooked up with your friend, but spent the next two months trying to repeat it?

He didn't love me. You didn't treat someone you loved like he had treated me.

Resolutely, I put a smile on my face and looked at Darwin/ Jonathon. "Thanks again, Jonathon. Have a good night." I started to walk away, wanting a private moment to myself.

"I'll walk out with you," he said easily, falling into step beside me.

Damn it.

"Are you okay?" he asked, as he held the door open for me.

Cold air hit me in the face. I winced. "Fine. I'm stressed, but I'll do the best I can on the exam. If I fail, well, at least I tried."

"I'm not talking about the exam."

Puzzled, I glanced over at him, hovering on the sidewalk, not sure which way he was going. "What do you mean?"

"Whatever was on your phone upset you."

That it was that obvious made tears instantly rise to my eyes. "No, it's fine." I gestured to the left. "I'm this way. Have a good night."

"You're walking?" He frowned.

"It's just a block."

"It's dark. I'll walk with you."

"No, no, it's fine." I started walking, anxious to get away from him. He was being too nice and I felt vulnerable, like a loser. I couldn't keep a boyfriend or understand basic chem. What he considered chemistry for dummies.

But he continued to walk with me. "You're a junior, right?" he asked casually, like I wasn't struggling not to cry.

I nodded.

"What's your major?"

"Education. I want to be a kindergarten teacher." I gave him a wan smile. "I don't need to know chemistry to teach that."

"I bet you'd be good with kids."

"I love kids."

There was silence between us as we walked, the heels of my boots sounding extra loud in the dark; the street, which was normally filled with students, mostly empty. It was a bit of a creepy walk at this time of night, and I'd known a girl who had been mugged. I would pee my pants if I were mugged and if I wasn't feeling so bummed, I would be more grateful for him walking with me. But mostly I just wanted to get home.

Then I realized what I was going home to—a dark, silent room.

And the tears I'd been holding back fell along with a sob that burst out unbidden.

We were in front of my building and I just about ran to the door, digging in my bag for my key.

"Kylie." Darwin/Jonathon touched my arm. "Hey. Look at me."

I shook my head.

"Do you want to talk about it?"

I shook my head harder.

But then, because I'm not someone who stuffs my feelings down, and because all my thoughts come out like a toddler commentating from their car seat on every car, cow, and house they see out the window, I blurted out, "My boyfriend cheated on me with my best friend."

"*What?*" He sounded horrified. "Are you fucking kidding me?"

It gave me a sense of relief that his reaction was so strong. "That's what I thought. I mean, it's like the worst thing ever."

"I hope he is your ex-boyfriend."

"He is. Because the thing is, okay, so it was a drunken hookup, which is really bad, but I don't know, maybe I could have forgiven him for that. But I found the texts he sent her for months afterward, creeping for a repeat. He said it was the best blow job he'd ever had and that she had a . . ." I shook my head. "Never mind. It just was obvious he wasn't even remotely sorry."

"Wow. That's rough. He sounds like a complete asshole. I'm sorry."

My shoulders fell as my breath expelled. I ran out of words for a second. It was the right thing for him to say, but every time I heard someone offer sympathy, I just felt worse. Because while they were all genuinely sorry for me, they were also a little bit glad it hadn't happened to them. "Thanks." I finally found my key and I noticed my hand was shaking a little as I tried to unlock the exterior door to my building.

Darwin/Jonathon put his hand over mine to steady it. For a second, I just stood there, drawing in a breath to calm down. He waited, then helped me turn the key to the right.

He was close behind me when I looked up at him, my hip shoving the door open. "Thanks," I whispered.

"He's an asshole," he repeated, his voice serious, eyes earnest.

"Do you want to come in?" I asked, because I really, really didn't want to be alone. My thoughts were too scattered, my anxiety high. Failing chemistry, moving out of my old apartment, hating my jealousy over my friends' relationships . . . it was hitting me hard. I didn't want silence.

His eyes shuttered for a minute and I felt silly. He was, like, twenty-five years old, a grad student with labs and research and probably a brainiac girlfriend who did physics for fun. Why would he want to spend the rest of his night with an undergrad who didn't know biochemistry from her butthole and kept threatening to cry? "Sorry, I don't know why I said that. I'm sure you have better things to do. Things that don't involve me boring you with my pathetic love life." Shame wasn't an emotion I'd felt a lot in my life, but the last three months, it had become a familiar feeling. One I hated.

I stepped into the vestibule, intending to close the door behind me, letting Darwin off the hook. But he came with me. "I'd love to."

Oh, God, he totally felt sorry for me. The shame increased, but at the same time, I still didn't want to be alone, so I didn't hold firm and send him home like I should have. I trudged up the stairs to the second floor and he reached out and put his hand on the small of my back when I stumbled a little on the third step.

Darwin was clearly a nice guy. Whatever he was getting paid by the university to tutor wasn't enough. How many hours a week did he spend coaching crying undergrads? Probably half the freshman class was failing chemistry. Yet here he was, being pretty damn sweet when it was obvious he could be doing about a million more interesting things.

"Do you have a roommate?" he asked.

"No, it's just a studio. I moved here in September after classes started, so I had to take what I could get and this was it. But I couldn't live in an apartment with Robin after what happened, so this was the best solution." I unlocked the door and shoved it open. Flicking on the light, I felt depressed all over again looking at the gloom. "It has terrible lighting."

He wandered in to the small room and bent over to inspect my two lamps. "You only have twenty-five watts in here. You could get brighter bulbs."

"Oh." Of course I could. But that had never once occurred to me. I was too busy feeling sorry for myself to be logical. "Yeah, I guess I could do that."

He dropped down onto my bed, which also acted as my couch, because I had no furniture and no space. "It takes a while to settle into a new place."

"I never wanted to be here. So it's hard to care." Setting my backpack on the floor, I sat next to him, crossing my legs and tucking my feet under them. "Do you have a roommate?"

"Yeah. My friend Devon. I'd rather live alone, honestly, but I can't afford it."

"And I would rather live with people. I'm social." My phone buzzed in my pocket.

I wasn't going to look at it. I didn't want to look at it. It could be nothing. It could be Jessica or Rory or my mother. But compulsion drove me to pull it out and check. I was sorry I did. A pit formed in my stomach as I read the text from Nathan.

This wouldn't have happened if you had stayed here this summer like I asked you to. We would still be together and happy.

My lip curled. So it was my fault that he had fucked my friend? Because I wasn't around for a few weeks?

"Why don't you block him?" Darwin asked.

"I don't know. Maybe because I keep wanting and waiting for a better apology."

"I don't think there's a better apology for what he did. I don't think he can ever really give you a good enough reason for why he had sex with your best friend."

I nodded. "You're right." I knew it. "I also know it's not my fault, but I can't help but feel like if only I'd done something different . . ."

He held his hand up, palm out. "Stop right there. There is no way that you could have done anything different so that it would have prevented this. If a guy is willing to cross that line, you could be perfect and it still wouldn't matter. Don't put yourself through that."

The tears started again. I nodded, my lips trembling.

"It's not your fault he's selfish, stupid, immoral, and an asshole."

"Well, I don't know if he's stupid." I could concede the rest, but for some ridiculous reason I felt the need to defend Nathan, even just a little.

"He got caught, didn't he? That makes him stupid. Besides,

any guy who would waste his time hooking up with a chick when he has *you* is an idiot."

I smiled. "Thanks. Even if you are just saying that."

But he shook his head as he peeled off his jacket. "I'm not just saying that. You're beautiful, Kylie, and more than that, you're sweet."

I did like to think that I was nice. "I try to be a decent person. But it seems like that's worked against me."

"Don't let one guy's dickheadedness change who you are. Don't let him ruin you. You're attractive just the way you are."

Confused, I wasn't sure what to say. I knew he was just being nice, and I hated that it even mattered to me what anyone's opinion was, but I felt needy. It had me seeking validation in a way I hadn't since probably middle school. "You think I'm attractive?"

It was an embarrassing thing to ask. I wanted to choke myself for letting it slip out.

Darwin nodded, though. "I find you very attractive. So attractive that I have to admit to being distracted the whole time I was tutoring you."

A shiver inched up my spine. "You were not." He hadn't looked at all like he'd been undressing me with his eyes. But then again, maybe nerds were smart enough to hide it, unlike the douchebags I usually hung out with.

"Oh, yes, I was." He was leaning against the wall, hands resting on his knees, and his expression was hooded. "I can tell you that you wear two necklaces—one is a cross, one is a heart with a ruby in the center. You have on a braided bracelet and if I had to guess, you are a 34C bra size. You have a tiny mole on your neck, you're really fond of lip gloss, you always twirl your hair with your left hand, never your right, and you are a natural blond."

Oh, my. A blush covered my face and it was partly from embarrassment and partly from a sudden arousal that caught me completely off guard. "How do you know I'm a natural blond?"

"You don't have any exposed roots and your eyebrows are the same tone as your hair."

Were all intelligent people this observant? Rory was the same way. Though Rory had never nailed my bra size. I wasn't sure what to say.

"Is that creepy?" he asked. "I only told you to illustrate my point that I find you attractive."

"It's not creepy. It's flattering." It was. And he was very sweet to massage my damaged ego.

"Good. I want you to remember that, whenever you start to doubt that you had anything to do with Dickhead cheating on you. It was his problem, not yours."

I felt like I should give him a fee for the therapy. "Thanks, Darwin. I find you attractive, too."

He gave me a smile, the corner of his lip turning up in a way that made me focus on his mouth, made me wonder what it would feel like to have it on mine. I kind of really wanted him to kiss me, just to see.

"Now you're just flattering me."

"No." I shook my head, feeling myself leaning closer toward him, without even intending to. "The first thing I noticed when I sat down next to you was how good you smell."

His nostrils flared a little. "How I smell?"

"Yes. You smell masculine."

"That's evolution," he told me. "A female instinctively responds to the scent of a male and she is subconsciously drawn to the specimen she thinks will ensure her progeny's survival."

Whatever. "I think it was more that you don't smell like sweat or cologne."

"It's still the chemistry of attraction."

He had shifted closer too, and I could see that he had an erection. It hadn't been there before, and now it was. Bam. The sight of it so clearly outlined beneath his jeans had me tingling in places I had thought no longer existed. I hadn't had a single sexual urge at all since RAN, and now a warm sensation was pooling between my thighs and spreading out to all my limbs. My nipples felt constrained in my bra. My 34C bra.

"Can you just show me instead of explaining it to me?" I asked, and I was shocked to hear the flirt, who I thought had taken a permanent vacation, return to my voice for the first time in four months. "I learn better hands-on."

"With visual aids?"

I nodded, biting my bottom lip.

"Come here," he urged, holding his hand out to me.

I did, crawling up between his legs, breathing in his scent, taking in his narrow lips, his eyes, so dark behind the lenses of his glasses. He reached out with his thumb and wiped the tears that were still lingering on my face in itchy, wet streaks.

Then he kissed me.